Praise for Alex Brown

'Warm and witty'	*Hello*
'Adorable, comical and magical'	*Closer*
'We love it!'	*Now*
'Defies the chick lit cliché'	*Heat*

'The perfect, feel-good summer read'

Woman's Weekly

'A wonderfully crafted masterpiece'   Melanie Blake

'Very lovely'   Jill Mansell

'A lovely book to curl up and unwind with'

Milly Johnson

'Warm, wonderful characters – a really lovely read'

Sarah Morgan

'Intriguing and heart-warming'   Katie Fforde

'Kept me turning the pages'   Trisha Ashley

'Charming, witty, heart-warming'

Carmel Harrington

A
Postcard
from
CAPRI

Alex Brown is the international No. 1 bestselling author of thirteen books, including *A Postcard from Italy*, *A Postcard from Paris*, the Carrington's series, the Tindledale series, *The Secret of Orchard Cottage*, *The Great Christmas Knit Off*, *The Wish*, and the Bicycle Bakery series. Her books are loved worldwide and have been translated into twenty languages. Alex lives by the sea on the south coast of England with her family and two glossy black labradors. When she isn't writing, she can be found walking on the beach, binge-watching a boxset or enjoying a French martini.

If you'd like to find out more about Alex, visit her website www.alexbrownauthor.com, and sign up to her newsletter to receive *The Beach Walk*, a free short story. Alex loves to hear from her readers, and you can chat to her on social media:

f /AlexBrownBooks
@ @AlexBrownBooks
🐦 @AlexBrownBooks

Also by Alex Brown

The Carrington's series

Cupcakes at Carrington's
Christmas at Carrington's
Ice Creams at Carrington's

The Tindledale series

The Great Christmas Knit Off
The Great Village Show
The Secret of Orchard Cottage
The Wish

The Postcard . . . series

A Postcard from Italy
A Postcard from Paris

The Bicycle Bakery series

A Cosy Christmas at Bridget's Bicycle Bakery

Short Stories

Me and Mr Carrington
Not Just for Christmas
The Great Summer Sewing Bee

A Postcard
from
CAPRI

ALEX BROWN

HarperCollins*Publishers*

HarperCollins*Publishers* Ltd
1 London Bridge Street,
London SE1 9GF

www.harpercollins.co.uk

HarperCollins*Publishers*
1st Floor, Watermarque Building, Ringsend Road
Dublin 4, Ireland

First published by HarperCollins*Publishers* 2022
1

A catalogue record for this book is available from the British Library

ISBN (PB): 978-0-00-842201-1

Set in Birka by Palimpsest Book Production Limited,
Falkirk, Stirlingshire

Printed and bound in the UK using 100% Renewable Electricity by
CPI Group (UK) Ltd

To Dr Caroline Cauchi Smailes, for being
the very best friend.

'Hollywood is a place where they will pay you a thousand dollars for a kiss and fifty cents for your soul.'

Marilyn Monroe

PROLOGUE

Capri, Italy, 1953

The glamorous young woman with platinum waved hair cascading over bare shoulders signed the postcard with a flourish, using her real name and secretly delighted not to be using the name the studio bosses had given her. She replaced the cap of the fountain pen and, after allowing the ink to dry, she hid the postcard away from prying eyes. Slipping her feet into a pair of satin-lined marabou feathered mules, she stepped through fluttering white voile curtains onto the veranda. An evocative scent of salty sea air, mingled with an exotic, intoxicating aroma of delicate yellow-and-white pomelia flowers, teased her nostrils. She closed her eyes and tilted her face up towards the sun, her body relaxing, a tautness in her shoulders easing as the rich melodic sound of a deep, male voice singing 'O Sole Mio' floated up in the gentle warm breeze to greet her. Back-to-back filming for the last three years had taken its toll, although worth it in so many ways to achieve her acting ambition and catapult her life into an unfamiliar world of glamour and opulence since leaving Tindledale, the little English village where she had grown up. She missed her home and family dearly, and there was always a tinge of sadness as she pined, on occasion, for the simplicity of the humble way of life that she had left so far behind. Uncomplicated and free. Now she was on the cusp of achieving her lifelong dream, having landed a coveted role in *A Moment to Cherish*, the next big Hollywood blockbuster film – or at least the studio had assured her it would be. The critics were already speculating about Oscar nominations after previewing her screen test. Until then she was to enjoy a well-earned, carefree summer break before filming commenced.

The exclusive hotel was everything she'd dreamt it would be, and as a personal guest of the owner – the legendary Gracie Fields, who lived here in Capri and whose home was nearby – she had been afforded every luxury, including her own personal butler. Taking a sip of the refreshing peach wine cocktail the butler had mixed for her, she dropped her shades over her eyes and surveyed the sumptuous scene beyond the veranda. To her left she could see the Faraglioni rock stacks rising majestically from the sea, the rays from the hot, Mediterranean sun dazzling on the crystalline azure and emerald waves, creating a trillion tiny diamond flecks, floating and twinkling as if to welcome her to this magical island paradise of Capri. Lush green trees and pink bougainvillea mingling amidst the white stucco architecture meandered her gaze down the cliff and out to sea, where something caught her eye. She wandered closer towards the wrought-iron balustrade at the edge of the veranda and, after leaning forward for a better look, keen to ensure her eyes weren't deceiving her, she allowed herself a momentary gasp of pleasure on seeing him standing there on the deck of a yacht. He was wearing a white linen shirt and trousers, showcasing his tall, suntanned physique, his aquiline nose and distinctive strong jaw. Glossy black hair swept back from a high forehead framed his famous movie star looks. There was no doubt! Suddenly afraid she would be spotted looking out for him, she dipped back behind the curtain out of view. Always cautious. Yet with so much to lose the stakes were high . . . and she simply couldn't take the risk.

They had first met on the set of her last film in Los Angeles and the attraction as he had smiled and graciously introduced himself, even though everyone knew who he was, had been instant, a sizzling bolt of electricity, quite unlike anything that she had ever experienced before. His affable charm and deep-set smouldering black eyes had been irresistible – and strictly off limits. The studio had her tied into a five-year contract with pages and pages of draconian rules – no dating, no marriage and definitely no babies. Yet here he was, in a Riva speedboat travelling across the white froth-capped waves of the mesmerising, sapphire sea towards the hotel's private jetty . . .

1

Tindledale, rural England, present day

Maddie Williams loved this time of the day. The golden hour. Perfect for capturing the best images to add to her photography portfolio. Sweeping her sister's amber-flecked ebony hair into place around her shoulders to catch the glow from the late afternoon sunshine, Maddie positioned her against the trunk of the red apple tree at the end of the garden. Sofia stood patiently as Maddie gently swathed a chiffon scarf to the side of her baby bump before taking a few steps backwards to check that everything was arranged the way she wanted it. Satisfied that her pregnant sister looked completely gorgeous, as always, Maddie lifted her camera, adjusted the shutter speed, and snapped several times, determined to take the very best collection of pictures to show off her photography skills.

'Are you nearly done, Mads?' Sofia called out, like a ventriloquist trying not to move her lips or head in case she ruined the shot. Any minute now, Ben, her husband, would return from the local nursery with their two-year-old twins, Ryan and Sonny, and chaos would ensue.

Six months ago, Maddie had won the camera, tripod, reflector boards, and pretty much everything she needed to be a professional photographer, in a magazine competition, together with a cash prize. The lucky break couldn't have come at a better time. Maddie was still reeling from the blow of being made redundant and then dumped by Brad, her boyfriend of eleven years, in the space of a week.

Her life until then hadn't exactly been perfect. Since the age of eighteen, Maddie had been working as an administrator in a variety of dull office jobs in London that had left her feeling as though she had been swimming upstream, forever trying to fight off the wanderlust, the constant yearning to travel the world and take pictures for a living instead. And she might have followed her dream if she hadn't needed to pay her half of the extortionate rent and living expenses. Brad had insisted they split it all down the middle; that way it was fair, he said, even though his half was mostly covered by a trust fund he had inherited from his wealthy grandfather. Whenever she broached the subject of travelling, Brad had ruled it out, saying there was no way he could take time off work to go with her and she would hate travelling on her own. No, she was much better off staying at home – or so he'd told her.

Then one fateful day her whole world had fallen apart. It had started with Maddie's boss, Toby, calling her into his office to explain that the company was downsizing, and it wasn't anything personal, and if he could keep her on then he would in a heartbeat, but to cut a very long story short it was last in, first to go, which meant there was no big lump sum pay-off coming to her. Inside she had been panicking, swimmy with nausea as she wondered how she was going to manage to pay her half of the bills.

As fate would have it, she found out the next morning that she had won a photography competition with a thousand-pound cash prize plus all the equipment necessary to set her up as a professional photographer. It was a dream come true for Maddie. She was a big believer in things happening for a reason, and so figured the redundancy was a sign, a kick-start to make her go for it and create the career change that she had hankered after for so long.

Her euphoria at having 'lost a penny and found a pound', as Sofia put it when Maddie FaceTimed her to share the news, was extremely short-lived. That very same evening, in fact mere moments after she had ended the call with Sofia, Brad had arrived home and, cutting her off as she was about to tell him about her win, announced that he had been offered, and had accepted, a promotion. A big step up with a significant salary increase. In New York.

As Maddie had dashed forward to congratulate him with a hug and a kiss, ecstatic for him and at the prospect of them moving to New York together, Brad had taken two steps backwards and, without meeting her eye, informed her that he was, 'just not feeling the wedding vibe any more'. Maddie's world had stopped spinning, suspended in space as if time had stood still, as he carried on talking, telling her that while he didn't want to hurt her, this was something he just had to do alone: 'It's a fresh start for me, Mads!'

Her heart had cracked in two as she wondered when it was exactly that Brad had started hankering after a 'fresh start'. Because she was sure he'd been the one who had initiated the talk about them getting married, and he'd definitely been the one who'd proposed. He had always wanted them to have children too – something Maddie hadn't felt ready for, not until she'd had a chance to pursue her dreams. He had countered by telling her she would be mad to start all over again in a new career as a photographer, especially at her age. She had only been twenty-five at the time, and for all his eagerness to have a family, Brad had been happy enough to postpone until his own dreams of promotion were fulfilled.

When the slo-mo moment of silence had subsided, Maddie had slumped to the floor, stunned and trembling. Brad had left ten minutes later with his pride and joy Player of the Match football medal, Xbox, golf bag and a carrier bag of clothes under his arm, saying she could keep the engagement ring as a token to remember the good times by.

Maddie had limped on for a while on her own, struggling to eke out her prize money for as long as she possibly could, even resorting to selling her beautiful engagement ring, before she conceded defeat. Feeling like an absolute failure, she'd moved back to Tindledale, installing herself in the spare bedroom of Honeysuckle Cottage, her granny's tiny, ramshackle, thatched cottage overlooking the village green. The place had been standing empty since Granny had fallen and fractured her left hip. Maddie and Sofia's dad, who lived in Spain, had been worried that the three-hundred-year-old house would fall into disrepair if left empty, so he was only too happy for Maddie to move in. Granny was delighted too, as she had politely declined Sofia's offer to come and live with her and Ben after the fall, saying she didn't want to be a burden. Instead, she'd booked herself into the Evergreens supported living complex, insisting that she'd be happy there with her friends, Joanie and Sandra.

'I met them through the Tindledale Tappers knitting circle. They say it's ever so nice living at Evergreens, having all your washing done for you and your meals cooked,' Granny had told Maddie. 'And they have plenty of trained nursing staff on hand in case I have another fall. There's no end of social activities to get involved in, with trips out for afternoon tea or a stroll around the local garden centre – they even offer yoga and power walking for those that fancy it.'

Maddie had thought it sounded perfect for a sprightly octogenarian like Granny. Apart from the fall, she was generally in good physical health, but her memory was showing signs of fading and the family had been worried about her.

'Mads, can we call it a wrap . . . or whatever it is you say at the end of a shoot. I've had enough now,' Sofia bellowed. It was getting chilly as the afternoon sun had sunk down behind the summer house and she longed to go indoors and get warmed up.

'Just one more!' Maddie called back, flicking a lock of curly auburn hair away from her eyeline. 'You look utterly stunning by the way.' She gave her sister a thumbs up before finishing off, grateful to her for agreeing to do the shoot. Maddie had hopes of securing a fashion photoshoot in Italy, although her chances were slim with the competition so fierce. Unlike the other photographers vying for this particular shoot, Maddie didn't have any well-placed connections, not even a friend who was the make-up artist, like she had for her last assignment in Cornwall for an online fashion store. That had been a few months ago and so she badly needed to keep the work coming in.

Eventually she had chanced her arm and called her old school friend, Cynthia, who was a make-up artist on many of the big fashion shows and London's West End theatre and global film productions.

'Sure, I'll see what I can do to help,' Cynthia told her. 'There's nothing like a good recommendation in this business.'

Cynthia had advised her to keep phoning booking agents directly in the meantime, but the usual response was a dismissive suggestion to submit a selection of images from her portfolio and they would get back to her. One had added airily, 'We'll call you in the event a rare opportunity opens up where we may require a photographer with your level of experience.' Ouch, the implication had stung! Maddie knew she was a good photographer, but she was very much a self-taught amateur and, having come to the world of travel and fashion photography far later than her contemporaries, she didn't have a large professional portfolio of accredited paid work to share.

Since the spilt with Brad, Maddie had worked hard to drag her self-esteem off the floor and put herself back together again. She'd helped out with the twins, volunteered at the local charity shop, photographed a couple of local weddings – all while working as many shifts as she could in the village pub, the Duck & Puddle. In short, she'd done everything possible to keep her mind occupied and away from wondering just how brilliant a time Brad was having in New York. She knew she had to move on, but it wasn't easy given that Brad had been her first real love and the only long-term relationship she'd had.

She walked over to join Sofia, turned the screen of the camera towards her so she could see the pictures. 'See how beautiful you look,' Maddie said, handing Sofia the kaftan.

'Hmm, you're lucky I love you and want you to have the career you've always dreamed of, because I wouldn't be standing up against a tree all afternoon for just anyone, you know,' Sofia said, feigning exasperation and shaking her head before giving Maddie a quick hug. 'But yes, I can see it was worth getting backache for. I don't suppose you would print a few for me to keep please?' she asked. 'I'd like to have some to show this one when he or she is grown up.' She stroked a loving hand over her bump.

'Of course, I'd love to. And thank you for today. Sorry it took so long. You've been amazing.'

'Well, amazing is a stretch! I've done a pretty good job of being tired and irritable though. And I want to put my feet up.' Sofia let the kaftan slip over her head and float down around her naturally tanned body.

'There you are!' It was Ben, his kind eyes twinkling as he came through the white wooden gate at the other end of the garden, waggling a phone in the air and with a twin hanging off each outstretched arm. 'I just got home, and your mobile was ringing on the hall table – I saw it was Evergreens so thought I'd better answer it in case something had happened to your granny again.' He handed the phone over to Sofia, simultaneously planting a kiss on her lips and saying, 'You look gorgeous, by the way. You too, Mads,' he added with a brotherly grin. Then to the twins, 'Hey, enough climbing, you two . . . I'm not a flaming tree!' He shook his head as the twins let go and ran to hug Sofia, then Maddie, before making a beeline towards

13

her silver camera case. 'Ah, I don't think so!' Ben said, intercepting them just in time. 'Right, I'm off to put the lasagne in the oven. Sofia, don't rush, babe, I've got it all under control,' he yelled back over his shoulder.

Maddie smiled, tenting her eyes with a hand to shade them from the sun as she watched Ben wade through the wildflower meadow that had sprung up in that section of the garden which had been left to nature, with a twin under each arm. Sofia and Ben had been together since their teens, having first met one summer when Sofia came over to visit her English granny, then falling in love and eventually marrying in their twenties. They were the quintessential teenage sweethearts; they just went together, like toast and jam, sweet and kind to each other.

Sofia motioned to Maddie to bring her a wooden garden chair from over by the summer house.

'Yes, that's right, it's her granddaughter, Sofia, here,' she said into the phone, giving Maddie a look of concern as she mouthed her thanks and gratefully lowered herself into the chair. Maddie stopped packing away her equipment and moved in closer to hear what was being said, fidgeting with her butterfly necklace as she always did when worried.

Sofia paused and glanced again at Maddie. 'I see. Are you sure she doesn't have concussion?' Sofia nodded as she listened some more, seemingly taking it all in. 'Oh yes, she has mentioned that name several times . . . No, I'm afraid we don't know.' More silence. 'If you're sure, then we'll come in the morning, but please do call if anything changes.'

After saying goodbye, Sofia turned to Maddie and told her: 'Granny has had a fall. Nothing too serious – she tripped over a ball of wool that had fallen from her knitting bag. She grazed her face when she landed on the carpet. The doctor checked her over and gave her the all-clear, then they helped her up to bed. She's sleeping now. They don't want to wake her but thought we should know as she's been upset and has been talking about someone called Audrey again.'

'Oh dear . . .' Maddie creased her forehead, concerned for her grandmother. The same thing had happened with her last fall when she fractured her hip. In the distress and confusion, and immense pain, no doubt, she had become very anxious, wringing her hands and asking after Audrey, desperate to know where she was and whether she was OK. Maddie had found it very difficult to witness her beloved grandmother so upset, especially when they were utterly helpless to make it better for her because the simple truth was . . . they had absolutely no idea who Audrey was. 'Poor Granny. At her time of life she shouldn't have a care in the world, other than which pudding she'll choose for dessert, or what she'd like to knit next, or the best book to select from the library trolley. You know, all the lovely things in life.' Maddie thought of their dad's gentle, unassuming mum, who loved knitting and reading and sharing a bag of her favourite Liquorice Allsorts with her friends over a good chinwag and a cup of tea. The last thing Maddie wanted was for Granny to be upset and tearful. She resolved that, first thing in the morning, she was going to make it her mission to find out who Audrey was, and put her granny's mind at rest . . .

2

'You're going to be a star!' Rose O'Malley's twin sister, Patsy, whispered, her voice full of glee as she momentarily lifted her ear away from the glass that she had pressed up to the panel in the sitting room door. Inside, their father – a farmer who was far more at home milking cows than talking to a vice president of production from a film studio in Los Angeles – could be heard pacing up and down. The metal Blakeys on the soles of his best Sunday shoes clip-clipped across the wooden floorboards before softening as he moved onto the well-worn rug in the centre of the room. Louis Baxter, the vice president, was puffing on an extra-large cigar, the fumes of which filled the hall of Honeysuckle Cottage. The two sisters had grown up in the cottage and it had been a happy home until six years ago, when their older brother, who'd gone off to be a pilot

17

in the dreadful war, had been shot down over enemy territory. Not long afterwards their devoutly Catholic Irish mother had succumbed to a bout of influenza, which meant it was now down to their father to navigate this exciting but wholly unfamiliar turn of events for his daughter, Rose.

At seventeen years old and with her eighteenth birthday only two weeks way, Rose considered herself grown up and perfectly able to take care of herself. Nevertheless, if her dream of becoming an actress was to come true, she needed her father's blessing. He would never let her go otherwise. Realising that she was holding her breath, she exhaled silently and nudged Patsy away from the door, determined to hear for herself. The two men had stopped talking, and this worried Rose, so she found herself holding her breath once more, consumed with thoughts of her destiny hanging in the balance behind the sitting room door.

'What am I to do if Dad says I can't go?' Rose mouthed, her eyebrows knitting in concern as she searched her sister's face, desperate for a clue as to how she thought this potentially life-changing moment would play out for her.

Patsy, who was far more pragmatic than Rose, rolled her eyes, let out a long silent huff of air and whispered, 'Of course he will let you go!' She was hankering after moving into Rose's bedroom at the back of the house, which overlooked the fruit farm where her sweetheart, George, tended the apple orchards. In her mind's eye she pictured him, stripped to the waist on a hot summer's day with a fine sheen of sweat glistening across his splendidly solid chest and rather broad shoulders. So, Patsy too was willing their father to let Rose go to America, even though she was baffled by her sister's ambition to be a movie star. For her part, she was perfectly content to remain in Tindledale, marry George and have lots of babies. But her twin sister had always been a dreamer. Though she was as shy and quiet as a mouse, the moment Rose stepped on a stage she came alive, vibrant and vivacious, captivating the audience with her dramatic skills. Yes, Rose certainly had a gift for acting. A 'deep well', their mother used to say, 'serene on the surface with rippling depths only to be revealed when Rose plucked up the courage to become someone else'. Patsy wasn't the least bit envious of her sister's talent; George had told her he liked the fact she was a 'what you see is what you get' kind of girl because it meant he knew where he stood with her, and if George was happy then so was she. Her only dream was that one day soon he would be her husband.

The brass doorknob on the sitting room door turned so suddenly that the sisters barely had time to dash away and busy themselves in the kitchen, selecting cups and saucers, along with a sugar bowl and milk jug, and arranging them on a tray. Rose's hands were shaking in anticipation and excitement mingled with nerves as she smoothed a lace doily across the gold-handled tray. Patsy placed Rich Tea biscuits on one of their mother's best Royal Doulton china plates with a pink and purple floral pattern, a wedding present that was only brought out for visitors and special occasions.

'Rose,' her father called out as he came through the door, his Sunday-best shoes now clipping across the linoleum kitchen floor as if counting down to announce her fate.

'Yes?' she stopped fiddling with the doily and momentarily closed her eyes, murmuring a silent prayer of hope to herself before looking up to the framed picture of the blessed Virgin Mary before turning to face him. Patsy, finished with the biscuits, was now positioned behind their father, and had her hands up under her chin too in a prayer of hope, her eyebrows arched so high they were almost joining her hairline. She winked at Rose, who didn't dare wink back or even smile until she had heard her father's decision.

'Do you want to go to America?' He cut to the

chase, placing both hands, palms down, on the blue Formica counter. His eyes were sharp with a seriousness she hadn't seen before as he looked directly at Rose.

'Yes. Yes please. To act in films is all I've ever dreamed of,' she replied dramatically, as if her life depended on it, then winced at the plea in her voice as it jumped up several octaves, making her sound utterly shrill. Her father didn't like shrill – it was unbecoming and off-putting in a young lady, Mother had always told her and Patsy.

Rose smoothed down her new dress, made especially for today. She had seen Vivien Leigh wearing a dress just like it, with matching gloves, on the cover of *Picturegoer* magazine, and so had wanted to emulate the exquisite film star's look. Her buttercup yellow gingham swing dress had been good enough to audition for the role of Cordelia in Shakespeare's *King Lear* at the theatre in the nearby town of Market Briar, but a meeting with a Hollywood scout was a once-in-a-lifetime opportunity and as such it required the kind of dress that her idol, Vivien Leigh, would be proud of. So Rose and Patsy had set about making the emerald-green satin sheath dress and then she'd experimented with make-up and hairstyles, conducting a dress rehearsal in her bedroom every evening to be sure of getting it

21

right for when Mr Baxter came to see Father. Now, with her flame-red hair carefully styled, crimson lipstick and wing-effect black eyeliner to accentuate her green eyes, a boat neckline to show off her lightly freckled collarbones, Rose felt sure she looked the part.

'Mr Baxter said there will be a five-year contract to sign.' Their father nodded, as if mulling over all the details that had been explained to him. 'And stipulations you have to stick to.' He folded his arms across his chest and the room fell silent.

Unable to bear the suspense for a moment longer, Rose lifted the tray, in the hope of taking it into the sitting room and seeing Mr Baxter for herself. If she could just look him in the eyes and explain how much this opportunity meant to her, she was sure that he would give her a chance. Miss Henderson, her drama teacher, had told her that, having travelled down from London to catch a matinee, he'd been so taken with her performance and 'star quality' that he was considering offering her a contract. She only hoped he wouldn't reconsider after meeting her today.

'That's all right, Dad, I can stick to the rules,' Rose told him, gripping the tray so tightly her knuckles had turned as white as the milk inside the small china jug. Patsy, with an impatient look on her face, ducked out from behind their father's back and marched across the kitchen to stand alongside her sister. After taking the tray from Rose, Patsy smiled sweetly and tilted her head to one side.

'Rose has always been a sensible girl,' she reminded him. 'She can stick to the rules, whatever they are – most likely it'll be trivial things like being at rehearsals on time and not stealing the costumes.' Patsy laughed and shrugged, waiting for him to agree. Silence followed. 'Oh, go on, Dad, we'll never hear the end of it if you stop her from going. Please say yes and then we can all get back to normal,' she stated in her typical no-nonsense way. She was bored now and wanted to know, was she to have the back bedroom or not? More silence followed as Rose looked at her father, willing him to say yes.

'America is a very long way away,' he hesitated, his face weary now with the burden of decision.

'I can write letters. Postcards too, so you can see the marvellous sights!' Rose assured him in earnest, taking a step forward.

'Every week, you'll write . . . won't you, Rose?' Patsy joined in, nodding fervently and giving her sister a sharp nudge with her elbow.

'You will need to go to Mass every week, your mother would insist upon it.' Her father looked at Rose and then Patsy and then back to Rose again, a

23

bead of sweat forming at his temple. Taking his handkerchief, he dabbed at his forehead.

'Yes, yes of course, wearing a Sunday best dress with hat and gloves,' Rose agreed right away, her mother's Dublin accent ringing loudly in her ears.

'And you would travel with Mr Baxter's secretary,' their father stated, as if suddenly remembering this fact. He relaxed slightly, folding his handkerchief and returning it to his breast pocket. 'Your mother would insist on a chaperone – a female companion. It's not proper for an unmarried young lady to travel all that way alone with an older gentleman.'

'Yes, that's fine, Dad.' Rose recalled the glamorous woman with a butter-blonde chignon, exhaling elegant plumes of smoke from a cigarette in a holder, seated next to Mr Baxter in the theatre. She hadn't appeared to be much older than Rose, although she looked very businesslike in her pastel pink Chanel two-piece suit and blue winged secretarial glasses. But Rose had seen her laughing when Mr Baxter leaned across and whispered something in her ear, so she hoped she would be fun to travel with.

'That's settled then,' Patsy jumped in. 'Shall I take the tray through to Mr Baxter now?' She lifted her elbows and Rose allowed herself to revel momentarily in what was surely going to be good news. But her father didn't say anything more. Instead, he clipped across the kitchen and pulled open the door to the cupboard where they kept the glasses, and after taking two crystal tumblers from the shelf, he turned to face Rose and her sister. With a glass in each hand, he lifted them up.

'Put the tray down, Patsy,' he instructed, and Rose caught her breath. Surely not . . . he couldn't say no. Not now, not after everything she had done to get to this point. The hair, the make-up, the dress! Not to mention the hours of rehearsing her lines to make sure her portrayal of Cordelia was perfect. Plus, all the years of going to auditions and then playing parts in numerous local amateur dramatics productions and pantomimes, dating back as far as when she was five years old and had debuted as Mary in the school nativity play. It was then that Rose first knew she could come alive on a stage underneath the sparkling bright lights, and her tendency to shyness seemed to fade away. As Rose held her breath, it was as if her dream was slipping away like sand seeping through an egg timer, and she feared she'd never have a chance to turn the timer upside down again. This was it! Her moment. To leave Tindledale and head to Hollywood. Just like her idol, Vivien Leigh. Rose let out a long breath, swallowed hard and was about to give the performance of her life in an attempt to persuade her father, when his serious face turned into a smile. 'This calls for something stronger than tea,' he declared, indicating with his head towards the sideboard. Patsy immediately pulled open the door and lifted the bottle of best brandy out and gave it to her father. 'I'll let Mr Baxter know that you will accept his generous offer and will sign the contract.' He nodded, and Rose gasped and clasped her hands underneath her chin as her father left the kitchen with the bottle in one hand and the two tumblers in the other.

Stunned, the two sisters stood and stared at each other for a moment. It was Patsy, of course, who eventually broke the silence and recovered first.

'You're going to Hollywood!' she whisper-screamed triumphantly and promptly pushed a whole Rich Tea biscuit into her mouth before embracing Rose in a jubilant hug, feeling utterly delighted for her sister, but secretly far more delighted for herself and the new dreamy view that was soon to be hers.

3

Maddie and Sofia had arrived at Evergreens the following morning and were looping the visitor lanyards over their heads when Janice, the on-site carer assigned to their grandmother, came bustling towards them, her white plastic apron making a swishing sound as she moved.

'Morning!' Janice greeted cheerfully, 'How are you both today?' Before either Maddie or Sofia could answer, Janice ploughed on and with her hands on her ample hips took a step back, broke into an enormous smile and declared, 'Ooh, you are positively blooming, my dear! A new baby is always a blessing and I'm sure your granny will be over the moon too to have another little one to fuss over,' Janice beamed. 'Anyway, shan't hold you up! You know the way – and I'll ask Sammy to bring the tea trolley along to you. Finger slices of lemon drizzle sponge and mini chocolate cookies are on today's elevenses menu!' And giving them another big smile, she swished off towards the day room.

Sofia knocked on the door to Granny's flat, waiting a moment before pushing it open and, with Maddie close behind, they made their way down the narrow hallway and into the large, sun-bathed room with a big bay window overlooking a pretty garden full of colourful flowers. Their grandmother was sitting on the settee with her knitting and Frank Sinatra was crooning soothingly from the CD player. The air was delicately scented with Granny's familiar Dior perfume.

'How are you, Granny?' Sofia asked, letting the strap of her handbag slip from her shoulder as she pressed a hand into the small of her aching back and sank into the armchair opposite. Maddie placed the bouquet of her grandmother's favourite pink peonies on the coffee table in the centre of the room and went into the little kitchenette area in search of a vase.

'I'm very well, my dears. How are you?' Their grandmother rested her knitting in her lap before giving her elegant snow-white chignon a little pat, then checking her lavender-coloured cardy was tidy. Always wanting to look her best, Maddie thought.

'We're fine, thanks. Here to see how you are after your fall. What happened?' Sofia got straight to the point as always.

'You had us worried, Granny.' Maddie had found a vase, filled it with water and was busying herself with arranging the peonies, feeling hesitant as to whether they should push Granny to talk about what had happened last night in case it upset her all over again.

'Aren't they beautiful?' Granny indicated the flowers, acting as if she hadn't heard a word they'd said. She leaned forward to touch the flowers but couldn't quite reach, so Maddie handed one of the plumpest peonies to her instead. 'Thank you.' Granny took the pastel pink bloom in her papery, near trans- lucent hand. 'You know, roses have always been my favourite flowers,' she declared, after lifting the flower to her nose to draw in the scent.

'Oh, but they aren't—' Sofia started to correct her but, giving her sister a look, Maddie quickly jumped in:

'That's why I brought them for you,' she said, not wanting to contradict her granny. She looked so happy to see them, her rheumy forget-me-not- coloured eyes twinkling keenly and her delicate face smiling in joy. She looked vulnerable too, with a bruise ripe on her forehead next to a plaster, presum- ably there to cover the graze.

29

'You always were a kind girl.' Granny handed the peony back to Maddie, giving her granddaughter's hand a fond pat as she took the flower from her, trimmed the stem and popped it into the vase with the others. Lifting the vase, Maddie smiled and went to place it on the table, moving a place mat into position at the centre of the table so as not to mark the polished walnut surface. Maddie knew how fond her granny was of her old furniture, some of it inherited, like this vintage gate-leg table. Dad said most of the furniture pre-dated the Second World War, but he couldn't be sure because Granny never really spoke about her life. She was a very private person, one of life's supporters – always more interested in others and never the main character.

'Thank you, my love.' Granny lifted her gold-clasped black patent leather handbag from where she always kept it on the seat of the settee in the generous space between her tiny frame and the side of the armrest. 'Would you like a sweet, dear?' And after snapping open the handbag, she pulled out a big bag of Liquorice Allsorts and offered it to Maddie.

'Oh, um . . . thank you,' Maddie hesitated. She wasn't a fan of liquorice, but on seeing Granny's eager face and wanting to please her, she chose one of the round sweets covered in pink sprinkles. 'Take one for your friend too!' Maddie saw Sofia's eyes widen with concern as she handed the bag of sweets to her and then sat down on the settee next to Granny.

'Granny, she's not my friend,' Maddie started gently, but the old lady had picked up her knitting and was busy looping the wool around her index finger, ready to carry on with her knit-one, pearl-one routine.

Before Maddie could go on, Granny interrupted. 'What's she doing here then? Who is she?'

'It's Sofia, your other granddaughter, my sister.'

Their grandmother looked hastily away and busied herself by fiddling with the clasp of her handbag as if pondering on what to say next. 'Oh yes, silly me. Were you in the family way the last time you came to visit me?' she said, as if to change the subject, her wrinkle-lined face crumpling in confusion as she pointed a spindly index finger towards Sofia's baby bump.

'I was here last week, don't you remember?' Sofia flicked her eyes towards Maddie.

'Maybe it's the fall, Granny . . . you did graze your head . . . so it may have shaken you up a bit.' But even as she spoke, Maddie knew this was more than a graze to the head. She remembered the last time she was here, and the time before, and the one before

31

that too, and Granny had been forgetful on all those occasions, but never to the point of not knowing who her sister was.

Her grandmother stopped knitting and moved her left hand up to her head, her fingertips trembling slightly as she delicately traced the outline of the plaster before moving back to curl them around the knitting needle. 'Yes, I had a silly fall, nothing to worry about. It's all fine now, dear, so don't you be worrying yourself. Tell me about your photographs – have you taken any more good ones to show me?'

'Um . . . yes,' Maddie said, thrown off-kilter by the sudden change of subject, but encouraged that Granny could remember this piece of information about her. 'I took some gorgeous pictures of Sofia in the garden yesterday, next to the apple tree – I'll bring one for you next time.'

'I'd like that.' Granny smiled over in Sofia's direction, but Maddie could see the vagueness still there in her eyes and she could also see that Sofia wasn't convinced that her grandmother really remembered who she was. Sofia coughed to clear her throat, clearly keen to cut to the chase.

'Granny, who is Audrey?' The question hung in the air as Sofia helped herself to another liquorice sweet and put it in her mouth. Maddie glared at her sister, annoyed at her typical bull-in-a-china-shop approach to everything.

'Audrey?' Granny repeated, oblivious to the sisters' silent exchange as she carried on with her knitting, the rhythmic click-clack of the needles filling the now ominous atmosphere.

'Yes, you were asking about her after your fall,' Sofia persevered, seemingly unperturbed by Maddie's glare.

'It doesn't matter though . . . if you can't remember,' Maddie jumped in, shooting another look at her sister.

'It would be nice to know though, wouldn't it?' Sofia said through a smile as she chewed the sweet and then swallowed. 'Have a think and see if you can remember while I go to the loo.' After hefting herself forward in the armchair, she placed a hand on each of the armrests and levered herself into a standing position. 'And it's very hot and stuffy in here . . . that certainly won't help you keep a clear head.'

Maddie inhaled sharply through her nostrils before letting out a long 'keep calm and carry on' breath.

As soon as Sofia had left the room, Granny put down her knitting and leaned towards Maddie. 'Why does she want to know who Audrey is?'

'Oh, we were just curious after we heard you'd been asking for her again. You seemed a little upset about it after your fall and you've mentioned someone called Audrey a few times since . . .' Seeing a look of wariness mingled with sorrow in her grandmother's eyes, Maddy trailed off.

Granny didn't say anything and seemed to be weighing the situation, but then in a soft voice, after glancing at the door where Sofia had left the room, she said with urgency, 'Will you help me find her?'

'Of course I will, Granny.'

'Before it's too late?' Granny added quietly and looked away before adding, 'I'm not getting any younger and I want to know what became of her. It really would mean a great deal to me, my dear.'

'Oh, Granny, please, it will never be too late, I'll always help you if I can . . . and besides, the doctor said you're in excellent health!' And Maddie gently placed a hand on her granny's arm in comfort. It was true, Granny was in remarkably good shape, physically; it was just her memory that was failing her. 'Is Audrey a friend of yours? Or someone you used to know and lost touch with, perhaps? If you'd like to see her, then I could call her or write to her for you . . . if you have a phone number or an address?'

'Oh no, dear, she isn't a friend,' Granny said hesitantly, then sat quietly, her eyes losing focus as she stared out into the middle distance over Maddie's shoulder. Then creasing her forehead and clasping her hands in front of her as if in anguish, Granny refocused, leaned in closer to Maddie and said in an even quieter voice, 'she's a baby . . .'

4

The following day at Honeysuckle Cottage, the two sisters, their curiosity piqued, were eager to find out more about the mysterious baby. Granny had clammed up completely after Sofia had returned from the bathroom, changing the subject when Maddie had delicately mentioned Audrey again to see if she could garner some clues to help her decide where to start the search. Was she still a baby? Or was Granny getting confused and Audrey was a baby in a memory from many years ago?

Now, sitting at the kitchen table, Maddie and Sofia were drinking sweet tea and mulling it all over.

'I still can't believe she didn't remember me!' Sofia said, lifting the saucer and taking a sip from one of Granny's delicate bone china teacups.

Seeing the wounded look on her sister's face, Maddie reached across the table and gave her arm a quick pat. 'Are you OK?'

'Yes, I'm fine,' Sofia said, followed by a short silence. 'Well, I suppose Granny is bound to remember much more about you than she is about me. She hardly ever saw me when I was growing up, so maybe that has something to do with it.' Sofia pursed her lips and placed the saucer back on the table before flicking her hair over her shoulders.

'Ah, I'm sure that isn't the reason, and besides, you've lived here in Tindledale for a long time now . . . since you and Ben got married.' Maddie instinctively knew to tread carefully with this particular line of conversation as Sofia, her younger half-sister, had grown up in a beautiful, whitewashed Spanish villa by the sea in Valencia with Maddie's dad and his second wife. She'd been five when her parents divorced and her dad went off to Spain. He'd married a Spanish woman, and Sofia was born a year later into what Maddie's mum referred to as 'a charmed life of sunshine and luxury', in stark contrast to the inclement English weather and unhappy childhood that Maddie endured. Never allowed to visit her dad, but always yearning to be a part of his seemingly magical, idyllic life in Spain. Yet Sofia seemed to think she had missed out on years of cosy visits to Granny's cottage by growing up in Spain, when the reality was that she hadn't got the short straw at all. Quite the opposite, in fact, as far as Maddie was concerned.

After the divorce, Maddie had a rocky childhood alone with her volatile mum who drank too much. Over the years, her mum had grown even more insular and emotionally distanced from Maddie, keeping Granny – her ex-husband's mother – very much at arm's length. So Maddie hadn't been able to enjoy cosy visits with her lovely Granny. Both sisters had missed out, Granny too. In fact, Maddie's memory of those childhood years with her mum were mostly of feeling isolated and alone, interspersed with the highlight of her week – a phone call from Dad. He made her laugh with his groan-inducing jokes, never knowing how much Maddie missed him because she hadn't wanted to say and run the risk of spoiling the precious conversations that meant so much to her.

Pushing the painful memories away, Maddie took a pastel pink macaron and popped it into her mouth, savouring the sweet taste. 'Maybe Granny's memory issue is just a temporary thing. The shock of the fall, as it were. It could have made her anxious to the point she just can't think straight.' Her voice tailed off; they both knew this was wishful thinking.

Sofia sighed. 'There's no getting away from the fact that Granny has been forgetful for a very long time now. A few months back, when Ben and I took Ryan and Sonny to see her, she had no idea who anyone was. At one point she thought Ben was Dad and called him Jim. She laughed it off when I corrected her.' Sofia paused and Maddie winced, replaying in her head how this might have made Granny feel. Sofia was never subtle about these things. 'Yes, she's been very good at covering it up, but I actually think she has dementia and this latest fall has made it even more apparent,' Sofia concluded.

'Maybe,' Maddie said slowly, pausing for a mouthful of tea to give her time to think. 'You could be right, but it doesn't make it any easier to see her like this. I can't bear the thought of losing her.' She dipped her head and fell silent.

'You haven't lost her! Granny isn't dead yet,' Sofia said, and Maddie winced again.

'Fade, then. I don't want to see Granny lose her energy, her essence, and become a shell of her former self with no memory of her life,' Maddie explained. 'There's so much we don't know about her. The girl she once was, the woman in her twenties, thirties and so on. The history of her life. I'd like to find out before it's too late. Before she loses her memory entirely. Don't you think it would be a shame not to know?'

'I guess so,' Sofia shrugged, 'but there isn't much we can do about it.' Both women sat quietly, each with their own thoughts. 'You know, we could just phone

Dad and ask him . . .' Sofia suggested, helping herself to a fruit scone – they had called by the Spotted Pig Café and Tearoom in the village high street on the way here after she'd had a sudden craving for a cream tea. Unable to eat all the generous feast that Kitty, who owned the café, had prepared for them, they had packed up the leftovers into a big cake box. Sofia, not wanting to share the leftover sandwiches and scrumptious scones and cakes with the twins, or Ben, was determined to finish them herself. She was eating for two, after all, she had told Maddie, followed by telling her too that this wasn't actually a thing these days, according to the midwife. Sofia cut the scone in two and slathered it in strawberry jam and clotted cream before licking a blob of jam from her fingertips and taking a big bite. 'Mmm! This is so good,' she murmured, momentarily closing her eyes as if she was in some kind of cake paradise. Maddie laughed on seeing her sister with jam and cream all around her mouth like a child as she devoured the scone in record time.

'Why are you laughing? I'm just getting started,' Sofia told her, laughing too as she wiped her mouth and went for a miniature Battenberg slice next.

'Don't let me stop you,' Maddie said vaguely, her mind elsewhere.

'What is it?' Sofia gave her a prod. 'I know that look on your face . . . you're pondering, overthinking it all as usual.'

'Well, I was wondering if we should have a look around here in Granny's cottage?' It was true, Maddie's mind was working overtime. Granny had asked for her help and now she was determined to find out who Audrey was and what had become of her.

'You mean go through Granny's things? Like a pair of nosey parkers?' Sofia laughed.

'No, not exactly . . .' Maddie shook her head. 'I just thought it might help put Granny's mind at rest if we could find some information about this Audrey she keeps mentioning. She's clearly concerned about her whereabouts, and it's sad to see her fretting about it. You're right though, we shouldn't snoop, it was a bad idea.' She lifted a hand as if to bat the thoughts away before helping herself to a mini profiterole.

'No, it isn't! Come on, let's start with the sideboard in the dining room – I know there are photo albums in there, do you remember? Granny got them out to show us when we were children . . . so it wouldn't be like we were snooping, because we've already seen them before. If they were secret then she would never have shown them to us, would she?'

'I guess not,' Maddie agreed. Sofia polished off the last of the Battenberg, wiped her hands and lips on a napkin and, pressing her palms down on the arms of the chair, she heaved herself up into a standing position.

'Mads, think I may have overdone it on the cake, after all!' she groaned, smoothing down her dress and straightening her back. 'I'm completely stuffed! Any chance you can roll me along the hallway and into the sitting room?'

Thirty minutes later, they had been through all the photo albums but hadn't come across any pictures of babies, apart from some of Sofia as a newborn pressed to Dad's bare chest soon after birth in the hospital, and then plenty at various stages of her childhood in Spain, right through to when she was a teenager and came on trips to Tindledale. There were a few of Maddie too, but only up to the age of five. Her mum hadn't taken many photos after the divorce, and she wouldn't have shared them with her mother-in-law if she had. There were some from when Maddie was a teenager and able to visit Granny of her own volition without her mum needing to be involved, or indeed able to stop her, as she had done during her earlier childhood, apart from the odd Sunday afternoon tea that Maddie had been allowed to go to at Granny's cottage when her dad had been visiting. Those times with Granny in her cosy cottage had been a highlight for Maddie, so she felt that trying to find out about Audrey was the least she could do to repay her grandmother for giving her glimmers of happiness when she had needed them most.

'Oh well, I guess it was worth looking.' Sofia snapped the last album shut, making Maddie jump from her reverie, and then frowned from the comfort of the armchair where she had been sitting while Maddie passed the albums over to her. 'No baby pictures, apart from Dad, and then us two. And a few black-and-white photos of people neither of us recognise, dressed up in old-fashioned clothes.'

'Hmm, strange, isn't it?' Maddie said. 'How come there aren't any pictures of Granny's life before she had Dad? There aren't any of her as a young woman, or with her parents. And why are there blank sections in the albums? It's as if somebody has taken pictures out; you can see where corner mounts are still in place where they used to be.' Maddie gathered up all the photo albums strewn over the carpet and neatly stowed them back in the sideboard.

'Guess it would have been such a long time ago, maybe they just didn't have cameras in those days?' Sofia shrugged. 'And as for the missing pictures, maybe the family fell out and someone tore them up. You know, like they do in those old black-and-white movies where the heartbroken heroine is seen ripping photos from albums or cutting her lover out with a large pair of scissors before falling back on a chaise to sob.'

'Are you talking about the silent movies of the Twenties? Because Dad's not that old!' Maddie laughed. 'And there were definitely cameras long before he was born.'

'OK. Well, I don't know . . . I was never any good at history.' Sofia let out a bored puff of air.

'I'd love to see what Granny looked like when she was a young girl; it fascinates me seeing moments in history captured in a photo. Just like the photos we took of you yesterday . . . one day they will be a moment in history for your great grandchildren to cherish.'

'Oh, don't get all sentimental or my hormones will go into overdrive, and you'll make me cry.' Sofia shook her head. 'If you're that interested, why don't we have a proper snoop?' She raised her eyes to the ceiling where Granny's bedroom was directly above them. 'I know there's a suitcase on top of her wardrobe, one of those old-fashioned brown leather ones with two metal locks on, because when Ben and I were helping her pack up some personal things for the move to Evergreens, I asked her if she wanted it down to take with her. She went quiet and didn't answer, as if she hadn't heard me . . . but I'm quite sure she had as when I turned back around, I saw her in the dressing table mirror, and she was looking up to where the suitcase was stored and had a very odd look on her face.

'What do you mean, "odd"?' Maddie frowned.

'You know . . .' and Sofia lifted her eyebrows and creased her forehead to show Maddie an exaggerated version of what Granny's face looked like. 'Sad. Or worried . . . a bit afraid, maybe. Could there be something in the suitcase that she didn't want anyone to see?'

'Maybe we shouldn't snoop then. If Granny has a secret hidden away in the suitcase, it's not right to go looking.' Maddie shook her head.

'But of course it is – especially if it's going to help her! And you said that's what you wanted to do: put her mind at rest. Come on,' Sofia added before her sister had time to contemplate further.

Upstairs, Maddie gingerly pushed open the door to Granny's bedroom, the scent of her Dior perfume still hanging faintly in the air, even though she had been living at Evergreens for well over a year now. Maddie only came into this room occasionally to hoover the carpet and clean the windows as she always felt as though she were intruding in Granny's private space. But perhaps Sofia was right, and today was different;

they were here to find something to help put Granny's mind at rest, after all.

Moving into the room, Maddie instinctively went to loop a tieback that had fallen from one of the heavy brocade curtains. Granny liked the cottage to be kept nice and tidy, so she knew that the curtains needed to be just so. The same for the magnificent old kidney-shaped dressing table with triple mirrors and matching pink velvet-covered stool where Maddie had vague memories of her much younger self sitting on the bed and watching Granny dust face powder over her cheeks before applying a coat of crimson lipstick and teasing her hair with a wooden paddle brush. Maddie had thought her granny looked so glamorous and sophis-ticated, like a princess, always serene and elegant too and she wished one day, when she was a grown-up, to look and be just like her. There was a light layer of dust coating the dressing table's glass top and some of the cosmetics and pots of face cream were still there as if waiting to be used.

Sofia went to move the dressing table stool over to the wardrobe. Maddie gave her younger sister a look and swiftly swiped the stool away. 'You can't climb on this,' she said as Sofia slipped her shoes off and prepared to step on the stool. 'It's too risky with a baby onboard.'

'Oh, I'm sure it'll be fine,' Sofia brushed her off, reaching out a hand to take the stool back. 'I was up a step ladder painting the nursery on the day I went into labour with the twins!' she added nonchalantly.

'What?' Maddie put her hand to her mouth, horrified.

'And Ben doesn't know, so don't you be telling him.' Sofia pouted.

'Exactly!' Maddie glared. 'Because you know he would tell you off too.'

'It's only a tiny stool. But OK, if you insist.' Sofia held up her arms in acceptance. 'Be quick though, I'm dying to know what's inside the suitcase.' And with a big sigh she flopped into the armchair by the window instead.

Maddie climbed the step ladder and retrieved the suitcase from the top of the solid mahogany wood wardrobe.

'I wonder if this is the reason Granny didn't want you to get the suitcase down,' Maddie said, sneezing several times in quick succession. 'It's covered in a thick layer of dust, and you know how particular she is about keeping things neat and tidy.'

'Just open the suitcase, Mads, I can't bear the suspense any longer,' Sofia sighed.

'OK, here goes.' Maddie put the suitcase on the end of the bed and pushed the little buttons underneath the locks and held her breath, inwardly willing them to open, which they did with a satisfying snap. Sofia was out of the armchair now and peering over Maddie's shoulder.

'Oh, is that it?' Sofia elbowed her way around Maddie to get a better look. Both women saw the suitcase was packed full of old newspaper cuttings, bundles of letters and postcards, photos and cinema or theatre programmes. Everything was faded and looked as if it had been soaked in water at some point as the pages in the programmes on one side were all crinkled and stuck together, so at first glance it was impossible to read the words where the ink had smudged. The first programme on the top of the pile appeared to date back to the 1940s, or 50s even, as on the cover there was a jaunty picture in technicolour of a teenage girl with vibrant auburn hair in a vintage style buttercup yellow gingham full circle dress cinched in at the waist with a wide belt and long gloves up to her elbows.

'I can't see anything at all about a baby,' Maddie said as she sifted through the contents, before lifting out a cardboard framed photo. She turned it over. 'Oh wow! There's a picture of an extremely glamorous woman though, she looks like a movie star from the 1950s, Marilyn Monroe or Jayne Mansfield . . . with

platinum blonde waved hair and immaculate make-up.
It looks like a professional shot too. And there's another
picture here . . .' Maddie leaned over and handed the
headshot to Sofia, then picked up what appeared to
be a holiday snap. 'Look at this one of a woman in a
sundress – she looks really happy with a big smile.'
Sofia pulled up the pink stool and lowered herself
down on it. The woman in the photo was wearing a
headscarf covering her hair and big shades, but it was
hard to tell if it was the same woman as the one in
the headshot. 'She looks so glamorous reclining on
the side of a boat with the most wonderful backdrop.
Look at that rugged shoreline with rocks rising from
the sea. It's quite sensational.'

'Could any of these women be Granny?' Sofia asked,
picking up the headshot photo to scrutinise it. 'The
glamorous woman in the picture does actually look a
bit like her . . . a much, much younger version of
Granny perhaps, she's definitely familiar, but it's hard
to be sure . . . she sort of looks the same, but different,
if that makes sense. It could be the old-fashioned
make-up and styling that's making me wonder. Was
she famous? Was Granny a movie star in the olden
days?' Sofia laughed.

'I'm sure we'd know about something like that. Dad
or Granny would have mentioned it, wouldn't they?'

Maddie shook her head. 'The woman in the headshot picture looks utterly gorgeous. She's famous for sure, so if this is Granny back in the day, then why on earth would she keep a secret like that? I'd want to make sure my grandchildren knew just how cool I was,' she laughed. 'It's exciting!'

'Let me see that one.' Sofia took the picture that Maddie had in her hand and tapped the corner of the photo. 'There's a name written in swirly old-fashioned writing. K-e . . . something and a surname starting with S-i-n-c. Can you make out what the rest says, Mads?'

'It looks like it could be Kelly and possibly Sinclair.' Maddie took the photo back and lifted it up to the light to get a good look. 'Oh, hang on a moment . . . there's another word with a date underneath, it's very faint, but I can just make out a C and an A and a P—'

'Capri!' bellowed Sofia, right in Maddie's ear. 'I thought I recognised those rocks. The famous Faraglioni rocks in the sea around the island of Capri! I love it there. I remember when I went on holiday to Capri with Dad. The first time was when I was about six or seven, and then when I was ten or so and loads of times after that. My mum loves it there too, going sailing and seeing all the rock caves around the coastline and the blue grotto. I used to think it was magical, and then there was the shopping in those gorgeous white-canopied boutiques in the cobbled, winding lanes. All the most exclusive designer shops are on a little street called Via Camerelle.' She paused, lost in memory, placing the tip of an index finger to her bottom lip before carrying on: 'What with the sunbathing and the seafood and the scenery, it's all so incredible and picturesq—'

'I'm sure,' Maddie jumped in, a bit too quickly, trying to push away a horrible dart of jealousy on hearing how wonderful Sofia's childhood sounded, compared to her own one where she couldn't remember ever going on holiday, certainly not to a foreign country. And Mum had always refused to let Maddie go to stay with her dad in Spain, not even when he offered, one summer, to pay for her flights. Fast-forward through the years and it still hurt that Dad barely visited her back then, just those occasional 'afternoon teas' at Granny's on the rare occasions he came back to Tindledale. Maddie was never able to tell her dad what she really felt for fear of upsetting her granny. Maybe she should ask him about it one day.

Inhaling sharply, she let out a long steadying breath and scrutinised the picture some more. 'There's a one and a nine in the date, and then a five and then another number, possibly a zero, so it looks like the picture might have been taken in 1950.'

'Interesting! But it can't be Granny in that case,' Sofia said, 'her name isn't Kelly, for a start . . .'

5

Later, when Sofia had left, Maddie called her dad to tell him what they had found.

'How are you, Maddie . . . everything OK?' he asked on answering.

'Well, yes and no . . . Granny had a fall yesterday.'

'Oh no,' he immediately said, his voice full of concern. 'Is she all right? Why didn't anyone call me?'

'Yes, she's fine, Dad, just a little graze on her forehead,' Maddie assured him. 'But the staff said Granny was asking about someone called Audrey. It isn't the first time she's done that, and when I asked her who Audrey was, she couldn't remember at first, then she told me Audrey's a baby and asked me to help her find her . . . Granny wants to know what became of her. I don't suppose you know who Granny's talking about, do you?'

'A baby?' There was a short silence as he pondered, and Maddie wondered if he was folding his elbows and frowning as he usually did when deep in thought.

'No, sorry I don't know. Is this what you're trying to find out?'

'Yes, Granny seemed quite upset about it, so I want to put her mind at rest,' Maddie told him, knowing it was more than this. She was curious to know as well; she was interested in people, it's why she took photos, she presumed, and loved people-watching, and now she had an opportunity to discover more about her own grandmother's life story. Maddie so hoped her grandmother felt that she had lived a fulfilled life, and if there was a way to ensure the last part of her life was pleasant and worry-free then Maddie was going to do all that she could to make that happen.

'I know, love, and it's a shame. She shouldn't have to be worrying about anything at her time of life,' Dad said, echoing Maddie's thoughts. 'I'm glad you called actually – I phoned Evergreens earlier on for the weekly update and Janice said your granny was far too upset to talk to me. Apparently she kept saying she should have been more careful all those years ago, that she should have stopped me and that I never would have left if she had done so. Janice didn't mention anything about a fall, though.'

'Oh Dad. Janice was probably just busy, plus Granny seemed perfectly fine when we saw her yesterday – a bit forgetful, but physically OK. Maybe Janice didn't see the need to mention the fall and worry you unnecessarily, not when Sofia and I had already visited. But it's strange that Granny would think it was her fault you left – what could she mean?'

'When I left Tindledale to move to Spain, I presume.'

'Ah,' Maddie started, unsure of what to say next because they had never really spoken about Dad leaving. Not even when it had happened all those years ago when she was a little girl. She had no memory of ever being sat down and having it explained to her. The two of them had always skirted around the subject until it had just become the way things were – her dad lived in Spain. Everything her Mum had to say on the subject was very negative, and so Maddie had always avoided the topic. Just as she wished to right now, so she added a vague, 'but that was a long time ago.' And swiftly changed the subject with, 'I wonder what she means by "should have stopped you . . . and been more careful." Careful about what?'

'I've no idea.' Dad let out a long breath. 'Your grandmother never did anything wrong; she's always been kind and very caring, and she was all for me moving to Spain. In fact, I distinctly remember her saying to go for it and create a wonderful life because love can disappear in the blink of an eye.'

'Oh, that's a lovely thing to say . . . but a little bittersweet, don't you think? I wonder if Granny had love that disappeared . . .' Maddie pondered.

'Yes, it is a lovely thing to say. It was years ago, of course,' Dad noted, 'but I remember it like it was only yesterday. Granny has always been very private, very unassuming, and never one for expressing strong emotions, which is why it's completely out of character for her to be upset to the point of not wanting to speak to me.' Maddie heard her dad sigh as if he was trying to work out what on earth was going on.

'You know, Granny doesn't mean anything by it, she's getting confused, that's all.' Maddie sat down on the bed.

'Maybe, but I'm a bit troubled by it all myself, Maddie. I wonder if it might be best if I come over for a visit as soon as I can. I know her memory isn't what it used to be, so I want to sit in front of her, hold her hand and bottle the moment while she can still remember who I am,' he finished quietly. There was a short silence as Maddie contemplated telling him about Granny not remembering who Sofia was yesterday, but quickly thought it best not to; he'd only worry more and feel even more guilty.

'That would be great, Dad, I'm sure Granny would love to see you . . . and the rest of us would too.'

'That's settled then, I'll sort out the arrangements and see when I can visit.'

'OK, Dad. And please, if you remember anything at all that might help us work out who Audrey is, then let me know. I'm intrigued to find out.'

'Of course, but nothing good ever came of raking up the past, love . . . maybe she's just got muddled up and Audrey is an old friend she lost touch with years ago.'

'But why would she say she's a baby?'

'Well, she could be someone else's baby. Perhaps she belongs to a family visiting one of the other residents at Evergreens. That'll be it.' Her dad was beginning to sound a bit impatient.

'Are you sure you can't remember? If she's an old friend, I might be able to find her . . . or perhaps a distant cousin or whatever . . . someone you never met.'

'Mum was never one for having lots of friends – she's always kept herself to herself. And as you know, she's not one for dredging up the past either. "No point in dwelling, best to look forward," she used to say before her memory started failing. I don't have an aunty called Audrey, or a cousin. I'm an only child, remember, and my dad was too, and he died when I was a teenager, so I don't have any recollection of ever really knowing that side of the family. And I never met Granny's parents – they died before I was born – but I seem to remember she had a twin sister—'

'Ah, yes,' Maddie jumped in. 'That would make sense. I remember Granny saying twins run in the family when Sofia first told us that she was expecting Ryan and Sonny. Do you remember? It was while we were all spending Christmas together. Granny said it but then wouldn't elaborate. Instead, she poured herself a glass of prosecco and practically downed it in one – and she doesn't usually drink alcohol. It was very strange.'

'That's not like her at all,' Dad sighed. 'And I can't think why she would react in this way. I think she also had a brother who died in the Second World War. But I grew up with a sense of there having been a family rift of some kind. Maybe that's why she clammed up: she fell out with her twin sister and didn't want to talk about it or be reminded of something painful. If that's the case, it would probably be best if we just let it be, Maddie. We don't want to upset her.'

'Guess so. But, Dad, when she told me that Audrey was a baby, Granny looked upset, wary – frightened even, like she was going to get into trouble.'

'Maddie, please. Like I said, better to let it rest, love. Especially if Granny looked wary and frightened; I

don't want you making things worse. Your grandmother has had her fair share of heartache with my
dad dying when I was such a young lad, so it could
really upset her if we start asking questions about the
past and bringing it all up again. I mean it, I'd like
you to stop.' Her dad had a tremble in his voice that
Maddie had never heard before, and it brought her up
short.

'Yes, OK, I guess you're right,' she agreed reluctantly,
feeling deflated as she really didn't want to let her
grandmother down after she had made a promise to
see if she could find Audrey. But her dad sounded
resolute, and the last thing she ever wanted to do was
cause her granny any upset, so maybe it was better
to let sleeping dogs lie.

6

Maddie had finished her shift at the Duck & Puddle pub and was back at the kitchen table with the suitcase on a chair beside her and a notepad and pen with which she was writing down anything that might possibly be related to the mysterious Audrey, all the while looking for clues to the identity of the beautiful woman with the platinum blonde hair. Since talking to her dad, she had been thinking more about what he had said. While she agreed with him about not upsetting her grandmother, she couldn't stop thinking about her grandmother's angst when she had asked for her help. Surely it couldn't do any harm to have a look at the contents of the suitcase?

She saw a bundle of letters tied with a pink ribbon; maybe the answers were here, and she should try to find something definite . . . yes that's what she would do, discover a fact that couldn't be disputed, then her dad would have to listen to her. And there were plenty of old newspaper cuttings too, yellowing and curled at the edges, about a woman, a Hollywood actress in the 1950s, so it seemed their guess about the woman in the little framed picture earlier had been correct. Kelly Sinclair. Maddie had written that at the top of one of her pages and underlined it. But so far, the rest of the page was almost blank except for the names of some of the shows – amateur dramatics or pantomimes by the looks of it, dating back to the 1940s. She hadn't come across anything linking to her grandmother, although it was hard to see much at all with the water damage having washed away many of the words. And some of the notes, and what looked like an official letter of some sort, with typed words and an insignia at the top, weren't written in English, so Maddie had no idea what they said.

Sifting through the contents of the suitcase again, Maddie's fingers touched on something hard inside a brown envelope. She lifted out the envelope and, after opening it, tipped out the contents. A gold chain with a small cross on the end puddled on the table. Looping the chain over the tips of her fingers, she let the cross dangle as she pondered who it might belong to. She knew her grandmother had her faith and went to Mass, and she always wore a small cross on a chain around her neck. If this cross did belong to her, why was it hidden away inside a brown envelope in a suitcase on top of her wardrobe? Maddie carefully stowed the cross back in the envelope and put it inside the suitcase then turned her attention to some old-fashioned magazines with quaint titles such as *Picturegoer* and movie stars on the covers. One in particular caught Maddie's eye, a glorious image of Vivien Leigh, the iconic actress who starred in *Gone with the Wind*. Maybe her grandmother had just been a film lover in her younger years. It could just be as simple as that. She was a fan of this Kelly Sinclair, whoever she might be.

And then Maddie had an idea. She dashed up to her bedroom to grab her laptop and, after racing back downstairs, she flipped open the lid and typed *Kelly Sinclair* into Google. Seeing pages of social media accounts with that name, Maddie scrolled through them all before giving up and changing her search to see if she could get a list of old movie stars. Again, the search returned many pages of information. Maddie started tapping her way through and was about to give up when she spotted something halfway down a page about stars of the 1950s.

The beautiful blonde English actress Kelly Sinclair returns from holidaying in Capri at Gracie Fields' exclusive hotel to commence filming her first lead role, starring alongside Hollywood big hitter Clarke King. Already there's talk of an Oscar nomination . . .

Maddie glanced at the top of the page and saw that the article was written in 1953. Intrigued, she searched on through pages and pages detailing stars of the Golden Age of Hollywood: Elizabeth Taylor, Marilyn Monroe, Grace Kelly, Audrey Hepburn, etc. Men too: Maddie lingered on a smouldering picture of the actor, Clarke King, mentioned in the previous article. *Mmm, now he is hot!* She could see why the article had referred to him as a big hitter – she imagined he most definitely was a hit with moviegoers. She wondered where he was now . . .

Checking the time on her phone, and now conscious of having spent an hour on the contents of the suitcase and scrolling through Google, she got up to put the kettle on, still deep in thought. Even if Granny was just a super fan of Kelly's back in the Fifties, why wouldn't she want to take the suitcase with her to Evergreens? Surely it would be a comfort to look through the old memorabilia? And why had she been so coy when Sofia spotted it on top of the wardrobe? Whoever Kelly Sinclair was, it still didn't get Maddie any closer to finding out more about baby Audrey.

The kettle boiled. Maddie opened the fridge and, on seeing that she had forgotten to buy milk, poured herself a glass of wine instead, lit a sandalwood scented candle to help her relax and found a packet of kettle crisps, figuring she might as well make an evening of it. She didn't have anything else to do, other than her knitting or binge-watching a boxset, and had declined Sofia's invitation to pop round to hers after she finished work at the pub, because she had a feeling that Sofia would be telling Ben all about her childhood holidays to Capri. Though she knew it was ridiculous to feel jealous of her younger sister having had a far happier childhood than she had, full of travel and laughter, parties, shopping in exclusive boutiques and exciting opportunities, it was hard not to sometimes.

Swallowing a sip of wine, she wondered how her mum was. She lived in Liverpool now and Maddie hadn't seen her in ages. They talked on the phone occasionally, when Maddie called and Mum actually picked up and spoke to her with a degree of coherency, which was a rarity, but that was about it really. Maddie had also tried over the years to instigate a conversation with her mum about seeking help for the excessive drinking, but it always ended the same way: with Maddie being told off for interfering and being put firmly back in her place.

Maddie polished off the crisps and, after wiping her hands, not wanting to spoil the bundle of letters with her greasy fingertips, she untied the pink ribbon keeping everything together and glanced again at the rest of the suitcase contents. She wondered whether her dad had ever opened the case and sifted through the many letters and photographs and theatre programmes. Then again, maybe he had more restraint than she had and never felt compelled to snoop through his mum's things . . . But having opened the suitcase, Maddie was committed now. Always a great believer in things happening for a reason, she decided that it would be a good thing if the contents of the case led her to find Audrey. Perhaps her dad could then get onboard.

She paused on a postcard. On turning it over, she mouthed 'wow' to herself at the sight of Capri spelled out in colourful lettering at the corner of an exquisite picture of dazzling blue sea surrounded by lush green, mist-capped mountains dotted with pink bougain-villea and mimosa trees. It looked amazing. No wonder Sofia had gushed about going there. Maddie could see that it was breathtakingly beautiful and wished she could visit Capri too. The postcard was dated 1953 but water damage had smudged part of the writing, so it was impossible to see who had written the words.

> *Here with my darling sweetheart in a lemon-scented paradise! We had dinner in the gorgeously romantic Lemon Tree restaurant with a view of the beautiful sea and sipped limoncello cocktails and ate grilled lobster while listening to the gentle ebb and flow of the waves as we watched the sun set . . .*

Maddie quickly made a note to google *Lemon Tree restaurant, Capri*, because she was already longing to see what it looked like. And there was something else too . . . a photograph that was folded in half. Maddie had spotted it tucked inside one of the old programmes at the bottom of the box. She opened it carefully. And ran her eyes over the image in front of her, holding her breath as she saw that it was a black-and-white picture of a baby lying on a blanket in a garden. The baby had a kiss curl on her forehead and was dressed in an old-fashioned cotton romper suit, with knitted bootees on her feet and a bonnet tied with a ribbon underneath her chin. Quickly turning the image over again, Maddie read the words written in swirly old-fashioned cursive letters on the back: *Darling Audrey*.

'I've found her!' she couldn't help crying out to herself in triumph: she had a photograph of Audrey in her hand! Her first thought was to take it to her grandmother in the morning, hoping it would jog her memory. But then Maddie remembered what her dad had said, and the firmness in his voice. He was right, there had to be a reason why her grandmother never talked about her past, why she had clammed up that Christmas when the conversation had turned to there being twins in the family . . . After all, what did any of them know about her past? Very little indeed. There were no photos of Granny as a young woman in those old albums, so it was almost as if the past had been erased. And there had to be a reason for that, so maybe she should tread carefully after all. Maddie sighed, running a finger over the picture before placing it back inside the suitcase. If only her dad knew a bit more, or was at least open to her trying to find out. After all, Granny clearly wanted to know what had become of Audrey, and Maddie didn't think it was fair to ignore her plea for help.

She was reaching to pick up a bundle of letters when her phone buzzed.

'Hey, camera girl!' a voice bellowed in her ear.

'Cynthia!' Maddie glanced at the screen to double-check before pushing it back to her ear; a chat with Cynthia always lifted her spirits. 'What have you been up to?'

'Oh, the usual: pub work and taking pictures. Oh, and discovering a mystery baby in the family.'

'What?' Cynthia roared. 'Is this for real? Or a wind-up?'

'Yep. All real. Can you believe it . . . I found a box full of old photos, letters and postcards. It seems my granny had some connection to an actress called Kelly Sinclair back in the Fifties and there's a postcard from Capri dated 1953. The island looks magical. There's also mention of a romantic dinner at the Lemon Tree restaurant overlooking the sea. I don't know who sent the postcard from Capri but I'm finding it all fascinating. Living history, as they say, and there are lots more letters and other memorabilia still to go through, so who knows what else I might discover. I'm beginning to wonder if my granny might actually *be* Kelly Sinclair. They do look a bit alike, even after all this time.'

'That would be incredible,' Cynthia said. 'How is your lovely granny?'

'She's doing OK, apart from a graze on her face from another fall—'

'Ouch, your poor granny.'

'It's a shame, isn't it. And mentally . . . her memory is fading,' Maddie sighed.

'Ah, that can't be easy for her . . . or you,' Cynthia said.

'No, it isn't . . . it's hard seeing her decline and getting confused.'

'I'm sure,' Cynthia said kindly, then a few seconds later, added, 'Now, talking of Capri, in *Italy* . . . She paused momentarily and, given the emphasis, Maddie's pulse quickened in anticipation of what Cynthia might say next.

'Italy? Cynthia, is this what I think it might be – what I've been hoping for?' Maddie held her breath, mentally crossing her fingers for the dream photoshoot in Italy, her first proper job for a big brand, to become a reality.

'That's right. The shoot. Do you fancy it? The Italian job is yours if you want it—'

'YES! Yes, yes, yes, I want it. Of course, I'd love to.' Maddie's heart soared, but then a dart of doubt crept in. 'Are you definitely sure? I called the booking agency directly and the woman I spoke to didn't seem at all interested in my work—'

'Well, someone there loved your portfolio because it was the first thing they mentioned when I called. "Doesn't your friend want the job?" is what the guy said. Apparently they sent you an email raving about

69

your latest look – rustic, romantic pics with perfect lighting and contrast of colours and just the vibe they are going for with the Italian shoot. It's going to be outdoors in a vineyard in Naples . . . but you hadn't replied, so—'

'What?' Maddie yelled, aghast. 'How could I have missed it!' She frantically tapped the screen to flick through to her inbox. After doing a search she found the email and all her doubts immediately faded and her confidence soared – it was there in black and white: the perfect opportunity to launch her career as a proper photographer. She felt as if she had won the lottery.

'I can't believe it! You're right, there's an email . . . in my junk folder.' She inhaled sharply, feeling like a fool for missing it, but elated all the same to have won the job on her own merit, without having to rely solely on Cynthia putting in a good word for her. 'Honestly, Cyn, I can't tell you how much this means . . . it's a dream come true.'

'Good. You deserve it. You're a brilliant photographer. And you had better pack all your camera gear right away because we leave tomorrow! I took the liberty of presuming you would say yes and so got my assistant to book a flight for you as well. I can meet you at the airport.'

'Tomorrow?' Maddie froze. 'But I can't go tomorrow!' She felt panicky now. 'Dad is planning to come over to England; what's he going to think if I'm not even here? And what about Sofia . . . she might need me to look after the twins, I don't want to disappoint her and, well . . . I promised my grandmother that I'd help her find Audrey, and I can't let her dow—'

'Maddie! This is your moment. Stop looking for excuses. You'll be back in plenty of time for the baby. It's not your job to make sure everyone else is taken care of and feeling happy!'

'Hmm . . . I know, you're right,' Maddie agreed. 'But what if my photography skills aren't up to it? It's one thing putting together a portfolio with pictures of my sister in the back garden . . . but working with professional models and a high end fashion designer is something different entirely.'

'You're a fantastic photographer, that's just nerves talking,' Cynthia said. 'There's nothing, nobody, holding you back. And you could even go and see the Lemon Tree restaurant mentioned in the postcard from Capri for yourself. I know you've always wanted to travel so now is your chance . . . you could literally relive history from the 1950s.'

'Could I?' she asked, looking down at all the correspondence in the suitcase; there was so much more still to discover.

'Of course. The shoot is in Naples, which if I'm not mistaken is only a boat ride away from the island of Capri; you could do it in a day trip!'

Maddie felt her pulse quicken. Then remembering how she had felt earlier when Sophia had been talking about her magnificent sounding holidays in Capri . . . well, she thought it really would be wonderful to go there too.

'And Capri is such a small island so there can't be that many Lemon Tree restaurants. You never know, if you ask around you might find someone who remembers this Kelly Sinclair. It's entirely possible, if she was a movie star, as they all went there in the 1950s, and she could be connected somehow to the baby Audrey in the photo. So, you could still be helping your granny out after all.'

'Yes, you're right, Cyn, it would be wonderful . . .' Maddie said, mulling it all over. She was thrilled of course and loved the thought of going to Capri, thinking she could have a fantastic holiday after she finished the photoshoot in Naples. It would give her a chance to have a proper read of the letters in the suitcase to see if there was some concrete link to Audrey, something irrefutable that her dad would then have to get on board with. But Maddie had never been very good with spur-of-the-moment decisions.

'Maddie!' Cynthia yelled, snapping her back to the moment. 'Do you want to come to Italy or not? Do you want to be a fashion photographer for real? For it to be your job, your career, the thing you've always dreamed of?'

'Yes, yes you know I do.'

'Then, for crying out loud, stop dithering! Grab your camera gear and let's go! Designer fashion shoots for high-end magazines in Naples don't come along every day, so you are coming – and that's the end of it.'

An overwhelming sense of excitement surged through Maddie. This was her moment. She may not have had the holiday lifestyle as a child with her dad that Sofia had, but Maddie was going to make up for it now. She was going to Naples, and then she fully intended on having a holiday and taking a boat to Capri and seeing the glorious sights that Sofia had talked about. Maybe she would manage to find some clues and discover who the mysterious, glamorous Kelly Sinclair really was. And if she turned out to be her granny, then why had she kept it a secret? Where was the Lemon Tree restaurant perched on the cliffside with the sumptuous view? Maddie was going to start there, and she too was going to sip limoncello cocktails and eat grilled lobster while listening to the gentle ebb and flow of the waves in the distance as the sun set. Yes, Maddie could not wait for her Italian adventure to begin . . .

7

Capri, one week later

The fashion photoshoot was in the can and Maddie was overjoyed to hear the designer was so impressed with her work that he had specifically requested her to do the pictures for his autumn collection too. She was delighted at the prospect of having more work lined up, and now with her confidence growing, she fully intended to make sure she kept the momentum going by creating an exclusive summer collection of exquisite Mediterranean island escape photos all taken here in Capri to add to her portfolio. She was on her way, having enjoyed the photoshoot in Naples immensely. And it had certainly taken her mind off wondering what Brad was up to in New York, with no more unsettling dreams, as she'd had back in Tindledale in the months following the break-up. Now she just had an exhilarating sense of achievement for

the carefully curated collection that she had created
. . . and been paid well for – certainly enough for her
to enjoy her holiday in Capri. It was all the validation
she needed to feel like a proper fashion and travel
photographer at last.

Having said goodbye to Cynthia, who was on her
way to the airport now, heading to San Diego for her
next job, Maddie was standing on the deck of a ferry
with her camera poised, wanting to capture it all as
she headed for the island of Capri, the hazy
Mediterranean air giving her view a veil of fantasy. As
the mist parted, Maddie could see the majestic rise of
the rugged cypress and myrtle tree-capped mountains
in the distance, and wondered if whoever had written
the postcard from Capri that she had found in her
granny's suitcase had arrived on the ferry too. Had
they seen this exact same view all those years ago?
And then, remembering the photograph of the glamorous woman draped on the side of a boat, maybe
she travelled on one of the many private yachts and
tenders that Maddie could see serenely sailing by. She
had taken several shots of the armada of yachts, and
the sailboats, stunning with their crisp white sails set
against the backdrop of a crystal-clear cerulean sea
that seemed to merge as one with the perfectly cloudless sky. It really was quite breathtaking, and Maddie

loved how this moment seemed to draw her and the woman in the picture closer together over the decades dividing the time when they were each here in this exact same spot. Had the woman wondered back in 1953 what the future would hold for her six decades later? Maddie pondered on it all and her thoughts moved to her own life and what it might have in store for her in sixty years' time. She would be in her nineties by then, if she was fortunate to live to such a grand old age. She hoped that she might have a legacy of some kind to leave behind, although she was never going to be as glamorous as that woman in the photo on the side of the boat!

No, being firmly behind the camera with someone else taking centre stage was much more in Maddie's comfort zone. To be a photographer of some renown would be incredible, with a collection of stylish and technically sophisticated photographs to leave behind when she was gone. But who would she leave them to? Maddie mulled the prospect over in her head as she focused on the waves rippling alongside the hull of the boat, the gentle rhythm comforting and calming as she wondered why it was that she had always been so averse to having a family of her own. Digging deeper, her mind meandered to how she had always felt whenever Brad brought up the 'baby thing', as he called it, in conversation, and how she had instinctively shied away from the idea.

Before Sofia had the twins, Maddie's only experience of parenting was her own unhappy childhood; could that be why she hadn't ever considered it as an option for her? What if she took after her mother and messed it up somehow? Or maybe it had been Brad's insistence, continuously going on about it, implying there was something wrong with her for not wanting it too? Or could it simply have been that she didn't want a baby with him? Now there's a thought!

In the moment, here on the deck of the boat, with the warm breeze making her auburn curls flutter around her face, she felt calm and content, relaxed even, and able to hear herself think . . . really think, so she could consider what it was that she truly wanted for her own life, without Brad's carping voice living rent-free inside her head. And she was sure a frisson of something swirled within her, curiosity perhaps, to explore the possibility of what it might feel like to be solely responsible for another human being. It certainly didn't feel as daunting as it had done in the past. Maybe she did want it. Maybe she could do it. Maybe it would be exciting. Definitely a challenge, she knew that from helping out with the twins. And parenthood needn't be how Brad had always presented it: stay at home and basically give up your own life, is what he'd had in mind for her. Yes, if it ever happened for Maddie then she could see herself with one of those baby carrier slings strapped to her chest as she travelled and showed her child the world and took lots of incredible photos of the memories they would build together.

Maddie had very few photos of her own childhood, a handful at best, kept within the pages of the albums in Granny's sideboard so she would make sure not to repeat that mistake. She would try to be attentive and interested, and most of all she would make sure her child felt loved . . . something that had often been lacking in her own childhood. But she was sure her mother hadn't set out to intentionally distance herself from her daughter and make her feel this way. Maddie knew that the drinking had been a factor and, in her lucid moments, her mum would express regret and promise 'I'll make it up to you'. But Maddie had learned over the years not to get her hopes up as it rarely happened, or there would be some effort for a little while but never sustained, invariably ending up with a late-night phone call full of condemnation and accusations of it having been Maddie's fault for 'complaining so much about missing her dad' or 'going on all the time about wanting to go to Spain to see him'. Maddie had listened to a podcast a while ago, all about taking control of your own life and not repeating recurring patterns, waxing lyrical about the healing power of letting the past go instead of allowing it to define your future. She had been cynical at the time, but maybe there was something in it after all. Weren't we all in charge of our own destiny? Maddie felt as if she'd lost sight of hers for far too long, but she was doing what she had always wanted to, at last: travelling and indulging her wanderlust instead of suppressing it, and it felt incredible, exhilarating . . . Coming to Capri and having a holiday, some time on her own, would give her the opportunity to figure things out and make changes so she could chart a new course. And she was ready! So ready to see what the future held, and whatever this magical island had in store for her . . .

8

As the ferry glided towards the shore, Maddie closed
her eyes and tilted her face upwards to the shimmering
sun to draw in the gloriously enveloping warm air
that was fragranced with a sumptuous scent of lemons
and happiness . . . similar to one of her favourite
perfumes containing juniper and myrtle too. She had
arrived. The prospect of exploring the island was exhilarating and exciting. Glamorous too, as on opening
her eyes she saw a catamaran setting sail with the
Cartier logo along the side and a group of gorgeous
socialites, by the looks of it, dancing on the deck to
upbeat party music. They were all wearing skimpy
designer bikinis and floaty kaftans, the men in shorts
and sliders with impeccable tans, one of them popping
the cork from a magnum of champagne and spraying
it into the crowd. Maddie blushed as an extremely
attractive man with curls the colour of rich, glossy
molasses, a stubbled chin and washboard abdomen

tapering down underneath red swim shorts saw her watching and beckoned for her to hop aboard and join them, yelling something in Italian and feigning a broken heart with both hands pressed to his solid chest when she shook her head to decline his offer.

The ferry came to a halt in the Marina Grande alongside the ubiquitous row of colourful wooden fishing boats bobbing gently in the tide of seawater as it lapped the shore. After disembarking, Maddie was swept along in a throng of tourists all marvelling at the sights and sounds of this beautiful island as they wandered past striped canopied cafes and restaurants. Diners sat at red-and-white-gingham-covered tables, chatting and laughing as they twirled their forks in delicious-looking bowls of linguine or colourful salads piled with shredded burrata, basil and red tomatoes. The air was heavy now with the tantalisingly sweet aroma of garlic and onions mingled with a sugary scent of gelato from a nearby ice cream parlour, pretty with its pastel pink decor. An older couple were sitting side by side at one of the tables admiring the view and sipping prosecco from mini goblets; the woman smiled, raised a glass and tilted her head in greeting as Maddie walked on by. She smiled back and gave the woman a wave, thinking what a wonderful, welcoming place this was.

A Postcard from Capri

Maddie stopped walking and rested her heavy rucksack on top of the silver wheelie camera case and pushed her shades up to see the screen on her phone to check the address of the little Airbnb place she had booked for her holiday. She was staying for a week, which gave her plenty of time to really explore the whole island and take lots of pictures for her portfolio, and hopefully find the Lemon Tree restaurant and someone who may remember a movie star called Kelly Sinclair visiting here in the 1950s. She had even scanned the photo of her to show to anyone who was interested, and the bundle of letters and postcards from the suitcase too, and they were now safely stored on her laptop so she could have a proper read through them all later. The shoot in Naples had been non-stop – working long days and then dinner and socialising late into the night had meant she hadn't had a moment to catch her breath, let alone read the letters. She was looking forward to having some time off to relax. And she needn't have worried about letting Sofia down – she hadn't seemed to mind at all when Maddie had explained about the job opportunity in Italy. In fact she had encouraged her to stay as long as she liked, reiterating what Cynthia had said: if the baby came early, she had Ben to help, and Maddie would be mad not to take the job. Plus, Sofia had thought it a great idea to take the opportunity to travel on to Capri, telling Maddie again what a fantastic place it was. 'Besides, you really do need a holiday, Mads – you've worked flat out since the break-up with Brad.'

Dad hadn't seemed in the least bothered that Maddie wouldn't be in Tindledale when he arrived there. He'd told her not to worry about Granny as he would be there to 'sort it all out'. It had crossed Maddie's mind that perhaps he was relieved she was going to be away working in Italy because it meant there was no risk of her getting too involved in Granny's quest to find Audrey and inadvertently upsetting her by bringing up the past. Maddie wasn't sure how she felt about that possibility, other than it hurt if it was true . . . but then maybe she was overthinking it. Perhaps Sofia and Dad just wanted her to have a good time doing a job she loved and then enjoy a well-earned holiday. In the end, Maddie had made a promise to herself to make the absolute most of being here. Capri was truly magnificent with much to see and experience, that was immediately clear, she thought as she looked all around in wonder at the sights, sounds and smells. It was breathtaking.

Despite Dad's reservations, Maddie was determined to carry on looking for Audrey. If her grandmother really was Kelly Sinclair, then could the baby Audrey in the photo be her daughter? Or a niece . . . a long-lost family member perhaps! Dad had mentioned Granny having a brother who died in the war, and a twin sister too. Or was Maddie just letting her imagination run away with her? There could be a much simpler explanation. But Maddie had an inkling this island held the key, especially after her last visit to Evergreens on the morning of her departure for Naples. Treading carefully, having taken Dad's advice not to mention anything about the contents of the suitcase, Maddie had merely told Granny that she would be away for a few weeks as she was travelling to Italy for work and would then take a short holiday on the island of Capri. As she spoke, she'd been gauging Granny's reaction, looking for confirmation that she really was the glamorous woman on the boat. It turned out Maddie needn't have worried about upsetting her granny by raking up the past, as she had immediately stopped knitting, her face breaking into a wonderfully blissful smile, her eyes softening as she gazed past Maddie and out towards the garden, as if remembering a happy time from long ago. Then, after a few moments lost in reverie, her granny had sighed contently, nodded her head, and looked back to Maddie, holding eye contact as she told her:

'Capri is a very, *very* special place, my dear . . . be sure to savour all the beauty and wonder that it has to offer, for the memory of how you feel when you are there will serve you well for many years to come.'

A bubble of excitement had rippled within Maddie as she wondered again if her grandmother was Kelly Sinclair. If anything, she felt even more certain of it now, but then excitement had turned to concern as the expression on her grandmother's face had changed. Suddenly she looked as wary and fearful as she had the day she asked Maddie to find Audrey. Though Maddie had tried to keep the conversation going, hoping her grandmother would elaborate further, share some memories from her past. Perhaps if she had brought the photos to show her, something in them might have jogged her memory. But, respecting Dad's wishes, she had left them in the cottage along with all the other papers in the suitcase.

Eventually Granny had closed her eyes and leaned back in her chair. Thinking she had fallen asleep, Maddie had gently placed a blanket over her grandmother's knees and was about to tiptoe from the room when she had woken up and muttered, 'Lucia, my dear friend, we had such a wonderful time together in Capri . . .' Then, clasping Maddie's hand, she had added, '. . . she lives in a lemon orchard on a hill, the most beautiful place I ever saw. Please tell her I'm sorry and I don't blame her for forgetting about me.' When Maddie had gently pressed for more by asking what she meant, her granny had faded further and looked blankly before closing her eyes once more. And so, Maddie had made a note of the name, Lucia, and decided to make it her priority to find her. As soon as she had unpacked and had a chance to read through the rest of the letters, she would set off to explore the island and find the lemon orchard on the hill, certain it would be a good starting point.

Her first stop was the kiosk in the harbour, where she bought a ticket and boarded the funicular train. As it slowly climbed the narrow single track up the steep cliffside, she took in the spectacular view of the island, with seagulls soaring and stone and stucco villas clinging to the hillsides while nimble goats roamed freely. On disembarking in Capri town, she made her way out onto a wraparound viewing balcony with several white pillars at the perimeter that were covered in trailing green foliage and pretty pink bougainvillea flowers. Marvelling at the mountainous terrain, with the sea beyond, Maddie wandered towards the edge of the balcony. Leaning against one of the pillars she took a moment to take in the breathtaking view of the island from this vantage point before lifting her camera to take several more pictures. She wasn't even thinking of her portfolio right now; the sheer splendour of the sight before her was simply captivating and made even better through the lens of her camera. It was like a private viewing, a kaleidoscope of wonder. She couldn't get enough of the island's beauty, pressing the shutter over and over as the adrenaline surged through her. The mountain air was pure and fresh, delicately scented with the now familiar citrus fragrance of lemon mingled with sea salt. Intoxicating. Mesmerising. And she had never felt so alive as she did right now.

Once she was certain she'd captured every conceivable shot of the scenery before her, Maddie stowed the camera away and studied the directions on her phone again, figuring she needed to make her way through the main square. La piazzetta. From what she could see the Airbnb was adjacent to a florist on a narrow street just off the far corner and so she headed that way. The sound of church bells from a honey-coloured stone tower with a mosaic-faced clock welcomed her as she wandered through the cobbled square past parasol-covered tables outside restaurants and cafes, past wide stone steps leading up to the old cathedral of Santo Stefano. She strolled on through a maze of narrow, cobbled streets bustling with tourists, past chic designer boutiques and on to a quieter street lined with lovely little three-storeyed townhouses and a canopy of pink magnolia trees giving shade, until she found herself in a small outdoor market.

The air was full now with the soothing sound of an accordion being played by an older gentleman sitting on a stool with a cap full of coins on a checked blanket at his feet, a toffee-coloured dog sprawled out contentedly beside it. Maddie stopped walking and took a minute to listen to the beautiful music and survey the colourful market stalls laden with wicker baskets of oranges and lemons piled high. The lyrical language of the locals milling around doing their shopping, the energy frenetic and exhilarating with their gesticulating and bustling and handshaking and hugging as they all seemed to know one another. Maddie could see bread stalls selling loaves and sweet pastries beside others with big barrels of black and green olives bobbing around in herb-infused brine, tall glass flagons of oils and wheels of cheeses, keepsake trinkets and traditional hand-painted wooden fans. She had never experienced anything like it. As the accordion player finished his song and took a sip of red wine from a small glass on a nearby table, Maddie found her purse and bent down to put a handful of coins, leftover from her time in Naples, into the hat, and gave the dog's head a stroke.

'*Le piace*,' the man shrugged and nodded, gesturing to the dog.

'Sorry, I don—'

'Ah . . . she like you,' the man translated in heavily accented English, as the dog did an indulgent stretch before sitting up and nuzzling her fluffy head against the side of Maddie's thigh.

'She's adorable. What is her name?' Maddie carried on petting the dog.

'*Fortunata*. It means lucky.' He nodded, slipping his hands through the straps at either end of the accordion, then stretching it into action in preparation for another tune.

'*Grazie*. And nice to meet you, Fortunata.' Maddie smiled and stood back up, feeling very lucky indeed as she gave the man a wave and wandered past more market stalls and towards another narrow street, stopping to check she was in the right place. Via Fiore. Flower street. *That's right.* Maddie saw it there carved into the brick wall and thought how aptly named it was as she saw tumbling purple flowers flanking either side of the road, cascading from each of the balconies on the terrace of tall, narrow buildings. And there at the end was the cutest little flower shop. She stopped walking and with her hands on her hips marvelled at the pretty sight – buckets of brilliantly coloured pink, red, yellow and orange roses and pots of white orchids. She inhaled and savoured the sweet scent of frangipani and honeysuckle from the plants growing up the walls on either side of a sun-faded shabby chic Tiffany blue wooden door.

'*Ciao! Maddie dall'Inghilterra?*' A sprightly old lady dressed all in black came dashing towards Maddie, her arms outstretched in greeting, a wide smile creasing her papery, lined face.

'Um, yes . . . I think so.' On hearing her name, Maddie parked her heavy camera case and put her rucksack on the pavement beside her leg and lifted her arm, intending to shake the elderly lady's hand but found herself enveloped in an enormous hug instead. 'Oh, it's lovely to meet you . . . Signora Romano,' Maddie said, into the woman's shoulder, quickly remembering her host's name from the booking confirmation email.

'Arjona. You can call me Jona, and welcome into my home.' Jona let Maddie go before making her way towards the blue wooden door, beckoning for Maddie to follow. Collecting her luggage together, Maddie entered the flower shop, relishing the refreshing cool air from the ceramic-tiled interior. They passed through a set of swing doors and up a narrow, spiral staircase to an open terrace that ran the length of the front of the building, overlooking the street. Jona produced a key from a pocket on the front of her dress and handed it to Maddie.

Inside her holiday accommodation, Maddie gasped in delight and relief. The little studio apartment was far nicer than it looked in the badly lit photos on the website. Cool traditional terracotta tiles on the floor and whitewashed exposed brick walls with a high arched ceiling gave the bedroom a wonderful light and airy atmosphere. Jona gestured to an archway at the far corner of the L-shaped room.

'*Sì*,' she smiled, walking through the archway, and sweeping her hand towards a small kitchenette area where there was a thoughtful welcome basket on the counter brimming with treats —chocolates, breadsticks, a couple of bottles of wine, olives and fruit. Then she indicated towards another door leading into a bathroom. The best bit of all was through the floor-to-ceiling shuttered doors that Jona flung open to reveal an exquisite little balcony with just enough room for a wooden slatted folding table and two chairs and an utterly breathtaking panoramic view of the lush green hilly island leading down to the sea. Maddie felt as if she had arrived in paradise and her heart lifted as never before. Her long-held desire to travel and experience new things well and truly satisfied.

'It's . . . it's,' she paused, struggling to find the right words to properly convey how she felt right now about her holiday accommodation, and then, laughing, she simply said, 'I love it! Thank you.'

'I see you later,' Jona smiled and dipped her head, clearly happy with Maddie's reaction to her beautiful guest apartment above the flower shop. After giving Maddie's arm a kindly pat, Jona left. Maddie closed the door and squeezed her fists together in glee before taking a running leap onto the bed where she landed like a starfish on her back with an enormous smile on her face, then cycling her legs up in the air she did a silent 'YESSSSS' scream of pure delight.

9

After unpacking her rucksack and powering up her laptop, Maddie changed out of her travelling clothes and put on a comfy kaftan that Sofia had let her borrow for the holiday. With it being very last minute, Maddie hadn't many options of summery clothes to pack, living mostly in jeans and jumpers back home in rural Tindledale. She poured herself a glass of wine from one of the bottles that Jona had put in the little welcome basket and sauntered out onto the balcony, relishing the refreshing warm evening air as it furled around her bare legs, making her feel light and optimistic and in true holiday mode at last. Though she couldn't wait to explore the island, she also couldn't resist settling into one of the chairs, her body relaxing as she slipped off her sandals and rested her bare feet on the other chair. She drank in the view of Capri, majestic and rugged and just so overwhelmingly beautiful. It was like no other place on earth, not that

94

Maddie had ever travelled to another country before, but that didn't detract from the sheer magnificence she could see over the balcony. She took in the greenery, the pastel-coloured villas, the vivid flowers – pink, red, and purple spilling over the corners of balconies and flat roofs. The narrow winding roads leading down to that sea, the breathtakingly, dazzling, stunning blue-green water dotted with yachts and sailboats. Serene and calm, making all the tension from the last few months since her split with Brad seem to melt away, leaving Maddie feeling content in this moment, but tired too. The shoot in Naples had been very full on, making her realise that all she really wanted to do this evening was sit here and soak up the glorious sunny surroundings as she read more of the letters and post-cards and planned the next few days of her holiday. A whole week to herself to explore and take photos was a treat indeed and she wanted to savour every second of it.

Taking a sip of wine, Maddie tapped the keyboard on her laptop to find the folder where she had saved all the photos of the postcards and letters, the envelopes too; some of them were pale blue airmail envelopes and she wanted to take a proper look to see where they had been posted from. The letters and postcards weren't in any date order; there hadn't been time to catalogue them properly or study them in detail, so Maddie just started with the first one. It was dated 1951 and the envelope had an American stamp on the front. She started reading. Soon she was holding her breath as the proverbial penny dropped when she saw the name at the end of the letter.

My dear sister,

Please ensure you are alone when reading this letter and then store it away in the suitcase on top of the wardrobe. Don't be alarmed – I am sure you will understand why when you read on! Firstly, I am still having the most wonderful time here in LA. The other girls are nice and ever so friendly, although there isn't much time to make proper new friends with the daily acting lessons and deportment, elocution too. It's hard work, but I am thoroughly enjoying myself and feel truly in my element learning all the rules – the spoken, and most importantly, the unspoken ones. The weather is simply marvellous too. Far hotter than we are used to at home, and I haven't needed a cardigan for the entire time I have been here.

I can't believe it is six months already!! So much has changed, not least my hair which is now a glamorous platinum blonde, as you will see in the small headshot I have enclosed. It was taken by a professional photographer during a shoot the studio arranged for me. My name too, has been given a starlet ring to it and I am now to be Kelly Sinclair! I wasn't sure about it at first, and know Mother would have disapproved dreadfully, but it has certainly grown on me and in fact it helps enormously for me to step out of my own character and play the part of a proper movie star – vivacious and charismatic. It's so much more fun than constantly being on best behaviour as I always had to be at home.

I have the most exciting news that you must swear not to tell a single soul. I have met the dreamiest man. He is devilishly handsome with thick black hair and eyes the colour of conkers shiny with autumn sunshine, and he is suitably tall as to tower over me. He is always impeccably dressed and quite the gentleman! He kissed the back of my hand on first meeting me, as if he were Prince Charming and I a princess, and I know that you would certainly approve! Father too, I'm sure. He is also a skilled raconteur with a quick wit and charm unlike any other man I have ever met, not that there have been many as you know. But please don't let on just yet as it is very early days. He's an actor as well and is playing the lead in my first film. It's a small production, a comedy caper romance and I have a walk-on part playing a shop girl called Sally with two lines to say. I am keeping my fingers crossed for my lines not to be cut in the edit. I long to play the lead opposite Clarke one day so that I might kiss him, but I will be sure to look away when Peggy, his counterpart, puts her arms around him and falls into his embrace. I find myself swooning and thinking of his handsome face every night as I put mine on the pillow and I simply know that, when the moment arises, I am not entirely sure I shall manage to resist. I long for him and he is all I can think of, and I am trying so desperately hard to channel the high emotion into my acting, for I fear Mother would turn in her grave at my gallivanting in such a way. I have been going to Mass every Sunday and confession too for my sins, but I have been unable to stop thinking about him.

Is this how it was with George at the start? Tell me, dear sister, how long you waited before doing it – if indeed you have. Forgive me if I am being presumptuous and simply burn this letter and forget I ever asked. But I feel quite alone here without you, my twin, and daren't confide in any of the

other girls in case it gets back to the studio bosses!
I'm sure you understand the rules are rather stringent
about this sort of thing.

Please do write again soon with your news, it
cheers me no end and eases my mind from feeling
homesick. I miss you and Dad terribly and hope
you are looking after each other and that Dad isn't
overdoing it as usual. I hope Dad is feeling better
now after his winter cold and George has popped
the question at last and that you are engaged to be
married.

Love
Rose xxx

Maddie stared at the screen and let the news sink in.
There it was in black and white. Kelly Sinclair aka
blonde bombshell of Hollywood's Golden Age. Then
Granny's name . . . Rose. So, she *was* a film star!
Maddie's hunch was right, but still, she couldn't quite
believe it. Her quiet, unassuming, gentle Granny Rose.
It was incredible. But how? And more intriguingly,
why on earth would her grandmother keep a secret
as big as this? She wondered if her dad knew, but
swiftly dismissed this notion as he would have said
so, surely . . . Keen to read on, Maddie closed the
letter and clicked on another.

Dearest Patsy
  This letter is most definitely one for your eyes only and must be put in the suitcase as soon as you have read it!!!
  I AM IN LOVE! Clarke is just the most wonderful man and such a considerate lover, to boot. He has asked me to be his girl.

Hang on a minute! Maddie sat upright and read the letter again. *Clarke.* A distinctive name, and she remembered having seen it before, back in the kitchen at Honeysuckle Cottage when she first decided to look at the contents of the suitcase. Tapping the keys on the laptop, Maddie opened her Google search history and retrieved the page with the picture of Clarke King on and found herself smiling as she wondered if it could possibly be the same devilishly handsome man with his slick of dark hair and smouldering eyes here on the screen in front of her. Surely not. But then again, why not? Until a few minutes ago, her grandmother was an ordinary octogenarian living in sheltered housing with her best pals from the knitting circle, but now, it turned out that she was in fact a film star from the Golden Age of Hollywood, so as far as Maddie was concerned . . . absolutely anything was possible. She took another look at Clarke and raised her wine glass to the screen as a tick of approval, thinking how blooming lucky her grandmother was, and Clarke too, for that matter. Because Granny, aka Rose, aka Kelly Sinclair was breathtakingly beautiful with her sparkling eyes and a magical aura that emanated from that black-and-white headshot photo that Maddie now knew for certain was her grandmother as a young woman. Maybe this is what they meant about someone having the X factor. Maddie had never met a real-life famous person, celebrity or actor, so had never experienced it, but she could just see from the pictures of Kelly and Clarke that they shone, or maybe it was just the spotlit background. Either way, she imagined what a handsome and charming couple they would have made.

Now with her curiosity well and truly in overdrive, Maddie was even keener to find out more. What had become of this golden couple? She needed to know. This had suddenly become much more than helping to find Audrey; this was finding out about her grandmother's life. The person Granny really was, the girl, the woman, the life she lived before she became Maddie and Sofia's grandmother. Managing to tear her eyes away from the heartthrob on her laptop, Maddie picked up the letter again and read more of Rose's words.

Of course, it must be hush-hush, especially with filming due to start on my return to LA. This is the chance I have waited my whole life for, my first proper part with lots of lines and the lead being played by Clarke, so I mustn't let anything mess it up. It's going to be simply marvellous, and I really cannot wait to show him off to you and Dad. Clarke has said he will fix it once filming has finished and I am free from my contract so we can be a proper couple and travel together.

Oh Patsy, life is so wonderful! For you too, my dear sister, a very suitable husband in George and a baby on the way is all you have ever dreamed of. Mother would have been so delighted for you, just as much as I am. You simply must write when Baby arrives, or perhaps a telegram to my apartment in LA, or here at the hotel in Capri if Baby comes early. You have both addresses and Dad does too, in case you are run ragged after the birth. I wish I could be there with you, my dearest Patsy, and hope you can forgive me not being able to. As always, love to Dad, I hope you are looking after him and not letting him work too hard in the garden so as to put his back out again!

Love
Rose

PS – I have met a truly marvellous new friend! An Italian woman, but her English is good, and I have offered to be a guinea pig for her to practise her conversational skills, which will be tremendous fun and something to occupy my mind when Clarke has to return to America ahead of me for his Broadway stage play in New York. My new friend is called Lucia and she kindly returned my handbag to me when I left it under a chair on Sunday. I found the prettiest whitewashed church on a hillside here in Capri. Originally built for the local fishermen, it's called Chiesa di Sant'Andrea and is little bigger than our sitting room at home but with an incredible view from the cliffside out over the sea, as one would expect for a lookout point for pirates, as the land the church is built on once was.

I felt like an utter chump when Lucia dashed up to me after Mass as I was leaving the church. My mind was a million miles away as I must confess to having allowed my thoughts to turn to Clarke during the service, which was conducted entirely in Italian, of course! A lyrical, passionate-sounding language, but my yearning for Clarke is all-consuming and I suppose this is how it is supposed to be when one is in love! It's just as well I have Lucia, and the beauty of it all is that I can be myself with her.

I feel so at home with her and her family who live in a traditional terracotta-coloured villa beside their very own orange and lemon orchard high up on a hillside with the most splendid view. It fills the warm Italian air with the scent of citrus mingled with mimosa from the tree-lined path that leads from their home to the orchard. There are fig trees too where one can simply pick a ripe fig and eat it! It is the most glorious thing to do and tastes incredibly sweet and warm from the midday sun. Patsy, it is so idyllic, and I wish more than anything that you were here with me to share in the beauty of this wonderful island. It really is the very best tonic, and I did so need a pick-me-up so that I can return to LA feeling refreshed for filming. I will miss Lucia and her family terribly, but we are to be pen pals in the hope that I can return to Capri again or that she might make it to America. She has an aunt and uncle and two cousins from Naples who live in Pasadena and have an Italian bakery in Lincoln Heights, so it is entirely possible . . .

Maddie sighed with pleasure on reading about the wonderful time Granny had had all those years ago. Living her best life in Capri . . . not to mention Hollywood, Los Angeles – it doesn't get any more glamorous than that! Maddie found her notepad and wrote a list of things she had found out so far:

Hollywood

Capri – church called Chiesa di Sant'Andrea (I can go there too, just like Granny did when she was here)

Clarke

Lucia – lemon and orange orchard on a hillside in Capri. Family in Pasadena – Italian bakery in Lincoln Heights

Maddie quickly googled to see that these places were in Los Angeles too, so she wondered if Granny ever went there and met Lucia's family with the Italian bakery.

Sister Patsy pregnant (I wonder if the baby was a girl, and she called her Audrey? Would make sense if Granny lost touch with her sister and so never knew what became of baby Audrey)

Maddie pondered on this possibility; it had also crossed her mind that her grandmother could have had a baby called Audrey . . . and maybe the baby died. But she had no evidence of this, whereas here was proof that her sister had a child, so Maddie underlined Patsy's name, twice, presuming this was the twin sister that Dad had mentioned, and wondered what they could possibly have fallen out over? Could this be why Granny clammed up during their Christmas dinner after introducing the subject of twins in the family? Maddie clicked on to another letter. This one hadn't been in an envelope and wasn't addressed to Patsy. Maddie sipped more wine and started reading.

Dear Dad

I hope you are keeping in good health despite all that has happened. It is as I thought, a hopeless situation, and I am to return home forthwith. I am so sorry it has come to this, and I hope that one day you will find it possible to forgive me, and for not making a success of the golden opportunity you allowed me to have. I will forever be truly grateful and will do all that I can to make you proud of me once again.

With love

Rose

Oh, no, poor Granny. Maddie creased her forehead in concern, wondering what on earth had happened to cause Granny to go from having a glamorous career in Hollywood, destined for an Oscar nomination – which, come to think of it, was actually a pretty incredible achievement for an ordinary teenage girl in the Fifties from a rural village in England – and in love with her extremely hot movie-star lover and having the time of her life in Capri, to utter sadness and dejection on having lost it all . . . from the sounds of this letter.

Maddie let out a long breath before finishing the last of her wine, a sadness descending for her granny and whatever upset she had been experiencing back then. And there was more to come. Putting the wine glass down, Maddie did some more Google searches, just in case she had missed any extra information about Kelly. As she scanned through the search results something else caught her eye. There was a page with a heading *Hollywood's Forgotten Stars . . . Where Are They Now?* There were lots of scanned copies of old gossip magazine articles. Maddie speed-read the page to see if it could give her any clues.

> *Kelly Sinclair faded from view after being dumped by the studio in Hollywood. Where is she now? Rumour has it she returned to England, heartbroken after the end of a love affair . . .*

Maddie added the date and a few more details to the timeline of events in her notebook then sat back in her chair and gazed out at the view of Capri as she contemplated all that she'd learned so far. Dad was right, she needed to tread very carefully before discussing any of this with Granny; the last thing she wanted to do was upset her by bringing back memories of heartbreak and faded dreams from all those years ago. Maddie also knew that it was going to be impossible to close the lid on the Pandora's box that she had now opened because it was fascinating finding out about her grandmother's extraordinary life, even if it didn't bring her any closer to knowing who Audrey was.

Maddie finished the last of her wine, closed her laptop and put away her notepad and pen. Deciding she had discovered enough of her grandmother's past for one day, she left the balcony and went through to the bedroom. In bed, she drifted off to sleep dreaming of Hollywood and glamour and movie stars, and Rose, or Kelly as she was then, with her heartthrob Clarke, in love and having the time of her life in 1950s Capri . . .

10

Kelly Sinclair caught her breath on seeing Clarke's handsome face as a cream-coloured scooter swept to a halt outside the hotel lobby that was for the use of private guests only. His elbow resting on the handlebar and jet-black hair a little windswept added to his charming appeal.

Tidying the pastel pink boatneck top with matching cropped pants that she had chosen for today's trip, Kelly made her way down the flight of mosaic-tiled steps, smiling at Clarke's thoughtfulness on seeing he had organised a picnic with a wicker hamper and a rolled-up tartan blanket strapped to the back of the scooter. He looked every inch the movie star; wearing a sky-blue, short-sleeved shirt with gaberdine trousers and brown-and-white brogues, he was dressed perfectly for a picnic on a secluded Mediterranean beach. A

109

tender touch, Kelly thought, excited at the prospect of a simple picnic, alone with her lover away from the dazzle of the hotel's dining room where the other guests commented in hushed tones on seeing them together. Not that the other famous actors were inclined to breach a confidentiality, but still . . . today was a chance to feel free and away from the spotlight for a change.

Popping sunglasses on, Kelly snapped the clasp closed on her Gucci handbag, a generous gift from Clarke, and slid it into the crook of her elbow. She paused to unravel from the handle of her bag an exquisite floral-patterned silk scarf with Capri embroidered at a jaunty angle on the corner, then wrapped it around her distinctive mane of platinum curls. She had bought the scarf on a shopping trip in Via Camerelle yesterday as a souvenir of her time here in Capri. It would be ideal for their trip today, allowing her to leave the haven of the hotel, where the privacy of the high-profile guests was protected, and travel incognito with Clarke, free from the prying eyes of the audacious press pack that appeared hellbent on snapping a photograph of Clarke and his 'mystery lover' together, preferably in a compromising situation. The bosses at the studio were very particular about this sort of thing and continually impressing upon her the importance of not tarnishing the image they were creating for her.

The sophisticated girl-next-door, classy yet sexy and most definitely wholesome and unencumbered. She was to be the woman the female moviegoers all wanted to be and all the men dreamed of being with. So, gallivanting in public around a paradise island with the man who would be headlining in her next movie, cast as her love interest, was out of the question and covered within point one of her employment contract. Plus, she had worked her whole life for this opportunity, with acting and singing lessons, not to mention the elocution practice to smooth out her English country girl accent, to make a name for herself. More than anything, she wanted Dad and Patsy to be proud of her, and Mother too would have been proud, even, with her high morals and cautious view of the acting fraternity. So it was completely out of the question for Kelly to jeopardise her once-in-a-lifetime chance. She had seen it happen to a couple of the other girls in her apartment block. Actresses starting out like her and with ambitions just as big as hers, fired from a film for wanting to marry their guy or for simply being too unwell to learn their lines or, worse still, too sick to turn up for filming. So, they'd been dropped, just like that! And replaced with the next bright-eyed young dreamer that caught the eye of Louis or any of the other studio bosses. Yet the rules, Kelly had learned very early on, did not apply to any of the men. She had been very naive at the start of her career. When Louis had come to Honeysuckle Cottage and made all her dreams come true, she had been a country girl with no idea of what it would be like living in Hollywood and being transformed into a starlet with walk-on parts to start with and an expectation that she would soon be ready to earn her keep with bigger roles in bigger movies. She supposed that she would have agreed to anything just to have her chance in Hollywood, although she often thought it a miracle that she had managed to keep her decency intact and circumvent any unwanted advances. And there had been a few. Yet she was quite sure Clarke wasn't a playboy, despite the studio's tendency to portray him as one. When they were alone, he was tender and kind and dependable. He was never brash or brutal or silky with his charm.

In the beginning it had been a stolen glance here and there, progressing to the delicate touch of a finger brushing against the back of her hand to create a frisson of delicious delight that, until then, she had only read about in magazines and romance novels. By the time her second film had started shooting, they were meeting in secret. Revelling in each other's company. They had stolen moments to be alone together, even managing to escape on a rare weekend off to a log cabin in Pine Mountain. There, a few hours' drive away from her apartment in Los Angeles, she had felt able to breathe, properly breathe, for the first time since leaving Tindledale. It had felt so good to once again enjoy being the carefree girl she used to be before leaving that life behind. Nestled amid the tall pine trees, the cosy cabin had felt like home as they had built a camp bonfire near the deck from which to watch the vibrant sunsets giving way to a seemingly endless canopy of stars. She had rested her head on his chest, his arms wrapped around hers, relishing the peace and tranquillity as she gazed up at the same inky night sky that she had looked out upon all those years ago from her childhood bedroom back home, whispering words of prayer to make her dreams come true. The dream that she was now living, although it hadn't quite turned out as she had ever imagined it to be. She often wondered whether, knowing what she did now, the young girl she once was would still have yearned for this life. Always performing, acting, dancing, and playing a part, all the while sacrificing herself to the whim of the studio bosses. Clarke felt it too, he had told her: trapped in the bubble of fame from the moment the lure of stardom had seeped into his pores during the first screen test.

Since that trip to the log cabin in the mountains, Kelly and Clarke had rapidly become inseparable, with eyes only for each other. Even if they still had to carefully plan every moment alone to ensure their privacy, each second that she was with him was divine and made her heart soar with joy. Kelly wondered if this was how falling in love was supposed to feel, for she had never experienced it before she met Clarke. Whenever they were apart she found herself longing to see him, yearning for his touch, her head full of dreamy thoughts of him. It was constant and overwhelming, and as a result she was becoming distracted and neglecting the other things that brought her pleasure, such as reading her letters from home, picturing Patsy and Dad bickering in the kitchen or in the garden sowing seasonal vegetables or helping George with the apple picking. Patsy was married now, with a baby on the way, and it had broken Kelly's heart to have to send flowers to her only sister's wedding, when she had been unable to be there in person because Louis wouldn't hear of her 'going AWOL' and ruining the filming schedule by missing the crucial last scenes. There were times when Kelly missed home with such severity that it gnawed away within her like a physical pain in the centre of her heart. But it was the price she had to pay to pursue her dreams because she was beholden to the studio bosses who controlled her career . . . and much of her personal life too, it seemed.

Louis Baxter's silky manner had vanished the moment he left the sitting room of Honeysuckle Cottage, replaced with a formidable force that his secretary, Sandra – twenty years his junior and who the others had told her was in fact his lover – was forever having to placate. Kelly wouldn't even be here in beautiful Capri if Sandra hadn't intervened when Louis refused to let her accept Gracie Fields' generous invitation. He grudgingly conceded when Sandra pointed out, 'It will boost Kelly's image to be seen mingling with the jet set in glamorous Capri, and besides, she so desperately needs a rest.'

It was true, Kelly had been feeling very tired, even more so than usual. Maybe it was the restlessness at night-time, tossing and turning with her dreams of being back home in the orchards without a care in the world, and then waking in a panic with tears on her pillow when the synapses of her brain kicked in and she realised that it was only a dream of a life that was no longer hers. But if she hadn't left Tindledale behind then she wouldn't have met Clarke. Plain Rose with flame-red hair and freckles would never have caught his eye hidden away in rural England. Tindledale seemed a million miles from the exclusive Bel Air residence where Clarke lived now.

It hadn't been her intention to abandon her Tindledale roots. In fact, she had been horrified when the changes to her image were first mooted. 'Ditch the ginger and do something about the freckles,' Louis had ordered as soon as she had arrived at the studio for her first screen test. It was only when the peroxide had been rinsed from her hair, and Gwen, the studio's top stylist, had expertly applied the movie star make-up and lifted the towel from her head, revealing the luxuriant dazzling blonde beneath, that Rose O'Malley truly became Kelly Sinclair, the new name Louis had come up with for her. He had also ordered her to remove the little gold cross that she had inherited from her mother, insisting it must be banished forthwith because 'the small guy on the street doesn't want to lust after a good Catholic girl, for chrissakes! The broad up there on the big screen needs to look stylish, to ooze sex appeal, to be unattainable yet desirable – but only in their dreams!' Louis had guffawed with a big, deep-throated smoker's wheeze, pausing to put his cigar in a nearby ashtray before spreading his arms up high and wide to demonstrate the sheer expanse of a movie theatre screen. The thought of appearing on such a screen had thrilled Rose right from the roots of her newly peroxide hair to the tips of her immaculately manicured toes. It was all she had ever dreamed of, the stardust having well and truly seeped into her pores. She felt alive when acting and wanted to shine and dazzle like a proper movie star as she delivered her lines to camera. And so she had immediately snapped the chain with the cross from her neck and pushed it into an old brown empty envelope inside her handbag, not even considering what her mother would make of such a thing, but silently praying to the Sweet Mother of God for forgiveness as she did so.

'My sweet gal, Kelly, your beauty takes my breath away,' Clarke said, drinking her in as he took a step back and let out a long whistle of appreciation, his American accent as smooth and warm as honey over peach pie as he reached out an elbow to escort her to the scooter.

'And your charm takes mine away, my darling,' she smiled, looping her arm through his.

After Clarke had mounted the scooter, she slid into position behind him on the sumptuous, buttery soft red leather seat, her pulse quickening on catching the intoxicating scent of his cologne. Her cheeks flushed at the memory of their first night together in the log cabin, when they'd celebrated his birthday back in

February – Valentine's Day, rather fittingly. She had gifted him the cologne and he had taken her to his bed wearing nothing but a generous splash of the sensual scent on his honed torso. They had made abundant love all night long. And she supposed the scent would for evermore remind her of that perfect moment. Her first time. His lips soft on hers as he had murmured words of desire, pleasuring her before gently and tenderly making love to her. As the night had drawn on, she had grown in confidence and her ability to pleasure him too, abandoning all her earlier inhibitions with a teasing strip, removing the petticoat that she hadn't managed to take off earlier. She had been unable to resist climbing astride him in her suspender belt and stockings, platinum waves sensual on her bare back as he kissed her nipples and made love to her all over again. There had been no acting that night; they had both been laid bare and vulnerable, and the feeling of love was mutual. From that moment on set when they had first met, she had known it would be impossible to resist him. How could she, when she had fallen in love with him at first sight.

Checking she was comfortable, Clarke drew her hands tightly around his waist and started the scooter's engine. The sudden speed was thrilling as he headed to the coastal road of a thousand bends, or so it seemed, each curve more exhilarating than the one before as he expertly handled the scooter. The sun-baked breeze cocooned her in warmth and happiness, a place where anything felt possible as she soaked up the picturesque scenery of lush, rugged, tree-topped cliffs on one side, giving way to the sumptuous sea on the other.

Soon the scooter slowed and, after unstrapping the picnic basket and blanket from the back, Clarke took Kelly's hand in his and led the way down a steep, narrow cobblestoned walkway flanked on either side by a canopy of pink bougainvillea, exquisite in contrast to the cloudless, aqua sky through which a hazy, plump sun radiated a golden glow upon them.

'Oh Clarke, this feels like paradise.' Kelly glanced all around, drinking in the view, so keen was she to remember every detail to dream about later and to include in her next letter to Patsy. Her twin sister was insistent she leave nothing out, living vicariously through her as the pregnancy had confined her to bed these past two months, and so the boredom was stifling, she had said in her last letter.

'Come on, there's more to see.' Clarke squeezed her hand in his and picked up speed until the pair of them were dashing towards a secluded cove, shielded from view by grass-capped rocky crags. The glistening blue-green waves rolled gently to the shore as Kelly slipped her sandals off and savoured the sensation of the sand, soft and undulating between her toes.

Clarke unrolled the blanket and placed the picnic hamper down, threw his shirt off and swept her into his arms.

'Clarke, we can't!' Kelly protested, though unable to resist slipping her arms around his neck. 'What if someone sees us . . . maybe we should hide inside that cave over there.' She pointed towards an arched opening in the rocks behind them where the sparkling sea water was trickling through a myriad of rock pools.

'I'm not hiding you away inside a cave!' His dark eyes sparked with defiance and passion. 'This place is private; nobody can see us here . . . there's only one way into this cove and that's down the path where we just came, and nobody in their right mind is going to risk venturing on to the cliff edge up there.' He tipped his head back and glanced up to emphasise the sheer height of the magnificent rock side above them. 'Yes, Lenny promised me it's safe and you know I trust him with my life . . .'

She nodded, remembering Lenny's reminiscences about growing up in Mississippi with Clarke. The two of them had been like brothers; when Clarke had been in danger of drowning in a creek after developing cramp, Lenny had been the one who leapt in to save him.

'And you know how fond Lenny is of you,' he went on.

Kelly nodded, her fear softening as she thought of Lenny. Dear gentle Lenny. Clarke's best friend had also had dreams of making it in the movies, and the two of them had come to Hollywood together. But the studios had deemed Lenny 'too effeminate', and after suffering one too many knockbacks he had decided to set himself up as Clarke's smooth-talking 'iron fist in a velvet glove' agent and right-hand man. Along with Lenny's business partner and secret lover, Ray, they had formed a tight trio, which had become a quartet with Kelly's arrival. She loved spending time with Lenny and Ray, laughing and joking over dinner or cocktails in the hotel's beach bar, living the high life, as Lenny liked to say. Both men were outrageous flirts in public – part of the pretence required to conceal their sexuality – but she didn't mind in the least. In fact she relished their company. She came alive when with them, her vivacious and energetic person-ality shining through, instead of being muted and restrained as she had been back in Tindledale. Yes, the jet set lifestyle of Hollywood, and now Capri, suited her tremendously.

'I do, my darling, and I'm so fond of Lenny too.' Kelly smiled, unravelling her arms from around Clarke's neck and letting him go. After shimmying free from her capri pants and flinging off her top to reveal the floral two-piece bathing suit beneath, she adjusted the head-scarf so it was tied turban-style around her head, just in case a camera guy was hiding out in one of the grottoes, and slipped her hand inside Clarke's. 'What are we waiting for then?' Holding the sunglasses in place so they didn't fall from her face, she ran into the tanta-lisingly refreshing waves with Clarke close behind her.

Soon they were laughing and fooling around, then swimming together towards one of the small caves where the sun was glistening on the crystal clear water lapping against the sand. As they reached the shore, Clarke held out a hand to help Kelly climb over the rocks until they were together inside the cave. The water there was as warm as a spa pool. He drew her towards him and they lay entwined in the water, letting it sway back and forth over their legs as they kissed and embraced.

'I wish we could stay like this here together forever,' Kelly said, studying his beautiful face, tenderly dabbing droplets of seawater away from his chiselled cheekbones as the love she had for him intensified within her.

'One day, my dear, sweet English rose, we will be here again, just the two of us – and without the need for any of this—' He grinned and tweaked the edge of her headscarf. 'The moment your contract is done and your five films are in the can, you can have Lenny take over managing things for you. The world is your oyster, my love, and he will make it work out so you get to call the shots and land the roles you want instead of dancing to that snake Louis's tune.' Clarke's face darkened.

'You think?' she asked, tracing an index finger along the dip at the centre of his chest before resting the side of her head there. The rhythm of his heartbeat mingled with her own, sounding comforting, like a mesmerising birdsong binding them together forever.

'I sure do, doll. And Lenny will fix it for us to be together, properly, without all the charades. Then you can show me around your beloved home in England too.'

'Oh, that would be wonderful, Clarke. Patsy's face will be a picture if I turn up at the cottage with you in tow,' she laughed. 'The whole village will be in awe . . . I can see it now. Breaking news! *Blockbuster heart-throb, Clarke King, here in tiny Tindledale,*' she said, lifting and slowly moving her right hand as if reading a newspaper headline.

'Ah, they'll be too busy going wild for *Kelly Sinclair, Hollywood's golden girl*,' he said, kissing the tip of her nose before lifting his hand too as if reading another newspaper headline.

'I've a bit of a way to go for that,' she said modestly. She hoped and prayed that the next film would be the one to really break her out. The movie to make her name, not just in Hollywood, but back home in England too. Market Briar, the nearest large town to Tindledale, had its own picture house with an impressive Art Deco facade and a billboard that she had grown up hoping to see her name on one day. Smiling at the thrilling prospect, she traced her finger around the curve of his hip. But then it dawned on her: it wouldn't be her name up there on the billboard underneath the spotlights. Well, not her real name, the name that her mother and father had given her when she was born . . . the name on her christening certificate. And a tinge of sadness slipped over her as the full implication of this sank in, of who she'd had to become to achieve her long-held dreams.

11

The following morning Maddie had enjoyed a lovely long and indulgent lie in and was about to head out after probably the best night's sleep she'd ever had, with the rhythmic sound of the sea and caw of the gulls soothing as she slept. She had been exhausted from working and travelling and then sitting up late last night reading through more of the letters, but was now feeling refreshed and raring to go on her first day here in gorgeous Capri. Delighted all over again when she had first woken up and flung open the double doors to her balcony and been greeted by that view. Now, brushing her hair and teasing the curls up into a bun, Maddie's mind went to the lovely letter she had read last night from Patsy to her sister Rose, thinking what a character her grandmother's sister sounded, forthright and straightforward, much like Maddie's own sister, Sofia.

Dearest Rose

It is such a joy to read about your life in America and your letters keep me company while I wait for the little one to arrive. I am so very excited to become a mother, it is all I have ever wanted, and George is taking good care of me. He insists that I rest and don't lift anything, not even the teapot! Can you imagine that happening? Of course, I told him that I am perfectly able to make him a cup of tea and his sandwiches too, and will continue to do so, thank you very much! In fact, I enjoy doing so, I am a married lady now and it is my pleasure look after him and so each day I prepare a packed lunch and take it to him in the field and simply ignore his protests . . .

Keen to pack in as much exploring and picture-taking time as she possibly could while she was here, Maddie was also hoping to find out a bit more about her grandmother's glamorous, yet mysterious past. It dawned on her that everything she knew so far hinted at there being a sad secret. And it wasn't as if her grandmother was able to fully consent to having her past raked over, not with the dementia taking hold. But Maddie was convinced that Granny would want her to press on in the search for baby Audrey – she had seemed so insistent and quite traumatised with angst from not knowing what had become of her. Maddie just needed to make sure any revelations were handled with the utmost care. She could see where her dad's urge for caution was coming from, but she hoped he would come round when she updated him on what she had found out so far.

Maddie closed the door to her holiday home and set off along the balcony leading to the stairs. From another doorway, Jona appeared with a small wicker basket covered in a pristine white linen napkin.

'*Colazione*,' she said. 'Breakfast for you.'

'Oh, that's so kind of you, Jona, but I was just on my way out—' Maddie stopped talking on seeing the disappointed look from her host as she glanced up from the basket. 'Thank you,' she said instead, not wanting to disappoint the elderly woman who had kindly gone to the trouble of bringing her a basket of freshly baked bread, if the deliciously doughy aroma was anything to go by. Slipping her smaller, more portable camera bag crossbody style over her head to have both hands free, Maddie carefully took the basket from Jona and lifted the corner of the napkin to peep inside, delighted to see a selection of traditional Italian pastries and bread with a ramekin of creamy, golden butter, a small pot of honey and several exceedingly plump strawberries and figs.

'My son, he works in the bakery and bring the cakes every day, but is too much for me to eat so I bring them for my guests. They are for you.'

'Well, I'm very grateful . . . and to your son too,' Maddie smiled as her stomach let out a very loud rumble right on cue.

'Hmm . . . is not good to miss your breakfast.' Jona lifted one eyebrow in disapproval as if Maddie were an errant child.

'Um, yes, this is very true,' Maddie acquiesced and went to put the basket inside her room, figuring she had plenty of time to eat before she left and then added, 'err . . . would you like to join me?' wanting to be polite.

'Ah, no . . . I have already eaten my breakfast and now must go to the flower shop.' And with that she gave Maddie's arm a kindly pat before leaving her to it.

Maddie went back inside her room and placed the basket on the counter in the kitchenette, smiling to herself at her host's kindness. She was looking for a knife in the drawer when it occurred to her that Jona was likely to be around the same age as her grandmother, if not in her eighties, then certainly in her seventies. It might be worth asking if she had ever met an English movie star called Kelly Sinclair, or indeed knew who Lucia with the lemon orchard on a hillside could be. Determined to act on the impulse, she ran back to the door and out into the terrace to look for her.

'Jona, I wonder . . . could I ask you something please?' she called, seeing her at the top of the spiral staircase.

'*Sì, mia cara.*' Jona turned around, concern clouding her eyes now. 'Is the breakfast not good?'

'Oh, yes, it's wonderful, thank you, it's just . . . well, the reason for my coming here to Capri . . .' Maddie hesitated, unsure now where she should start. Her grandmother's story was quite extraordinary and to say it out loud, well . . . she would sound like a ridiculous fantasist.

'*Sì* . . . you say is to have a holiday and you enjoy taking photographs . . . you tell me in the email.' Jona smiled and then leaned a little closer into Maddie. 'And is why I give you the room with the best view. The other room at the back is not so good, just trees and no sea view,' she waved a dismissive hand in the air. 'I put the guests in there who come just to go to the parties on the boats and not bother to see our beautiful island . . .' And she winked conspiratorially.

'Ah, I see,' Maddie grinned. 'It's true, I am here for a holiday, but there is something that I found out about my grandmother, and I wondered if you might be able to help me . . .' She pushed an errant chunk of curls away from her face. 'You see . . .' Jona's eyes softened as if prompting Maddie to confide in her. Pausing to take a breath and formulate her thoughts, Maddie then relayed the key facts of what she knew about Granny's time here as Kelly Sinclair in the summer of 1953.

'Sì . . . yes, yes.' Jona nodded, enthusiastically. Maddie's pulse quickened in anticipation of what she was going to hear next. Surely, it couldn't be as simple as this – or a lucky coincidence, perhaps? Had Jona met Granny all those years ago? Maddie realised she was holding her breath, but then felt foolish when Jona added, 'They all come here. The actors and actresses, their lovers . . . I see them all. But I never meet your grandmother . . . Rose, you say her name is?'

'Yes, that's right . . . or Kelly. Kelly Sinclair, that was her movie star name,' Maddie explained, hopefully.

'Ah, Kelly Sinclair?' Jona pondered, knitting her eyebrows as if casting her mind back through the mists of time. Maddie nodded, willing her host to say yes, she remembered her well, everyone was delighted when Kelly Sinclair and her famous heartthrob lover visited the island of Capri in 1953 . . . but it wasn't to be. '*No, mi dispiace* . . . I do not know her.'

'Oh, well never mind,' Maddie said, feeling a little disappointed, but then she'd only been here a short while and Jona was the first person she had spoken to, and of course Capri was famed for its glamorous, jet set visitors, especially in the Fifties when it was literally the playground for stars of the Golden Age of Hollywood. She would ask around; someone was bound to remember, if not Kelly, then Clarke perhaps. And then she remembered the other name in her grandmother's letter. 'She also made a new friend when she was here . . . Lucia, her family had a lemon orchard on a hillside.' Maddie thought it worth asking, her curiosity getting the better of her.

'*Sì!*' Jona clapped her hands together. 'This I do know . . . there is a lemon orchard on a hillside,' and she lifted her index finger to point across the terrace to a spot further up on the side of the island. 'Lucia, no . . . I do not know her. But you go to the restaurant, and they will know.'

'Restaurant?'

'*Sì . . . L'albero di limone.*'

'The Lemon Tree!' they said in unison.

'Yes, the Lemon Tree restaurant is next to the orchard. I show you. Come. Follow me to the flower shop and I write the address. You go in a taxi, is up a very steep hill.' Jona nodded, and Maddie was delighted to have found a connection to her grandmother's past. It was intriguing and very exciting to walk in her grandmother's footsteps decades later.

'Wow. Thank you,' Maddie followed Jona down the stairs and waited while she wrote the address on the notepad, tore the page off and handed it to her. 'This is amazing . . . you see, my grandmother was there in the restaurant . . . all those years ago, and she wrote about how marvellous it was in a letter to her sister,' Maddie told Jona, folding the piece of paper in half and stowing it carefully in her bag. 'She wrote about the grilled lobster and the magnificent view and, well . . . it's one of the places I planned on visiting while I'm here.'

'I am pleased for you. And the view is spectacular . . . the best on the island. You must take plenty of pictures to show to your grandmother, *si?*'

Maddie smiled, nodding in agreement. Maybe when she got home, she would show Granny the pictures from her holiday in Capri. She had been researching dementia and knew that it wasn't going to go away. Sadly, her grandmother's fading memory and confusion was only going to deteriorate further, but a lovely, happy memory of a magical evening with her handsome lover in a 'lemon-scented restaurant' could be a comfort for her. Maddie had read on one of the dementia websites that seeing photos of past events could be very therapeutic in sparking conversations about things people did remember from much further back in their lives.

On second thoughts, maybe not that exact memory, Maddie realised, remembering the heartbreak she had discovered for her grandmother too after the end of a love affair. If it was the love affair with Clarke which ended in heartbreak, then Granny was hardly going to want to be reminded of that. Oh well, but maybe a visit to the restaurant would be an opportunity to find out more. If someone there did know of the lemon orchard and Lucia, and Maddie was able to meet her, then it was possible she might remember her friend Kelly Sinclair, and everything that happened in the summer of 1953. Maddie couldn't wait to find out. Granny had asked her to find out about Audrey and, with very little to go on, this seemed as good a place as any to start. She would decide later what to do with the information, if she actually found any. For now, it was just about enjoying her holiday and revisiting the places she knew her grandmother had come to when she had been a young woman.

'Thanks again for this, Jona.' She patted her handbag, and the elderly woman smiled, inclined her head in acknowledgement before giving Maddie a stern look.

'But first – breakfast!' And she shooed Maddie back towards the stairs leading up to her room.

12

Maddie paid the driver and stepped out from under the convertible taxi's canvas canopy and into the scorching hot Mediterranean sun, the sudden, heady scent of lemons intoxicating as she smoothed down her floaty, floral print, cotton sundress. The taxi had slowed to a halt beside a pretty pergola-covered path, canopied in an abundance of lemons growing up and over from the many trees on either side. It looked sensational, and Maddie instinctively lifted her camera that was on a strap around her neck, and took several pictures, the exquisite contrast of a perfect blue sky framing the vibrant green leaves and yellow of the fruit making her heart sing. She knew these pictures were going to look stunning in her 'Capri Life' portfolio, the name she had decided on for the collection taken here, and she was looking forward to adding more of the view from up here on the clifftop overlooking the island.

Making her way down the pathway, grateful for the shade, Maddie could hear voices, laughter, and music, coming from the restaurant, she presumed, and quickened her pace. It felt surreal to be literally walking in her grandmother's footsteps. This was the only way into the Lemon Tree restaurant that Maddie could see, and so Kelly and Clarke would have made their way underneath this gorgeous, lemon-covered canopy too. Maybe they were holding hands, laughing, and talking, with Granny aka Kelly feeling happy and in love with her handsome movie star lover. Maddie hoped so.

'*Benvenuto, un tavolo per il pranzo?*' A man dressed in a smart white shirt underneath a black waistcoat and trousers appeared from behind a wooden podium to greet her as she reached the entrance of the restaurant. 'Ah, welcome, a table for you?' he followed with, as Maddie smiled and apologised in English for her limited Italian.

'*Sì, grazie,*' yes please, she managed to say with a reasonably acceptable Italian accent, and followed the waiter, delighted to see that he was heading towards the same curved balcony with a perfect panoramic view that Granny had written about in the postcard to her sister. There was a white linen tablecloth topped table with two seats tucked at the end, as if waiting especially for Maddie. A vase containing a lush sprig of hot pink bougainvillea at the centre with two pristine wine glasses and an array of silver cutlery gave the restaurant a very chic vibe. It was much grander than she had anticipated. For a moment, Maddie wondered if she could actually afford to have her lunch here, but swiftly decided that, if not, she could always opt for a glass of iced water and a limoncello cocktail with which to toast Kelly and Clarke, and their friends too – Lenny and Ray. She had loved reading about their jet set lifestyle of cocktail parties and private dining, the likes of which Maddie had only seen in films or read about in magazines. Yes, a limoncello cocktail seemed very fitting, given that was the drink Kelly had chosen all those years ago. Then Maddie would make her enquiries about Lucia with the lemon orchard, before politely leaving.

Settling into her seat at the table, looping her handbag over the back of the chair and placing the camera in its carry case carefully on an enclosed ledge beside her, Maddie thanked the waiter as he handed her a leather-bound menu booklet with a sketch of a gold lemon on the front. She took a discreet look around the restaurant from behind her big sunglasses, then turned to take in the sheer beauty of the view overlooking the grassy hillside and crystal-clear blue waves below. Maddie felt as if she was on top of the world.

The traditional al fresco restaurant with floaty white canopies for shade was full of people, couples, a few young, handsome Italian priests and many families too. Three or possibly four generations at each table. Several plump, elderly women clad head to toe in black were seated in white leather chairs and sipping red wine from small goblets, all the while chatting and keeping an eye on their grandchildren, she presumed. The young boys and girls were dashing around the table with slices of pizza in their hands, joking and laughing as they played chase. Their parents were eating meatballs and spaghetti or shelling garlic and parsley marinated langoustines from a three-tiered silver platter of seafood packed in ice while chatting over glasses of wine too. Younger women dined in pairs, sipping colourful cocktails and wearing chic, stylish jeans and white shirts, oversized shades, floral sundresses, and designer handbags with gold chain straps looped over their chairs. A group of older men at a big circular table appeared deep in debate, drinking espresso from white china demitasse cups with their shirtsleeves rolled up and lots of animated remonstrating with intermittent jovial laughter.

Maddie inhaled contentedly, as if to fortify herself with the happy, holiday vibe, and sat back in her own chair, letting the hot sunshine-infused air envelop her as she looked out at the panoramic view. It was truly spectacular. But she couldn't help thinking how wonderful it would be to have someone with her to enthuse over the magnificence of it all. A lover. Just like Kelly had. Someone to sit and share this moment with, to feel a part of the atmosphere as they lingered over a long lazy lunch. Connected. Maddie let out a long sigh as she picked up the menu and flicked through the pages to make her choice, pleasantly surprised to see that many of the dishes were well within her budget. The waiter appeared with a jug of iced water and a basket of bread and placed them on the table before turning his attention to her.

'Are you ready to order . . . *signorina?*' he asked, expertly flicking away a pink petal that had floated from the vase onto the table. 'The grilled lobster is no more . . . *finito!*' he explained, tapping the page. This made Maddie's decision for her – she had been hesitating over the grilled lobster salad, wondering if her grandmother had gone for the half lobster with fries or with a tomato and mozzarella salad, as she could see on the page here in front of her.

'Yes, please, I'll have the seafood linguine,' Maddie replied, the delicious-looking dishes she had seen yesterday in the marina still on her mind, 'with a salad too,' grateful to see an English translation written in small letters underneath each dish on the menu. Turning the page to see the drinks list, she selected the limoncello cocktail, of course.

'Sì, *grazie*,' and the waiter disappeared again.

Later, having polished off the last of the delicious linguine as she had soaked up the relaxed atmosphere of laughter and chatter and waves ebbing and flowing and seagulls soaring, Maddie mopped up the garlicky sauce and sipped the rest of the limoncello cocktail. She could see why her grandmother had mentioned it in her letter to her sister Patsy as it was delicious – fruity and sparkling and utterly refreshing. Applying more sun cream to her freckly, bare arms, Maddie contemplated ordering another cocktail, keen to savour her time here for a little longer.

Minutes later, and as if reading her mind, the waiter appeared again with a fresh limoncello cocktail on a tray balanced on his outstretched hand.

'For you.' He placed the glass on the table in front of her and then with a dramatic flourish he produced a paper straw from behind his back and popped it into the yellow liquid.

'Oh, *grazie* . . . but I didn't—'

'It is a gift! The *signor* over there, he sends it to you.' And the waiter turned and pointed to a man wearing a baseball cap and shades sitting at a bar area on the other side of the restaurant. 'I make the drink myself,' the waiter assured her, on seeing her hesitation over accepting a drink from a complete stranger. 'Is limoncello cocktail just like the first one.' He smiled kindly.

'Oh . . . um, thank you,' Maddie replied tentatively, and went to stir the drink, wondering why the man at the bar would buy her a drink and if she should be flattered or suspicious . . . she'd never had a drink bought for her before, certainly not like it happens in the movies – two strangers destined to meet.

'You are welcome,' the waiter smiled before walking away.

Maddie carried on stirring, unsure of what to do for the best. She wasn't a breezy, confident type of person who could take a situation like this in her stride and so was just about to ask for the bill so she could leave, when her phone buzzed on the table in front of her. It was Brad. She couldn't believe it! What was he doing calling her? They had agreed not to do this any more. And besides, with the time difference, she quickly worked out that it was the middle of the night in New York. What was going on? Was he playing some kind of game? Brad had liked games – or 'surprises' as he called them – and would berate her for being a spoilsport when she didn't see the funny side. Like the time he invited her to join him at a pot-plant themed fancy dress party with all his work pals, only for her to turn up to meet him there dressed as a yucca plant, complete with lurid green face paint, when everyone else was wearing normal 'smart casual' clothes because it wasn't a fancy dress party after all. Brad had cried laughing as she had hidden in the loo crying hot, silent tears of humiliation, simply unable to 'laugh it off' as Brad had said she should.

'Yes!' she answered, confused and frustrated that he was still messing with her heart. Memories of the anxiety dreams she'd suffered came flooding back, spoiling her happy lunchtime mood.

'Oh, well, that's nice. What did I do now?' he retorted.

'What are you talking about, Brad?' Maddie couldn't hide the frustration from her voice.

'The way you just answered . . . you seem annoyed with me. And I only called to see what you're doing.'

'What I'm doing?' Maddie repeated, thrown by him calling out of the blue after they'd agreed that it was just too painful to keep up this pretence of still caring deeply for each other.

'Yes, what are you doing – where are you? You sound different . . .' he said, an accusatory tone to his voice.

'Um, well . . . I'm on holiday. In Italy,' she said tentatively, wondering where this was going, and beginning to wish she'd let his call go to voicemail. She didn't want to do this. Not now. Not here in this gorgeous place. She wanted her memories of her time here to be beautiful and happy, not tarnished with negative vibes from having a tense conversation with Brad.

'Who with?' His accusatory tone was palpable this time. And Maddie heard him do a massive tut.

'On my own,' she said, following up with an impulsive nervous laugh. It irritated her that she had slipped so quickly into her old habit of wanting to appease him and keep things calm.

'OK, Mads . . . I was only asking, there's no need to be like that,' he huffed.

'Like what?' She could feel her cheeks flushing in tension.

'I don't know . . . weird. You've changed.'

Silence followed. Maddie let his accusation hang as she mulled it over.

'I guess I have changed. I do feel different these days . . . I'm working as a photographer, just as I always dream—'

'I was phoning to see if you were all right because I haven't heard from you in ages,' Brad cut her off. 'And well . . .' There was another short silence in which Maddie could hear him breathing, deliberating, '. . . I missed our chats.' Maddie pushed the phone away from her ear and onto the table. A little part of her heart had lifted on seeing his name on the screen of her phone and, for a split second, she had wondered – hoped even, if she was being perfectly honest – that he might be calling to fix things, to want to start over, like in a movie or something, with him having worked through his control issues and wanting to be better. But this wasn't a movie, and they couldn't just gloss over all the cracks in their relationship. This was real life. And it shocked her that she would feel this way after everything that had happened . . . after the way he had treated her, with such little regard, not even a proper conversation about 'not feeling the wedding vibe'. Eventually he had admitted that he had known for months that he was up for promotion and that it would mean moving to New York, so he'd been living a lie with her for all that time. Swallowing hard, Maddie took a deep breath.

'And I missed talking to you too, keeping in touch as we did when you first left, but maybe it's time to end the chats now. We've both moved on and so . . . I guess this is goodbye.' Maddie stayed quiet for a moment to let this sink in. She could see it all now, set out in front of her like a mini epiphany. He was playing with her, wasn't he. He wanted to keep her dangling, hanging on, and for what? So that if it didn't work out in New York and he decided to come home, he could pick up where he left off, or rather where he left her. He missed her missing him . . . if that made sense. And it was true, she had missed him like mad at first. She'd been lost without the familiarity of their relationship, after all they had been together for the majority of her adult life, and so she had called him and sent text messages . . . usually after a few too many glasses of wine on a lonely evening. Well, no more. Coming to Italy had given her headspace . . . pursuing the career she'd dreamt of in Naples, being away from her normal life, had helped bring things into sharp focus. So when Brad didn't reply she said, 'Goodbye, Brad,' and ended the call. Then she reached an index finger underneath her shades to wipe away a solitary tear, feeling like a fool for all the time and energy she had wasted on him. But she was relieved too, glad even, that it really was over now.

After inhaling through her nostrils and letting out a long breath as if drawing a line under it all, vowing to look to the future from now on, she focused her attention on the view once more, allowing her heart rate to slow back to a normal steady rhythm as she started to wonder who on earth the man at the bar could be.

13

'I didn't recognise you with your clothes on,' Maddie said, and immediately blushed on realising the inference. The exceedingly good-looking man from the bar was now standing at her table. Once he'd removed the baseball cap and shades to expose his black curls and show off his caramel-coloured eyes framed with the darkest, velvetiest lashes she'd ever seen, she could see he was the man in the red shorts from the deck of the Cartier party boat.

'Do you like the drink?' he asked, pointing to the limoncello cocktail.

'Um . . . yes, I do. Thank you.'

'I'm Giovanni, or Gio is what my friends call me. May I?' And he pulled out a chair.

Maddie's jaw dropped and she nodded her head, absolutely flabbergasted. She sat in stunned silence. Things like this just didn't happen to her in her real life. It was surreal. Everything about this moment

146

seemed like a dream; in fact, she'd go as far as saying she felt a bit euphoric, giddy, now that she'd gained a fresh perspective on the whole Brad situation, it was very liberating indeed. And because she was in one of the most beautiful places in the world with perhaps one of the most beautiful men in the world sitting in such close proximity. He smelled divine, of expensive aftershave, toasted almonds, sandalwood, and saltwater and all the gorgeously scented things she could think of. For a moment, she allowed herself a few minutes of fantasy to imagine they were together here on holiday, and she was having the time of her life with him.

'Are you OK?' Gio asked.

'Um, yes – I . . .' Maddie looked away, unsure of what to say next. She was still processing the conversation with Brad and her feelings of having drawn a line under it at last.

'You looked sad . . . unhappy. So, this is why I send you another cocktail,' he smiled.

'Thank you,' she said, still dazed and not really wanting to explain why she might have looked unhappy. Changing the subject, she added, 'But you can't just go buying drinks for random women you've never met before.'

'But we have met before . . . when you were on the ferry and I was on the party boat,' Gio pointed out in perfect English with a delicious Italian accent that gave Maddie butterflies. But she needed to get a grip and keep a clear head because who knew what he was up to . . . maybe this was a regular routine of his – send a drink over to a lonely, sad-looking single woman to see if she was desperate enough to be reeled in for a holiday fling, only to be left broken-hearted when it was time to go home, and he'd done a vanishing act. Not that there was anything wrong with having a no-strings-attached fling with an exceedingly hot man, absolutely not, but Maddie wasn't into that. For one thing, Gio was way out of her league. He looked like a supermodel, for crying out loud. And well . . . she didn't. Plus, she had read about men like Gio who preyed on vulnerable women; the next thing their victim knew, they were transferring their life savings to a 'digital wallet' to buy into his cryptocurrency empire. Ha! And this made Maddie smirk inwardly as she didn't have any savings, so Gio was wasting his time with her, if that was his game plan.

'Well, this . . . whatever this is, is not going to work with me, I'm afraid.' As soon as the words were out of her mouth, Maddie cringed at how prim she sounded.

'It's nothing, I promise. I saw you on the deck of the ferry yesterday and now here you are on your own and you look unhappy . . .' And to give him his due, Gio did look genuinely wounded by her rebuttal, but then instantly ruined it all by adding, 'No woman as beautiful as you should be sitting on her own in a restaurant.'

'Oh, come on, we're not in Victorian times here.' Maddie rolled her eyes, the frustration from her conversation with Brad still sizzling through her and the feeling of euphoria giving her a new boldness she wasn't used to. 'Do you really expect me to fall for this? Newsflash – a woman can do things on her own; she doesn't have to have a man to chaperone her or whatever.' She sat back in her seat and stared over the balcony, focusing her attention on the view instead as the sun cast a golden shimmer across the sea. It was mesmerising. And far more interesting than trying to navigate a conversation with someone who was quite clearly a massive player. He had been showing off on the party boat with all the socialites, indulgently spraying champagne around and then flirting and trying to cajole her to join him. Everything about Gio looked stereotypically 'bad boy', from his shirt that was unbuttoned just a little too far down so as to flash a glimpse, every time he leaned forward, of the ridiculously impressive muscular V in the centre of his chest, to the gold chain around his neck and leather and silver bangles on his left wrist, not to mention the eyebrow that seemed permanently cocked and the top lip that curled seductively whenever he spoke in his sexy Italian accent. Yes, Maddie had seen and heard enough.

'Look, it's very nice of you to buy me a cocktail, but I really must get going.' And she sat up and turned towards the other end of the restaurant where she hoped to catch the waiter's eye so she could ask for the bill.

'Please, at least tell me your name . . .' Gio said, standing up and going to help her with the chair as she went to stand up too.

'What for?' she asked, and he looked taken aback for a beat.

'Um, because I told you mine?' Lifting one shoulder, a line formed between his eyebrows in confusion as if he was a hundred per cent used to every woman he met falling for his charm and 'stunningly handsome man in a designer aftershave advert' looks. Maddie stared in baffled silence again, trying to work him out. 'Please,' Gio persevered, stepping forward now. Closer to her. Dipping his head to pick up his drink from the table, so he was looking up at her with warm, melting brown eyes, reminiscent of an adorable and quite irresistible puppy.

'OK . . .' *What harm could it do to just tell him my name? I'm leaving now anyway and will probably never see him again.* 'It's Maddie. And thanks again for the cocktail,' she told him, if only to not appear rude as she made a swift exit.

'It's my pleasure, Maddie. And the lunch . . . how do you say in England?' he paused to find the right words. Maddie quickly pushed the strap of her bag over her shoulder and found her purse. 'Is on the house.'

'But—' she opened her mouth and promptly closed it before some other prim retort tumbled out. A second later, she managed to add in a quiet voice, 'You can't do that.'

'I can . . . this is my family's restaurant. And I see now that I have made you sad and so I'd like to take care of the bill.' Gio shrugged and smiled kindly. 'I want to say sorry.' And placing a hand over his heart as if to pledge sincerity, he nodded and then walked away to the podium where the waiter had now appeared. Maddie raced after him to explain that she wasn't sad, she was just surprised, baffled, confused, and that nothing like this had ever happened to her before and so she had no idea what to say or do . . . and well . . . by the time she made it through the throng of children still dashing around playing chase,

Gio had vanished. And her moment for a thrilling rendezvous with an impossibly attractive man too.

'Please, can I have the bi—' Maddie started saying to the waiter, determined to pay for herself and besides, she could hardly just walk out, but the waiter pressed both his hands together a few times in quick succession and told her, 'There is no charge. Signor Bianchi tells me he takes care of it.'

'Oh, um . . . are you sure?' she checked, wishing she was the kind of person who could just take impromptu lunch gifts in her stride, be confident and not over-think it and convince herself it was some silly elaborate plan to have a joke at her expense, but she wasn't. She was still working on all that.

'Sì . . . very sure.' And he waved his left hand in the air with a flourish.

'Well . . . um, in that case,' and for some ridiculous reason, Maddie put out her hand to thank the waiter, which he obliged with a tentative handshake all the while giving her a very wary look. She had started walking away before remembering the whole purpose of her visit here today, and so swiftly turned back. 'Can I ask you something, please?'

'Of course.'

'Do you know a woman called Lucia by any chance?' Maddie paused on seeing the look of wariness return to the waiter's face. 'She was friends with my grandmother in the 1950s and, well . . . I just thought it might be nice to meet her while I'm on holiday here in Capri.' The waiter tilted his head to one side. 'She lives in a lemon orchard, or she did many years ago, and I was told there's one close by here. Jona, my Airbnb host said you might know here at the restaurant where the orchard is.' Her voice tailed off as a silence descended.

The waiter studied her momentarily, as if deciding whether to tell her or not, or so it seemed, before eventually saying, 'Ah, the orchard, yes is very close, you can walk to it.'

Once he'd given Maddie the directions, she thanked him and headed off to see if she could find Lucia still living there . . . hoping she might remember her English friend from the 1950s.

14

Maddie had almost reached the end of the lemon-canopied footpath where the taxi had originally dropped her off when she heard rapid footsteps crunching on the gravel behind her.

'Maddie . . . please wait.' She turned, surprised to see Gio striding purposefully towards her. 'You forget this.' And he held out her camera case.

Momentarily stunned, she stood in silence staring at the case, a mixture of disbelief dashing through her on realising that she had left her precious camera behind, followed by an enormous wave of relief to have it back. She took the case and clasped it to her chest. 'Thank you. I can't tell you how much this means . . . I'd be lost without it.'

'*Prego* . . . you are welcome,' Gio smiled and inclined his head. 'You were distracted. I made you sad. It's my fault.'

'No, please, it's not your fault, really I . . .' and she paused, inhaled, and after letting out a long breath as if to recalibrate herself and start again with him, she continued, 'It's true, I was distracted . . . but you weren't to blame,' she shook her head and flicked her eyes at the ground before looking back, 'err . . . somebody else was,' she settled on, figuring he didn't need to hear about the phone call from Brad. Besides, if she was perfectly honest with herself, she didn't want to talk about him any more. That part of her life was over now and had been for several months, she realised; the text-messaging chats and late-night calls were just leftovers and she'd certainly had her fill. 'Anyway, thanks again for this,' she waggled the camera case in the air and went to walk away, cursing herself as her toe caught on a tuft of grass and she stumbled, wishing she'd had the foresight to put her trainers on.

'Hey, are you OK?' Gio called out, and she turned back once again.

'Yes, thanks.' But Gio was coming towards her and so she stopped walking. On reaching her, he slid a hand through his dark curls before folding his arms across his chest and studying her. 'My waiter, Marco, he says you were asking about Nonna?' And he fixed his eyes on hers as if she was the one to be wary of now.

'Nonna?'

'Sì . . . Lucia, she is my grandmother!'

'Your grandmother?' Maddie repeated, astounded. '*Really?*'

'*Sì* . . . yes, really. Why do you ask about her?' and his eyes narrowed slightly as he lifted his chin.

'Oh, not for any sinister reason . . . she was friends with my grandmother many years ago in the Fifties.'

'Ah, yes, you say this to Marco, but Nonna never told us she has an English friend . . .'

'It's true, I promise you. They met at a little church called Chiesa di Sant'Andrea,' she told him, trying to get the pronunciation right. He smiled and nodded and so she assumed it was good enough.

'I know it. On the hilltop.'

'Yes, that's what I read in the letter from my grandmother . . .' Maddie made a mental note to make sure she went to see the church while she was here, another opportunity to step back in time and walk in her grandmother's footsteps. Hoisting the strap of her camera case over one shoulder, Maddie fished in her handbag for her phone so she could show him a photo of the letter that Kelly wrote to Patsy telling her about meeting her new friend, Lucia. After scrolling through to the part where Kelly mentioned the church and then the lemon orchard, she gave the phone to Gio. 'It's in English.'

'It's OK,' he confirmed. Shielding the screen from the sun with his hand, he took a look, scrolling to read the words, and then passed the phone back to her.

'She says very nice things about Capri.' Unfolding his arms, he pushed his hands into the pockets of his jeans but kept his scrutinising gaze fixed firmly on her.

'Yes. Yes, she loved it here and I can see why. It's a beautiful place.' She glanced around to indicate their magnificent backdrop. 'Would it be possible to meet Lucia? You see, my grandmother asked me to pass on a message to her,' Maddie added, remembering the last conversation they'd had before she left for Naples.

'But why do you come here now? After all these years?' Gio's eyes widened, the confident, flirtatious party-boy persona from earlier changing to reveal another layer, one of a concerned grandson looking out for his own grandmother. It warmed her soul and her wariness towards him waned a little.

'Well . . .' and she started to explain it all, the suitcase and Kelly Sinclair the movie star, she even mentioned wondering where Audrey was, all the while willing her face to stop flaming under his gaze. He was so damn hot. Hotter than any man she had ever met before, and he was definitely sizing her up. She could see his eyes studying her face, her hair . . . and now was he actually checking out her bust? She folded her arms and moved her head questioningly to one side.

'You have . . .' he gestured and fixed his eyes directly on her chest now, an amused smile dancing on his lips. Oh God. He was so obvious.

'Do you mind?' she lifted her chin.

'Are you sure?' he looked hesitant, but still with the smile in place. 'You want me to touch it?'

'Touch? Are you for real?' Maddie shook her head in disbelief. He really was something else. And her wariness from earlier was instantly fixed firmly back in place.

'It won't hurt, but I think it's better if you . . .' He nodded and lifted his eyebrows. Maddie followed his gaze. And yelped as Gio pointed at her bust. Perched on her left boob was an enormous bug. A beetle perhaps, with a petrol blue hard shell the size of a small, armoured tank. It was massive, and she'd never seen anything like it back home in Tindledale. Within a nanosecond, the giant bug was gone, flicked as fast as she could with her hand into a nearby hedge. She shuddered and checked all over her sundress, patting it down and swishing the material around her knees to be certain it had gone.

'Are you OK?' Gio asked, still looking amused.

'Um, yes . . . I think so. I've always hated big bugs,' she told him, her voice ragged.

'I see this,' he nodded, and to give him his due he did look a bit concerned now as he pulled a bottle of water from his back pocket and offered it to Maddie. 'For the shock.' He smiled and looked straight into her eyes as she took a few breaths and flapped a hand in front of her face to calm down. 'Sorry, I don't have anything stronger. Or you can come back to the restaurant for more limoncello?' She held his eye contact as they stood together in loaded silence.

'Oh . . . er,' Maddie came to, the panic fading as she tucked a curl behind her ear. 'No . . . I'm fine. But thank you.' She nodded and tore her eyes away from his. They each dipped their heads and studied the ground for a moment. Gio coughed and slipped the bottle back into his pocket before lifting his head. 'I should get going.' Maddie pointed with her thumb over her shoulder and turned to the left, then right, flustered and disorientated now.

'Please don't go . . . you say you want to meet my grandmother,' Gio said, stepping forward.

'I do, but I thought—'

'It's OK. You seem like a nice person . . . I think she will like you.' He smiled. 'And it's hot out here to wait for a taxi to show up.'

159

'Oh, are you sure? Yes, please,' and Maddie grinned, grateful for the chance to meet Gio's nonna, and she'd be lying if she didn't admit that she'd quite like to spend a bit more time in his company. Gio was interesting, an enigma; he seemed flashy, a player on the surface, but there was a depth, something more . . . the way he was looking out for his grandmother, his face when she had yelped on seeing the beetle, he had looked concerned.

'Yes, sure, you can meet her. Come, I take you there. You can tell me more while we walk. It's . . . how you say in English . . . *intrigante?*'

'Intriguing?' Maddie guessed, excitement building on this fortunate turn of luck bringing her one step closer to discovering more about her grandmother's extraordinary life. And with even more luck, Lucia might know about Audrey, and there would be a perfectly plausible explanation: she'd turn out to be an old friend that Granny simply lost touch with, not a baby at all, and Maddie would let her dad know so he could tell Granny. And everyone would be happy. No drama. No raking up of horrible memories from the past. Nothing for him to worry about upsetting Granny with after all. Maddie smiled to herself at the prospect of solving the mystery, and more importantly, putting an end to her grandmother's confusion and anguish.

'Sì. *Seguimi* . . . follow me,' And Gio indicated for her to walk with him along another more rugged path leading to a pair of tall wooden ranch-style doors that he pushed open to reveal an enormous grassy meadow full of orange and lemon trees in neat rows on one side and mimosa and cypress trees on the other, with a terracotta-coloured villa nestled amidst it all at the far end of the wide path down the middle. A golden retriever with a coat the colour of sun-bleached sand appeared from a shaded area underneath one of the lemon trees and came trundling towards them, her tail wagging in adoration on seeing Gio. 'This is Bella,' he told Maddie, crouching down to give the dog a playful ruffle and cuddle, circling both arms around her shoulders in affection. It was very appealing to watch, making Maddie warm to Gio even more.

'Ah, she is so cute,' Maddie smiled on seeing Bella lapping up the love from Gio before flopping down on to the grass and wriggling around on her back waiting for a tummy rub. Unable to resist, Maddie carefully placed her camera case on the grass and crouched down next to Gio, letting Bella sniff the back of her hand, and then petting her. 'How old is she?' Maddie asked on seeing Bella's greying muzzle.

'Very old lady – she is twelve,' Gio said, standing up and brushing flecks of sundried strawy grass from his jeans.

'Very impressive . . . I guess this Mediterranean sun must be good for her.' Maddie took in the lush surroundings, the sound of cicadas singing in the trees, a gentle mimosa-scented sea breeze fluttering over her bare arms and legs, and it made her feel light and relaxed. No wonder her grandmother had loved being here too and wrote to her sister telling her it was idyllic. It really was a special place, an oasis of tranquillity in contrast to the bustling vibrancy of the marina and La piazzetta on the other side of the island. Giving Bella one last tummy tickle, Maddie stood back up.

'Is good for all of us . . . but maybe not for you with your—' And he turned sideways to point at her left arm.

'Freckles?' she confirmed.

'Yes, this, freckles . . . and your gold hair . . . like a sun goddess,' he added, holding eye contact, and running a hand over his stubbled chin as if wondering whether to say something more, before changing his mind. 'Follow me, we go to the shade before you burn.' He walked on with Bella trundling along next to him. Maddie quickly gathered up her bag and camera case and dashed after them, his words replaying in her head, thinking how thoughtful it was of him to care that she might get sunburnt. Smiling, she lingered over his words – *gold hair, sun goddess* – loving how they made her feel lighter and a little more confident. Already her shoulders had lowered and her head was held higher; she knew a man's opinion of her looks shouldn't make her feel validated, but still . . . it felt good and so she was going with it.

'Do you live here too . . . with your grandmother, Lucia?' she asked, catching up and falling in step next to Gio, and Bella who was walking in between them with her tail wafting merrily from side to side.

'No, my home is a boat in the marina . . .'

'Ooh, that sounds nice,' Maddie said, instantly wishing she hadn't and had opted for something less 'small town' and slightly more sophisticated and worldly sounding instead.

'It's very good. I like the boat. My mother, my grand-mother and all my sisters live here, and it gets crazy and noisy. Is good to be quiet sometimes away from the restaurant, where it's also busy and noisy . . . and I take a break from the parties too.'

'Parties? Like the one you were at yesterday on the boat?' she asked, trying to figure him out. A player who also likes tranquillity and solitude. Interesting.

'Yes . . . I plan events and parties for the tourists. They come here and spend lots of money to have a good time and so I must entertain them.'

'Ah, I see, so you weren't there to have a good time yourself?' she ventured. 'Only it seemed like you were . . .' her voice trailed off on realising her curiosity was coming out all judgey and prim-sounding again.

'I make lots of money and the champagne parties and the girls are fun,' he said nonchalantly. Ah, so she was right after all: definitely a player! 'You should have joined the party,' he added, picking up a stick and giving it to Bella, who happily carried it the rest of the way in her mouth.

'Oh no, I couldn't.' Maddie shook her head.

'Why not? You do not like to party?' He stopped walking and turned to her with a curious look on his face.

'Well, yes . . . no, actually I'm not sure,' she admitted quietly, rushing through her memory in an attempt to remember when the last time was that she had been to a proper party. And to her horror, she realised it was Brad's work do, when she turned up as the pot-plant, and ages ago, years in fact. Brad had never liked parties, unless it was a work do, and he was there to impress with an eye on the next promotion, and her with strict instructions not to get drunk in case she showed him up. Apart from that time when she'd been dressed as a yucca plant . . . Brad hadn't minded her showing him up on that occasion!

'Not sure?' And Gio's expression turned to one of bafflement. 'But you are still young and sexy and—' He stopped mid-sentence when she looked away. 'What? You do not like me to say this?'

'Um, no . . . um, I don't know . . .' Her cheeks flamed so hard she could feel the blood pulsing under the surface of her skin. She wasn't sure anyone had ever said she was sexy before and so didn't know what to do with this comment. Silence followed. She coughed and swallowed hard and tried again. 'Well, it is a bit, err . . . forward. Flirty!' she settled on awkwardly, and immediately wished that she was the kind of breezy person who was used to a hot Italian man paying her a compliment and had a suitable response in her arsenal, but she was completely taken by surprise. 'Besides, we just met, and . . .' she stopped talking, and then after taking a breath, added, 'Sorry.'

'What for? Why are you sorry? It is true, you are sexy,' Gio said, as a statement of fact. Maddie opened her mouth to try to respond but was saved from saying anything more when a woman with grey hair wearing a black dress with a silver cross on a chain appeared on the veranda by the house. Clapping her hands together in what appeared to be glee, she shouted something in Italian before dashing down a small flight of steps and coming towards them, arms outstretched in greeting.

'*Gio, hai portato la tua ragazza!*' the woman exclaimed, clearly very excited and happy as she flung her arms around Gio and gave him a multitude of kisses on his left cheek, right cheek and then left again before stepping back and taking a good up-and-down look at Maddie, her face wreathed in an enormous smile. Then she stepped forward and placed a warm, welcoming hand on each of Maddie's arms before pulling her in for a lovely big hug that Maddie couldn't help but reciprocate as her face was squished up against the woman's ample bosoms. Letting Maddie go, the woman turned her attention back to Gio and cupped her hands around his face, her eyes sparkling and gazing at him adoringly.

'*Mama, per favore, non è la mia ragazza,*' and he shrugged off the woman's hands and gave Maddie a weary look before shaking his head. 'This is my mother . . . and she thinks you are my girlfriend . . . I tell her please, you are not my girlfriend,' Gio translated, rolling his eyes. Then he spoke in rapid Italian to his mum, whose shoulders drooped in disappointment as she appeared to be telling him off, even aiming an affectionate smack at the side of his arm which he managed to avoid by ducking out of the way just in time.

'Oh, um . . . no, no, sorry, I'm not his—' But before Maddie could finish the sentence two more, much younger women and a teenage girl came towards them and yelled excitedly in Italian to Gio, who held his arms out wide and glanced up to the sky as if in despair before yelling back in equally animated Italian until they were all talking and gesticulating louder and louder over one another.

'You see now why I go to live on a boat! They are crazy . . . and too loud,' Gio said out of the side of his mouth, leaning in to Maddie before shaking his head some more and casting out his arms again in further despair. The three women and the teenager dashed back towards the villa and Maddie wondered what was going on. 'They bring drinks and cakes,' Gio assured her. 'Come on, it will be OK.' And he placed a hand on the small of her back by her bottom, sending a spark of electricity straight up to the nape of her neck, to guide her past an enormous fig tree and onto the veranda shaded by a pastel pink and white awning. Gesturing towards a huge L-shaped rattan sofa covered in an assortment of cream-coloured cushions next to a low table and an array of other chairs and sun loungers, Gio waited until she was settled and then disappeared inside the house too.

Maddie placed her bag and camera beside her on the sofa and caught her breath. She had wanted an adventure, to see the world and to experience different things, so she wasn't complaining, but she never envisaged such a welcome, let alone meeting Gio and being invited to Lucia's home, the same place her grandmother had come to all those years ago. And what about Gio? He wasn't like any man she had ever met before. She thought again about the sexy comment and the gold hair, sun goddess, a smile forming on her lips . . . it was very flattering after all, but then she remembered her initial reaction, the not knowing how to respond, her immediate assumption that he was playing her, and for a moment it made her feel sad. Thirty-one, and she hadn't had the experience of feeling flattered and flirted with in such a way. And what about the hand on the small of her back making her tingle involuntarily – was there really such a thing as instant magnetism? It seemed so, but in such proximity to her bottom? Anywhere else, say on an ordinary day back home, and she would have thought it inappropriate and unwelcome. Certainly, if she had been working a shift in the local village pub and a bloke had come on to her, she most definitely would have thought it was sleazy if he placed his hand that near to her bottom. But here . . . with Gio, and his family, in this gorgeous place, it didn't seem off at all. If anything, it had felt thrilling. Yes, very thrilling indeed.

Moments later, and they all returned.

'Maddie, I sorry for saying you Gio's girlfriend,' his mum said with a very polite dip of her head in reverence as if on her best behaviour as she set a tray on the table and then looked towards Gio, who was standing by the door with his arms folded and his eyebrows raised, clearly checking to make sure she had done what he had asked her to. 'Please, I bring you a cold drink,' and she placed a glass in front of Maddie and poured a vibrant purple liquid with chunks of ice and orange slices in from a colourful blue and white flower-patterned ceramic jug before sitting down on the sofa too.

'It's cherry chinotto,' Gio said, pointing to the drink and coming over to the sofa to join them.

'Thank you.' Maddie picked up the glass and after surreptitiously sniffing the liquid, which she discovered smelt of oranges and cherries and cinnamon and cloves, she took a sip.

'Is refreshing, yes?' Gio's mum declared, before pouring a generous measure into another glass and handing it to him, then pouring herself a drink too.

'Yes, it is. And delicious.' Maddie took another mouthful, grateful for the ice-cold drink that tasted of sunshine and holidays and happy times.

'*Salute!*' Gio and his mum cheered, lifting their glasses towards Maddie.

'Oh . . . um, yes . . . *salute!*' She grinned, basking in their warm welcome.

'So, you come to see my mother, Lucia?' Gio's mum asked, leaning forward.

'Yes, that's right . . . please, if it's OK?' and Maddie glanced towards Gio to see if he was as guarded as he was earlier when she had asked about Lucia, but he seemed relaxed now with the glass in one hand and his free arm resting along the back of the sofa making his shirt stretch across his chest and accentuating that impressively muscular and well-defined V again. It was ridiculous, the charisma radiating from him. She quickly looked away on realising her eyes had ventured into staring territory, made worse when he appeared to have caught her looking and inclined his head slightly, his eyebrows knitting as if silently questioning her, a smile teasing at the corners of his lips. She willed her cheeks not to flame, even surreptitiously placing the palm of her left hand, which was cold from being around the glass full of the iced drink, up to the side of her face in an attempt to cool down.

'I explained it all to her.' Gio moved his head back and relaxed his eyebrows, but the hint of a smile remained in place. 'My mother—' He stopped talking when she interrupted to tell Maddie that her name was Valerie.

'Gio forget that I am a person as well as his mama.' Valerie laughed and went to give Gio another playful smack on the arm. Again, he leaned away just in time, giving Maddie the impression he was very used to being chastised by his mother. 'So, tell me yourself, Maddie, why you have come all the way from England to see us here?' Valerie smiled kindly, touching her fingers to the cross on the end of the chain around her neck.

And so Maddie went through it all again, explaining about the photoshoot in Naples and the wonderful opportunity to visit Capri. Then she got out her phone and showed Valerie the picture of Kelly Sinclair, who she now knew to be her grandmother, wearing a headscarf and shades on the boat with the iconic Capri Faraglioni rock stacks in the background.

'She is very beautiful,' Valerie declared, giving Maddie's arm a gentle pat as she passed the phone back to her. 'My mother is sleeping now, but you can come back another time to see if she remembers your grandmother. I am sure she will . . . her memory is

171

very good. She talks a lot about the "happy days", as she calls them, in the Fifties and Sixties, when she ran the restaurant, the wedding parties they hosted, and the food. My mother is a wonderful cook, and she loved to make the wedding cakes for the guests. These days she prefers to rest and potter in the orchard and read her books – she earned the easy life, she says.' And Valerie laughed.

'Oh . . . I can't wait to meet her, so yes, please, that would be wonderful if I could come back another time,' Maddie said, smiling to cover the dart of disappointment on knowing she wouldn't be meeting Lucia today. But then she reminded herself how lucky she was to have the chance to return to this oasis again. And maybe see Gio another time too. Then a thought came to her: 'Would you mind if I took some pictures of your beautiful orchard, please? If it's OK, I'd like to add them to my portfolio, but most of all I'd like to show my grandmother: her memory is fading and if she could just see the orchard for another time . . . I'm sure it would be a comfort for her. She wrote with such warmth and affection about her time here. And the photos might help her remember some things from the past too.'

'Ah, of course, yes, it is our pleasure for you to take pictures, and to show them to your grandmother,'

Valerie nodded as Gio's sisters returned, each with a plate of treats that they put on the table. 'But first you must eat.' And Valerie lifted one of the plates that was piled up high with plump fresh figs. Maddie selected one, delighted to discover that it was still warm from the sun as she bit into it, swiftly catching the sweet juice with a napkin as it trickled down her chin.

'Mmm, this is delicious.'

'You like to try?' one of the sisters said, lifting another plate. 'I'm Sara, by the way.'

'Nice to meet you, Sara. Mmm, thank you, what are these, they look amazing!' Maddie let her fingers hover over an assortment of pretty little pastry rolls, filled with a creamy paste and sprinkled with almonds and castor sugar.

'*Cannoli*. These ones are chocolate, here is lemon and then pistachio,' Sara pointed and then sat down opposite Maddie, helping herself to a couple of the chocolate ones. A phone rang.

'Ah, excuse me.' Gio stood up and with his phone pressed to his ear he wandered inside the villa. Maddie selected a lemon cannoli and savoured the sweet, tangy taste as she bit into it. Sara and Valerie opted for figs with rolls of ham wrapped around, while the other two sisters – Jenna in her twenties, Maddie reckoned, and Emmy, a teenager, tucked into the chocolate cannoli. A blissful silence ensued as they all enjoyed the food and sipped more of the chinotto. Licking sugar from her lips and feeling full from the delicious lunch and now snacks too, Maddie looked at her watch. Not wanting to overstay her welcome, she went to stand up.

'Please, no need to go yet . . . I like to hear about England,' Jenna asked. 'Is it as cool as it looks in the films?'

'Um, yes . . . it is pretty cool, in parts,' Maddie assured Jenna, sitting back in the seat, not wishing to spoil the illusion for her. 'But I think Capri is far cooler.'

'Does it really rain all the time?'

'Not all the time, but yes it can rain unexpectedly, usually you when you least want it to,' Maddie laughed. 'The weather isn't as nice as it is here.

'Have you been inside Buckingham Palace?' Jenna asked next, and Maddie shook her head. 'Have you ever met Prince William?' her eyes widened, 'Or Harry Styles?'

'No, I'd like to meet Harry, would you?'

Jenna nodded and grinned. 'He came here to Capri . . . but I didn't see him. Gio said I'm too young to come to the party on the boat to meet Harry.'

'Oh,' Maddie frowned in commiseration.

'Yes, so I go with my friend to the hotel where he stayed, but no luck.' And she frowned too. 'Are you staying in a hotel?'

'No, I'm staying in a lovely Airbnb above a flower shop in Via Fiore.'

'Ah, yes I know it,' Valerie joined in. 'Is *molto bella* . . . very pretty.'

'Do you have a boyfriend?' Emmy, the youngest sister, cut in, her eyes widening in wonder as she pushed the last of her cannoli into her mouth and waited eagerly for Maddie to answer.

'Um, no . . . not any more,' Maddie pressed her palms on her knees and studied the pattern of her sundress momentarily, before lifting her glass and busying herself by gently swirling the ice and orange slice mixture around.

'Why not?' Emmy asked.

'Well—'

'Is OK, it's private . . .' Jenna said to Maddie, then turned to her younger sister and glared before yelling something at her in Italian and then telling her to shush. Ignoring her, Emmy then added, 'Why don't you like Gio?'

'Oh . . . I do, I—' Maddie started, taken aback and unsure of what to say next. She didn't want to upset

175

anyone – it was clear they were a very close family, and all adored their brother and son, and she didn't *not* like Gio . . . in fact, her initial impression of him had been stereotyping and down to her own insecurities, that was obvious . . . but still, he was a flirt and could be a massive player, but either way, he was completely out of her league. She swallowed and drained the last of her drink. 'We just met and—'

'Gio needs a nice girlfriend.' It was Valerie who spoke this time. 'I tell him to stop going to the parties and to settle down. But he says you do not like him and tell me off for thinking you his girlfriend.'

'He likes you though. I notice it . . . and he said—' Emmy said, leaning forward, her voice a conspiratorial whisper and her eyes dancing with intrigue. Jenna nudged her as Gio reappeared on the veranda and they all looked in his direction.

Maddie, her face on fire now, squinted as she blinked in the sun. There was no denying the quickening of her pulse on seeing him standing there, casually leaning against the door frame with his muscular forearms folded across his chest, the dazzling, hot Italian sun radiating a hazy aura all around him. And he had changed out of his shirt into a more relaxed and effortless grey T-shirt that clung discreetly to his perfectly formed frame. The feeling was incredible . . .

and one she hadn't felt before as she slid a hand to her forehead to shield her eyes as she met Gio's gaze. Yes, he was incredibly hot, and she'd be lying if she said she hadn't been instantly attracted to him physically, but then she had been instantly attracted to Brad too, albeit in a far more measured way . . . and look where that ended up. Maddie didn't trust her own judgement when it came to the whole instant chemistry thing. It was hard to resist, but she wasn't about to make the same mistake twice. She caught her breath and busied herself with the pattern of her sundress, a million thoughts whizzing around inside her head as she wondered what had been said when they were all inside the villa. And what had Emmy been about to say before Jenna nudged her? Was Emmy just surmising, or had Gio told them all he liked her? Maddie mulled it over before quickly gathering herself . . . it was a fantasy in any case, nothing more. She and Gio had shared a very short conversation together, that was all; he wouldn't have told his family he liked her. He didn't even know her. Plus, she was sure that Gio was the kind of man who had many women to choose from.

'Come, I show you the best parts of the orchard for your pictures,' Gio offered, and after thanking Valerie, Sara, Jenna and Emmy, Maddie gave Bella's head a stroke and followed Gio up a hill towards the far end of the orchard, nearest the clifftop with the magnificent view of the Mediterranean. The hot breezy sea air was even more exhilarating up here, salty and citrus-scented. Maddie stopped by a heavily laden orange tree where there was an old wooden step ladder on the ground beneath it and an enormous wicker basket providing the perfect authentic rustic touches. 'You like this one?' Gio pointed to the tree.

'Yes, I do. It's beautiful.' As she walked towards the tree, preparing her camera as she went, lifting it and checking the light of the blue sky and sea backdrop against the orange and green tones of the leaves and grass, Maddie was in her element. She watched, spell-bound, as Gio effortlessly strode up to the top of the step ladder and plucked several ripe oranges, carefully carrying them in the crook of his elbow so as not to bruise them.

'I like to catch the fruit before it falls,' he explained as Maddie stood speechless, unable to take her eyes off him as she lowered the camera. He came down the ladder, pushing the branches aside, then casually lifted the bottom of his T-shirt, treating her to a quick glimpse of his toned abdomen, as he used the cloth to give each of the oranges an expert rub before gently resting them inside the basket.

'Sure,' Maddie squeaked, wondering who had just turned up the temperature; the Capri heat suddenly felt overwhelmingly searing. She could feel rivulets of sweat tracing a path from the nape of her neck all the way down to the small of her back, which still bore the sensation from the touch of Gio's hand.

'There is more,' he said over his shoulder, back up the ladder having spotted another selection of ripe fruit hanging from one of the top branches.

Coming to, Maddie lifted the camera again. 'Would you mind?' she asked tentatively, thinking what a fantastic shot this would be for her portfolio: an irresistibly attractive Italian man in jeans and a T-shirt picking oranges in his orchard overlooking the dazzling Mediterranean Sea.

'*Sì* . . . is OK,' he agreed easily, and turned his attention back to the tree to gather more oranges in the crook of his beautiful elbow.

Maddie took several pictures as Gio reached and stretched around the tree until he was satisfied that he'd picked all the ripe fruit. Walking again, he made his way to the next row of trees, keeping one of the oranges in his hand which he peeled, tore apart the segments and handed to her.

'Oh, thank you.' Maddie put her camera down carefully on the grass and bit into the sun-drenched orange still warm from the heat, a trail of super-sweet juice bursting on to her chin which she wiped with the back of her hand.

'It's good, yes?' Gio asked, devouring his half of the orange.

'Yes, very good. The best orange I ever tasted,' Maddie told him, nodding way too enthusiastically, and cringing slightly on realising she was still licking her fingers. Ducking down to retrieve her camera, she surreptitiously wiped her hands on the corner of her dress before standing back up.

'Are you OK, Maddie?' Gio asked, seemingly oblivious to the effect he was having on her.

'Oh yes,' she said, fiddling with her camera. 'I'm fine, I . . .' she paused. 'Um, shall we walk some more? I'd like to take some pictures to show my grandmother.'

'Of course. Let me show you the best place,' and he led the way.

As Maddie followed Gio through the long grass towards a grove of lemon trees set apart from the rest of the orchard, her thoughts turned to her grandmother. It was the most incredible feeling wondering if, as a young woman, she had wandered through this orchard and stood in this same spot and seen the same lemon trees that by the looks of their gnarled thick trunks had been here back then. And Maddie felt the moment seemed to draw her and her grandmother closer together, the decades between them disappearing. She couldn't wait to come back to this beautiful place again.

15

Feeling blissfully content from all the vitamin D she had soaked up yesterday in the orchard, and the kind hospitality Gio's family had shown her, Maddie was spending the day exploring the island, keen to photograph all the iconic landmarks to add to her portfolio. She had already visited Certosa di San Giacomo, the ancient, abandoned Roman monastery that had been built in 1371, and taken a selection of photos showcasing the spectacular white stone architecture, the open grass courtyards striking with their fuchsia flowering trees set against the cerulean sky. Up high on the hillside with the view of the Mediterranean, Maddie had loved wandering around in the blistering heat before retreating to the shade of the majestic colonnaded walkways, cooled by the refreshing sea air, and relishing the tranquillity and stillness of the place.

Then satisfied she had plenty of pictures showing the beauty of the monastery, the romance of the creamy white stone in such an idyllic location, she made her way to the nearby Giardini di Augusto, or Gardens of Augustus, taking her time as she wandered along Via Matteotti, another narrow street carved into the edge of a cliff with lush green foliage and olive trees. Pots of vivid red tumbling geraniums lined the wrought-iron railings to her left, framing the view down towards the sea. She stopped walking to look in the windows of the chic boutiques on her right, set into the cliffside with arched doorways and grey stone facades. Maddie smiled on seeing just how stylish they looked; even the gelato kiosk with its striped awning and creeping vine laden with lemons was picturesque. Moving on, she reached the iconic Carthusia perfume shop and couldn't resist popping inside to immerse herself in the irresistible scent and see the beautiful bottles lining the shelves: glass flacons filled with dried herbs and flowers, the ingredients that went into making the perfume here on the island, the information sign by the door had explained.

'*Lei vorrebbe provare il profumo?*' a handsome Italian man holding a bottle of perfume asked as she looked at all the different fragrances on the shelves.

'Sorry I don't under—'

He smiled and repeated in perfect English: 'Would you like to try the perfume?'

'Oh yes, please,' she replied, taking the strip of card that he had sprayed generously and handed to her. Pressing it to her nose, she inhaled and was immediately transported to that moment on the boat when she first arrived in Capri with the gloriously enveloping warm air that was fragranced with a sumptuous scent of lemons, holidays, and happiness . . . juniper and myrtle too. 'It's beautiful,' she breathed, looking at the label on the bottle. *Capri Forget Me Not.* She decided to treat herself to a bottle as a souvenir so she would never forget this perfect holiday – her first time abroad, travelling solo and having such a good time following her first assignment as a proper professional photographer. It was a special moment for Maddie, and she wanted to mark it, celebrate how far she had come since that horrible day in the flat when Brad had broken her heart. Inhaling again, she felt proud of having put herself back together. The prospect of further travel and building her new career had her brimming with excitement.

After paying for the perfume at the counter, delighted on seeing a few extra little sample phials popped into the gift bag, Maddie put her purse away.

'*Grazie*,' she beamed, and went on her way.

Walking along and swinging the perfume bag, she savoured the moment, feeling carefree and content as she smiled at people passing by and admired the surroundings. She stopped by a viewing balcony near the entrance to the Gardens of Augustus and sat on a bench covered in pretty yellow, blue, and white porcelain mosaic tiles. Leaning back and lifting her face to the sun, Maddie looped the strap of her camera over her head for safekeeping and rested her hands on either side of the bench, taking a moment to just sit and savour the feeling of stillness. She felt truly relaxed, for the first time in a very long time. And it was joyous. Coming on holiday really was just the thing she needed.

'*Fortunata. Vieni qui.*' Maddie opened her eyes. The toffee-coloured dog from the market appeared, wiggling her whole body from side to side in greeting, and the elderly man who had been playing the accordion was calling out as he tried to hurry along the path to fetch the dog away.

'Ah, it's OK,' Maddie waved and called back to him as she looped her finger through Fortunata's collar, which appeared to have disconnected from the lead still held in the man's hand.

'*Scusi . . .*' the man puffed on reaching the bench. Wiping his forehead with a white hanky, he slumped down on to the bench beside Maddie and attempted to clip the lead back onto Fortunata's collar.

'Can I help?' Maddie could see him struggling, his arthritic hands unable to open the clasp. Giving Fortunata a gentle stroke behind the ear, Maddie took the lead and clipped it to her collar.

'Thank you.' Fortunata pressed her paws up on to Maddie's knees and the man went to shoo her away. 'Sorry she interrupted your rest.'

'Oh, it's lovely to see her again . . . and you. How are you?' Maddie asked, then when the man looked at her blankly, she added, 'I saw you in the market . . . Fortunata lying on her blanket as you played the accordion.'

'*Ah, sì*,' he nodded. 'She remembers you and has a better memory than I do.' They both laughed on seeing Fortunata wagging her tail and pushing her little nose under Maddie's hand as a cue to carry on petting her.

'How could I forget her – she's adorable. How old is she?' Maddie stroked Fortunata's head and then swiftly scooted along the bench to make room as the dog expertly hopped up and snuggled down beside her, now resting her chin on Maddie's thigh.

'Sorry, please tell her to get down if she bothers you.'

'No, no, she's fine,' Maddie assured him, and made the most of her time stroking the dog. She'd always loved dogs and often thought that she would like to have one of her own some day.

'Are you waiting for someone?' the man asked.

'Oh no, I'm just enjoying this stunning view.'

'You come here alone?' he asked, looking surprised as he turned his face towards Maddie.

'Yes, for a holiday . . . I was working in Naples and well, my grandmother told me what a special place Capri is. She visited in the 1950s and so I wanted to see for myself. And she was right . . . it's spectacular.'

'Ah, Naples, my daughter lives there, but I like Capri more,' the man chuckled. 'And the 1950s, they were wonderful years. I was a younger man then, of course,' he said, nodding slowly as if recalling another time.

'Did you live here in Capri back then?'

'Sì . . . is when I first come here, from Roma . . . for my job to play the piano.'

'Amazing, where did you play?' she asked, keen to hear more about that time when her grandmother would have been here.

'Many hotels and restaurants. . .' He listed several before becoming distracted when his phone rang. Checking the screen and dismissing the call with an expressive, 'Pah' as he batted a hand in the air, he then slotted the phone back inside his pocket.

'My grandmother went to restaurants here . . . the Lemon Tree and La Canzone del Mare,' Maddie mentioned.

'Ah, yes . . . Gracie Fields . . . her restaurant with the swimming pool was the place to go back then. Lots of parties. I played the piano there too a few times.'

'Really? What was it like?'

'It was exciting. They were happy times of lots of fun and gaiety. I was a young man and all the ladies very beautiful. And generous too: they give big tips, leave bundles of notes on top of the piano. The key to their hotel room as well, sometimes,' he lifted his eyebrows. 'Rich people from around the world, the jet set. From Greece and America . . . they all come to do business and to have a good time. Is your grandmother from America?'

'Oh no, she's English. She was an actress though, in Hollywood,' Maddie said, the words still sounding surreal. 'Kelly Sinclair.' She held her breath. It could be possible their paths had crossed, so she'd thought it worth asking, but the man looked vague. 'I have a picture of her, if you'd like to see.'

'*Sì,*' he nodded. And he studied the image that Maddie showed him.

'She had a boyfriend called Clarke King. They were here together for a while in the summer . . .'

'Ah, Clarke! Yes, I know this name. A handsome actor . . . he came here in . . . 1953, I think. I remember because he asked me to play "That's Amore" – a romantic song and a big hit for Dean Martin at the time. Clarke, he left a huge tip and a box of finest cigars for me. And my wife . . . she was just my girlfriend in those days,' he explained, 'she swoons and then scolds me for not telling her when Clarke came into the restaurant. She was cross with me for a long time.' He laughed, making his shoulders bob up and down as he took another look at the picture of Maddie's grandmother. 'She's very beautiful, but sorry I don't remember her. She looks like Rita Hayworth – I met her once. And Liz Taylor too. They all come here.' And he lifted his hands up as Maddie listened, hanging on every word of this fascinating slice of history. A time in her grandmother's life, and she was hearing about it firsthand from someone who had been there.

After thanking the man for the lovely conversation and saying goodbye to him, and giving Fortunata another stroke behind the ears, Maddie walked on into the gardens. She was greeted with a burst of colour from the myriad of flowers, cacti and exotic tropical shrubs lining the pathways. A few minutes later she came to a tiled bench where she sat and gazed at the view across the bay of Naples, imagining her grandmother coming here too, maybe sitting in this same spot after partying the evening before with her dashing lover, Clarke. Maddie thought of what the man had told her, the insight into her grandmother's time here, and smiled to herself, pleased that Granny had experienced something incredible and had the time of her life, if only for a short time before her heart was broken and she went back home to Tindledale.

Oh Patsy, I am simply having the most spectacular time here in Capri with Clarke and his friends Lenny and Ray. Last night we dined in the prettiest restaurant tucked away in a secluded and exclusive enclave on the island. Lenny arranged it all and the place was jam-packed with the jet set. I spotted Clark Gable, who almost took my breath away with his debonair looks and smouldering charm. Audrey Hepburn, looking exquisite in an aqua silk dress, her hair effortlessly piled up in a beautiful chignon, and Grace Kelly too, wearing a chic tailored two-piece with a rope of pearls at her neck to match her earrings, and the most delicate lace gloves that she didn't remove until her meal arrived! I marvelled at how she managed her coupe filled with champagne, as I have tried this too but had to give up and remove my gloves for fear I would let the glass of bubbly liquid slip and spill and make the most almighty show of myself.

A Postcard from Capri

I must tell you, Patsy, that I am captivated to be in the company of all the Hollywood stars summering here. They are all perfectly charming and quite unassuming as they laugh and smile with the other guests at their tables. We drank champagne cocktails and dined on oysters last night, and I tried the most delicious bread called focaccia, sprinkled with rosemary and sea salt – I have never tasted anything quite like it before. Then we ate meatballs in tomato sauce, served with spaghetti that must be twirled with a fork for eating so as not to make a frightful mess.

After dinner we moved on to a piano bar and Clarke showed me again that he is simply the sweetest gentleman by asking the pianist to play my favourite song, 'That's Amore'. Of course, I blushed when he lifted the menu to shield us from the view of the other diners and kissed my cheek part way through the song. Lenny sat next to me and gave me a knowing wink, which only intensified my blushes, but he meant no harm. He too is a kind, gentle soul, for I saw how he discreetly touched Ray's hand under the table and shared a fleeting moment, only a glance, but enough to sustain their forbidden friendship for a few minutes as he insisted I join him in the first dance. Clarke didn't mind at all and clapped as Lenny twirled me around the little dance floor, later telling me how I shone and made his heart burst with pride on watching me dazzle under the sparkling lights. Later we were treated to a personal performance from Gracie, singing her marvellous 'Isle of Capri', which brought the house down with much clapping and whistling from the crowd.

Patsy, it was such a joyous evening, so full of gaiety with the most exciting people, the three very best friends I could ever hope to have in my life. I'm not sure Mother would approve though of my stepping out with three gentlemen on my own, but it is different here, it is the continental way, and nobody seems to mind in the slightest. All the stars of stage and screen mingle in the same way, the models, and businessmen too, and it feels like a million miles away from the life I had back home in Tindledale . . .

16

The next day, back at the path leading to the wooden doors of the orchard, Maddie was alight with curiosity, wondering what this was all about, what did Lucia want to tell her? Earlier this morning Jona had knocked on the door to Maddie's room and asked if she could come down to the street to talk to the man on a scooter waiting to see her. The man had turned out to be Gio; with an urgent look on his face, he'd explained, speaking fast in his irresistible Italian accent, that they had told his nonna about Maddie coming on holiday to Capri and wanting to find out more about her grandmother. When they'd asked Lucia if she'd known an Englishwoman called Rose, or Kelly Sinclair as she was also known, she had nodded. When they asked if she'd ever mentioned the name Audrey, Lucia had looked shocked. With her 'eyes springing open', as Gio described it, she had insisted on seeing Maddie right away. She'd sent Gio to, '*trovarla e sbri-*

gati . . . find her and hurry', because Lucia did indeed remember Kelly, though they had lost touch many years ago.

So Maddie had raced back to her room, grabbed her phone and camera case, having decided to ask if Lucia would let her take some pictures to share with her grandmother. Gio was waiting outside for her; he handed her a crash helmet then instructed her to climb on the pillion and hold on tight. Reaching her hands tentatively around his back, she held on, with her fingers tingling from the touch of his incredibly muscular body through the cotton of his fitted T-shirt. During the course of the journey she'd been a million times thankful that he hadn't been able to see her face, which she knew was flushed scarlet as she secretly savoured every second of the quite frankly sensational ride. She couldn't wait to tell Cynthia about meeting Gio, and wondered what her friend's perspective on him would be. She had been about to message Cyn earlier to see if she was awake yet – it was early morning now in San Diego – when Jona had knocked on the door. Maddie had called her dad yesterday evening to tell him that Granny really was Kelly Sinclair, Hollywood actress, and to let him know that she was hoping to meet Lucia. When she'd asked if he had managed to glean any more information from

Granny that could help them find Audrey, he said he hadn't. He'd sounded more anxious than excited, insisting that she call him before she spoke to her grandmother with any information that Lucia might share. She had agreed, but then he had said, on reflection, it would probably be best if Maddie waited until she got home so they could discuss it first. Of course, she was happy to respect his wishes, but as she hung up at the end of the call she couldn't help reflecting on his response when she told him about the orchard and meeting the man from the market and hearing his recollection of the Fifties . . . Her dad hadn't seemed in the least interested. In fact, she'd go as far as saying that he'd sounded sceptical about the prospect of Lucia remembering a friend from all those years ago. Something about his attitude had felt a bit off. Maddie couldn't think why her dad would be like this. Surely he'd want Audrey found, to put Granny's mind at rest and make her happy in her twilight years? Or maybe he was just disappointed not to have known about his mother's secret past as a Hollywood actress. Maddie had heard the hurt threading through his voice when he said, 'I'm a bit stunned, to be honest. Shocked. And I guess my first thought is, why did I never know? I wonder why she would keep something as big as this from me, her only son!'

Maddie's thoughts returned to the present as the bike slowed and the entrance to the orchard came into view.

'Thank you for coming back here so soon,' Gio said, taking his crash helmet off and running a hand through his mess of black curls. As the bottom of his T-shirt rose, flashing a glimpse of the dangerously taut abdomen her fingertips had traced mere moments earlier, Maddie had to turn away, her face a furnace. He took her crash helmet and stowed it on a handlebar next to his, seemingly oblivious to the effect he was having on her.

'Well, thank you for coming to get me, it's wonderful that Lucia remembers my grandmother.' She smiled, delighted to be back here so soon. 'Although, I hope I haven't alarmed her. I really don't want to cause her any upset.'

'I understand, but she says I must bring you right away . . . she wants to see you, so I do as I'm told. She knows her own mind – it is not for me to question her.' He shrugged, returning the smile, and Maddie liked his attitude, the way he respected his grandmother. But once again it made her question why her dad was being so 'gatekeeperish' . . . policing what she was to say to her own grandmother, as if not trusting her to be sensitive or tactful. Granny's memory may be fading, but she was still an adult woman who could make her own choices, so what right did her dad have to decide how much she should be told?

As Maddie went to walk towards the wooden gates. Gio gently touched her arm, his fingers warm as they brushed her bare skin. She caught her breath. 'Maddie, before we go to see her, I want to say sorry to you again.'

'Oh, really, there's no need.' She stood facing him as he dropped his hand, her skin still sizzling from his touch. 'It's fine, please . . . can we forget it. Like I said, I'm sorry too . . . I overreacted, I—' She stopped talking, conscious she was babbling from feeling flustered.

'Who is the other person to blame?'

'Er . . . what do you mean?'

'When I found your camera, you said somebody else was to blame for upsetting you. Is this why you were all alone on the ferry coming to Capri and then looked sad in my restaurant?'

'Um, no . . . no, well yes, I did come to Capri on my own and somebody else did make me feel sad and that's what distracted me. The phone call in the restaurant – it was one that I wasn't expecting.' She swallowed. Why did he want to know?

'Ah, yes, this is why I came to your table. I saw you talking on the phone, and I didn't like seeing you doing this . . .' He stopped talking to mime an unhappy face by lowering his soft brown eyes sadly, then lifting them back to hers. 'Is it your boyfriend?' The look on his face surprised Maddie. The confident persona from yesterday had slid away revealing another layer: curious, shy even.

'Yes.' A beat, as he waited to see if she was going to say more. She wasn't sure. 'It got complicated, that's all . . . it's over now and he's not my boyfriend any more,' she settled on.

'He hurt you?' Gio asked. Maddie fidgeted, stepping from one foot to the other, wishing he would leave it.

'Yes. Yes he did.'

'And this is why you are wary of me, why you didn't want to tell me your name? You think I will hurt you as well.'

'Gio, it's not that—' she started and then hesitated, taken aback by his perceptiveness.

'I do not know the English words to talk more, how do you say . . . *sofisticato.*'

'Sophisticated.'

'*Sì,*' he nodded.

'You're doing fine . . . in fact, sometimes, less is more,' she said, thinking of all the long, rambling conversations she'd had with Brad after he left, the lengthy WhatsApp chats where they 'talked' for ages and didn't actually manage to say very much at all.

'Less?' Gio tilted his head and creased his forehead, trying to work it out.

'Yes, it's just a phrase, a saying. It means sometimes you don't need to say lots of "sophisticated" words when a few short words can explain what you mean just as well.'

'Ah, OK, I see. So, like this . . .' and he took a moment, as if preparing the words he wanted to say to her. 'Maddie, I am interested in you. Right away when I first saw you on the boat. The way you look at the sea and the island . . . the, how do you say . . . *fascino?*

'Fascination?'

'*Sì* . . . the fascination in your eyes. You looked so happy to be here. Not like the wealthy party people who complain all the time.' He did a slight eye roll. 'And the way you look. Natural. Your hair, you are beautiful . . . it's like magic for me. Instant. But I know for you it's different, you do not feel the same. You think I am a bad boy. That I do not have good manners when I send you a drink and then come to your table.' And with one eyebrow raised, the corners of his mouth curled into a half smile, his eyes locking onto hers as he waited for her response.

'Gio, it's not that I don't like you . . . I don't know you; I don't know anything about you . . . but, um . . . I do think you're hot. Very hot in fac—' Maddie stopped talking and could feel her face frying. She instinctively looked away, unable to hold his gaze. Instant attraction. Beautiful. He said that. *This supermodel man in front of me who is so completely out of my league thinks I'm beautiful and nobody has ever said this to me before. Apart from Cynthia, but that doesn't really count, not really, it's not the same thing at all when it's your friend telling you you're beautiful after she's drunk near enough a whole bottle of prosecco to herself on New Year's Eve.* Maddie inhaled sharply through her nostrils and let out a long breath to try and clear the cacophony of thoughts racing through her head, but it was no use . . . she was feeling utterly overwhelmed. Yes, she was attracted to Gio, and it felt more than just a physical thing, it was insane and sounded cheesy inside her head to consider there was some kind of emotional connection too. Yet it was as if he could see right into her soul, and that made her feel *seen* in a way that she had never been until now. Maybe it was just wishful thinking, letting her fantasies run away with her because she was still on the rebound from the disastrous ending with Brad – which, let's face it, wasn't very long ago at all.

'We should probably get going . . . you did say your nonna told you to hurry,' she added as a way to change the subject and deflect attention from what she had just said. It was a little unnerving that Gio hadn't said anything in response to her telling him he was hot, very hot . . . but then he was most likely used to women, and probably some men, telling him this all the time. Which made it feel awkward as they both stood looking at each other. Then for some mad reason Maddie found herself wondering what it would be like to kiss him, like in a movie or something. To literally step forward and press her lips to his full, perfectly shaped mouth with the exquisite beauty spot just above the line of his stubble at the start of his cheek. She inhaled again and laughed, a ridiculous tinkly laugh, unlike any laugh she had ever uttered, because she knew she'd never have the nerve to do something like that. What was she thinking!

Gio swept a hand over his hair. Silence formed between them. The cicadas seemed to be strumming in time to the rapid pulse of her own blood pumping in her ears. And then the moment changed in an instant, saving her from herself. She swallowed hard and chewed the inside of her cheek, wishing she had responded to the compliments he had given her, said thank you . . . something at least, instead of gawping at him in silence. But wasn't it always the way: the perfect reply invariably eluded you in the moment when it was most needed.

'Yes, come on, I'll take you now to talk to Nonna. I'm interested too to see what she says, to hear about the past and what she remembers about your grandmother,' he said, and gestured politely for her to go first.

Walking side by side through the orchard, Maddie was conscious of Gio's hand mere millimetres from hers and it was all she could think of, like a magnetic field pulling her fingertips towards his. It was insane, the physical attraction she felt for him, and she wished she could tell him that she felt the same as he did, it had been an instant attraction for her too, lust at first sight . . . but the moment had vanished. She gripped the strap of her camera case.

'And one evening, I can take you for a date to the best place to watch the sun setting,' Gio said casually, and at first Maddie wasn't sure if she had heard him correctly or if she had daydreamed it. A date! 'Maddie, please, would you like to? And we can talk, so you can get to know me . . . and I want to learn more about you too.' He stopped walking and turned his head sideways, looking and gauging to see if he had overstepped the mark.

Maddie found herself nodding, giving herself a moment to figure him out. So maybe he wasn't playing with her after all. He'd have to be a pretty good actor to be making all this up, but still a part of her wasn't sure. It all seemed too good to be true: to come on a solo holiday and meet a hot Italian man who wanted to take her on a date, to talk and watch the sunset together. It was like a fantasy. Or a cliché, perhaps! She squeezed her hand a little tighter around the strap of her camera case as a way to focus and slow her overthinking.

Live for the moment, she told herself. She had wanted an adventure. It was one of the reasons she had come to Italy. And truth be told, she did want to spend more time with him, of this she was certain.

Her mind made up, she went for it: 'Yes . . . yes, I think I would like that very much.'

17

As they reached the villa, an elderly woman wearing a chic, floaty yellow silk dress with silvery grey hair in a bun at the nape of her neck was watching them from the veranda, one hand resting on a wooden cane. Bella, the dog, was next to her, wagging her tail and wriggling her body in greeting. The woman lifted her free hand in a wave towards Gio and Maddie. Gio waved back and quickened his pace. Maddie followed suit and soon they were standing on the veranda too, with Bella weaving her way around their legs before sitting in front of Maddie. She gave Bella's ear a stroke.

'*Le assomiglia.* You look just like her,' Lucia gasped, her English perfect with a soft Italian accent, as she moved her free hand up to the side of her face and scrutinised Maddie. Valerie appeared with a tray of drinks.

'Welcome, Maddie, and thank you for coming back.' Valerie smiled warmly, and after the introductions, they all sat down, with Lucia motioning for Maddie to sit on the sofa with her. Gio sat opposite in one of the chairs with Bella at his feet. He poured the drinks while Valerie disappeared inside the villa, only to return moments later with another platter of snacks: more of the homemade sweet cannoli pastries and bowls of olives, sliced meats, pears, oranges, and sun-ripened tomatoes, plump purple grapes with hunks of home-made bread and creamy burrata sprinkled with basil. A veritable feast, arranged exquisitely on a giant wooden sharing board. '*Buon appetito*,' Valerie declared, setting the colourful board in the centre of the table.

'Mama, please, sit with us,' Gio said, shaking his head as Valerie went to leave again, presumably to bring more food. 'This is plenty,' he said, arcing a hand over the table now laden with food. 'We are still full up from yesterday.' He patted his abdomen and exchanged a smile with Maddie. Valerie batted away her son's inference, clearly in her element when making delicious food for her family.

'Oh, Gio, Maddie is our new friend . . . eating together is how we strengthen relationships,' Valerie laughed, looping an arm around her son's shoulders to plant a kiss on the side of his face.

Maddie smiled contemplatively, uplifted to see how happy Gio's mum was. How close they all were.

A tight-knit family. Love . . . and food, welcome and warmth in abundance. And for a moment, Maddie thought of her own mother and how sad it was that they hadn't been able to forge a closeness like Gio clearly had with Valerie, Lucia, and his sisters. She mentally bookmarked the thought with a pledge to try again when she got home, to see if there was still time for her mum to turn things around, to choose herself and the life she could still have, and the relationship they could still have together, instead of the alcohol that Maddie knew was stealing her mum's happiness and quality of life. It seemed to Maddie that her mum had sacrificed enough to that . . .

After a brief conversation in Italian with Lucia, Valerie left them to it and went inside the villa.

'Please, Maddie, tell me about Kelly. How is she? Gio tells me she forgets the past.' Lucia shifted in her seat, so she was turned towards Maddie, who did the same to mirror her.

'Kelly?' Maddie murmured, swallowing a mouthful of tangy homemade lemonade packed with crushed ice, and momentarily forgetting her grandmother's film star name. 'Sorry, yes, of course, my grandmother is very well physically . . . but it's true, her memory is fading. She does remember you though. Very fondly.

And she asked me to tell you that she is sorry and that she never forgot you.' Maddie took another sip of her drink. 'She didn't say what she was sorry for though . . . I tried to find out more, so I hope this isn't difficult—' Maddie stopped talking as Gio leaned forward and took one of Lucia's hands in his.

'Nonna, what is it?' he said, his voice full of concern. 'You look sad.'

'No, no, I am not sad. I am happy that Kelly remembers me. We were the best of friends, my dear, sweet, kind, English friend . . . she taught me how to speak English with the correct words and the accent. A good teacher, *sì*?' Lucia looked at Maddie.

'Yes, a very good teacher, your English is perfect.'

'*Grazie.*' Lucia inclined her head with a modest smile and patted Gio's hand that was still holding hers. 'And we had so much fun that summer . . . sunbathing on the rocks by the seawater pool in the hotel where she stayed. Sailing and more sunbathing on the deck, swimming too in the sea and gasping in wonder at the electric blue water and green cave walls on our boat trip inside the Grotta Verde. We had dinner in many restaurants with different famous actors each night sitting around us at the other tables – I see Audrey Hepburn, Grace Kelly, Rita Hayworth, Richard Burton, Elizabeth Taylor . . . they all came here,' she paused, counting the film stars' names out on her fingers. 'All of them glamorous and sparkling. Kelly, she was different, though. Special. She had an aura, a fragility . . . no, not fragile, this is the wrong word . . . Strong. Yes, she was very strong. Is more how the other ones treat her. Vulnerable! Yes, this is it. She had a vulnerability. Like a little bird in the wrong nest.'

As Lucia fell silent, Maddie wondered what she could mean. Did someone take advantage of her grandmother? A dart of concern shot through her. Why would anyone do that? Granny was the loveliest, sweetest, kindest person she knew.

'Ah, yes the Kelly I knew was a lady, gentle and generous and loyal. And vivacious and vibrant when we were together having fun and sunbathing here in the orchard. She liked to play jokes and dare me to do silly things.' Lucia smiled and Maddie was fascinated on hearing about this version of her grandmother. The Granny she'd grown up with had always been unassuming and reserved.

'Really? I can't imagine my grandmother joking around and doing dares.' Maddie shook her head.

'Oh yes, she soaked me in water one time,' Lucia laughed. 'From the top of a ladder in the orchard she tipped a bucket of water on me. I didn't mind as the sun was so very hot and it was good to cool down.

But I did repay the joke by splatting her with ice cream on the way to church, so she had a sticky face and hands in Mass. Does she still have her religion?' Lucia asked, reaching to a small cross on a chain tucked inside the V-neck of her dress.

'Oh yes, she does, and never misses Mass on a Sunday. She lives in a care home now and there's a small church in the village nearby which she goes to with her friends,' Maddie explained.

Lucia smiled and nodded. 'This is how we first met. After Mass, she left her handbag behind and so I went after her to return it and we started chatting and never stopped . . .'

'Oh yes, I read about that in one of her letters to her sister – she said how happy she was to have met you,' Maddie told her, and Lucia's smile widened.

'Ah, it was a wonderful day . . . she came here, and we sat on the veranda, just like you are here now, and with my mama too . . .' Lucia stopped talking for a second to cross herself and look skywards. 'We bring out the trays of food and the cherry chinotto and we talked and talked for hours and picked oranges and figs too and then we went to the beach to see the sun setting on the sea. And then the next day too and every day on when she was here. The best summer. We spend all the time together, talking about Piero,

209

my husband,' Lucia crossed herself again. 'He was not my husband back then, we started courting and so it was a special time of romance and the giddy feeling of first love.' She sighed wistfully. 'And Kelly was so happy in love, and she talked about Clar—' Lucia stopped abruptly and after flashing a look at Gio, then Maddie, she looked downward, with a sadness in her eyes as she sighed and slowly moved her head from side to side. 'I wish she had stayed here . . . she said there is no place on earth like Capri. And it reminded her of home. The orchards and the grassy hills, the fresh air, the space, and the pace of life . . .' Lucia's voice drifted off and she looked ahead towards the fig tree as if remembering another time, golden days of long ago.

18

Capri, Italy, 1953

Kelly looked around the tiny church with the cool, whitewashed stone walls and open windows giving a breathtaking view of blue sky and sea, a refreshing salty breeze welcome as she listened to the priest delivering the service in lyrical Italian. Placing her handbag on the stone chapel floor at her feet, she settled on the wicker seated chair and allowed herself to daydream. Her thoughts drifted to the blissful night she had spent with Clarke in her bed, their lovemaking so passionate and . . . Kelly dipped her head to hide her blushes because this wasn't the place for such thoughts. Her mind meandered instead to earlier in the evening with Clarke, Lenny, and Ray. The fun they had had dancing and dining and laughing and larking around. Clarke had treated them to his incredibly slick tap-dance routine on the cobbles of a narrow, winding road that led them to the most exquisite little jetty carved from rocks in between two tall buildings with direct access to the lapping waves. The men had thrown off their lounge suits and dived in to cool down while she sat on the jetty and lifted her taffeta skirt to swirl her bare legs around in the warm water.

'Come in, my love, the water is warm like a bath,' Clarke had coaxed after swimming over to her, resting his elbows on the jetty where she sat, slicking his wet hair back, teasing her with his dazzling smile and twinkling toffee-coloured eyes and she had caught her breath on seeing his delight. A glimpse of the boyish charm he had in his younger years as he kissed her knees with his wet lips and glanced up pleadingly for her to join in and relish in the joyous moment too. 'It's just us four here, and why should you miss out on the fun because you're a girl?' Unable to resist, and with Lenny and Ray tempting her too as they swam and gambolled around in the water, she had thrown all caution to the wind and under the cover of darkness had discreetly unzipped her dress. In just her underwear and slip she had then lowered herself into the sensually divine water to swim under a twinkling starry sky. And she had truly never felt so alive as she had in that moment. They had all swum and laughed together, Clarke and Lenny taking it in turns to duck each other in headlocks just as they had as young boys back home in Mississippi . . . And then they had all sat on the jetty afterwards to dry off in the still-warm air before dressing and walking back to the hotel, Clarke slipping his arm around her shoulders on the quiet streets with nobody around to recognise him and spot them together, Lenny bravely letting the tips of his fingers touch Ray's as they strolled along side by side next to her.

Smiling at the memories of a marvellous night that she knew she was going to savour forever, Kelly let out a small sigh of contentment and gazed through the open window, grateful again to be summering on this magical island. Then on realising Mass was ending, she stood and drifted in her bubble of bliss from the church, following the other worshippers as they made their way down the hill, all the while daydreaming and looking forward to another evening with Clarke, creating more memories to treasure forever.

'*Aspetti per favore.*' Kelly felt a gentle tap on the side of her upper arm and stopped walking. '*La tua borsetta.*' She turned around to see an attractive Italian woman wearing a pretty pastel pink sheath dress with matching gloves and headscarf holding her handbag out towards her. '*L'hai lasciata in chiesa.*'

'Thank you so much. Sorry . . . *grazie*. I don't speak

much Italian,' Kelly explained, gratefully taking her handbag, and inwardly chastising herself for having left it in the church.

'Ah, I not speak much English,' the woman grinned. 'My name is Lucia,' she said tentatively, as if feeling her way, and then laughed. 'My nonna teach me a little English.'

'Hello Lucia. My name is Kelly,' she paused before adding, or 'Rose . . .'

'Two names?' Lucia queried, holding up her thumb and index finger and creasing her forehead.

'Err . . . yes, it's . . . well,' Kelly wondered how to overcome the language barrier to explain, but then settled on, 'Please call me Kelly,' figuring it best to use her professional name as this was her life now.

'Nice meeting you, Kelly. You have beautiful hair.'

'Thank you. I love your dress,' Kelly smiled, but Lucia frowned, clearly unsure of what she had just said. 'Your dress,' Kelly tried again and pointed to the skirt of her own dress and then to Lucia's dress.

'Ah . . . *il mio vestito*,' Lucia said, smoothing a hand over her dress.

'Yes, your dress,' Kelly laughed, nodding, 'and this is my dress.'

'I understand. You love my dress.' And Lucia laughed too. 'Two dresses!' And both women laughed together.

'Where you go to?' she asked as soon as they had both recovered.

'To the marina,' Kelly said, looking forward to a walk before heading back to the hotel and thinking she may have to translate, but Lucia understood and looped her arm through Kelly's. 'To see the boats. We walk together.' And so they did.

Having spent a lovely afternoon watching the boats and chatting over coffee in one of the quayside cafes with her new friend, Kelly had told Clarke all about her. He had been delighted to accept Lucia's invitation for them to dine at her boyfriend, Piero's, family restaurant, the Lemon Tree, and so here they were, overlooking the sea as they strolled beneath a pergola laden with lemons.

'Please, we have the very best table for you,' Piero said as they arrived, and Lucia came over to greet them immediately. As Clarke dipped his head to avoid being recognised, and quickly followed behind Piero to the privacy of the table tucked in the far corner of a wraparound balcony, Kelly checked her headscarf was in place and walked alongside Lucia.

'Your boyfriend is very handsome,' Lucia whispered excitedly, giving Kelly a subtle nudge with her elbow, not showing any sign of knowing who he was, which helped Kelly to relax.

'And yours too,' Kelly whispered back, having noticed Piero's handsome face and black curly hair with soft brown eyes. He looked kind and attentive as he had greeted them with open arms. The restaurant was clearly a traditional one with rustic wooden tables and chairs and tiled flooring, without any of the dazzle and chandeliers of the place they had been to last night. And there weren't any actors or jet set that Kelly could see as she walked through. But there were many families, several generations with lots of children darting around playing and laughing, and it made her think of home, in the village pub, or dancing around the maypole as a child as she saw three young girls skipping in a circle at the corner of the largest table in the centre of the restaurant.

'Oh, Lucia, this is perfect,' Kelly told her as she reached the table and took in the incredible view, the chairs thoughtfully positioned side by side so she and Clarke could both look out across the bay as they dined together.

'I am pleased you like it.' Lucia clapped her hands together, seemingly delighted at having replied in perfect English. The two women had been practising this afternoon, having an instant rapport, and making a pact to teach each other their respective languages. Kelly was over the moon to have found a female friend at last and was looking forward to spending more time with Lucia, especially with Clarke due to return to America ahead of her to star in a Broadway play. She was going to miss him dreadfully but was also determined to make the most of the time they still had here together in this beautiful place.

19

Maddie had been chatting with Lucia for over an hour now and was fascinated to find out about the friendship with her grandmother from all those years ago.

'Thank you for sharing this . . . it's amazing and quite wonderful to hear about my grandmother's life, and the younger woman she once was,' Maddie said. 'But I'm here for a few more days, so if you want to finish now, I could come back another time if you prefer?' Maddie could see a shimmer of sorrow in the elderly woman's eyes, a weariness, and didn't want to overtire her. Valerie came out on to the veranda with drinks on a tray which she set down on the table.

'No, it is OK . . . I like to remember Kelly. I was very fond of her, and I liked hearing about her home, in the English village. She told me our orchards reminded her of home, although with less sunshine.' Smiling now, Lucia focused again on the moment and turned to face Maddie once again. 'Gracie . . . Gracie Fields, she adored her too. She knew Kelly was special and she looked after her, she guided her. Kelly had dreamed of being a film star from when she was a little girl. It was all she ever wanted . . . but she had to learn to wear a tough skin to cope with the life for her in Los Angeles. And she did for a while when she went back there after leaving Capri, but then . . .'

Maddie sat motionless, spellbound as she listened to this version of her lovely grandmother, a young woman on the cusp of her life. It must have been an incredible experience for her. An adventure like no other. To be plucked from a rural farming village in England and transported to a whole other world in Hollywood, and then to come here, to the glamorous Capri of the 1950s, and mingle with all those iconic film stars. It must have been such an exhilarating contrast for her, from Tindledale to Tinseltown, countryside to concrete. And no wonder her grandmother liked being here in the orchard; Maddie imagined it reminded her a little of home as it must have been hard to leave all that she knew behind, to travel so far away, and it wasn't as if she could just pop back to see her family whenever she felt homesick. Or FaceTime or jump on Zoom for a virtual catch up. They didn't even have telephones in those days – at least, not in places like Honeysuckle Cottage – so her grandmother would have relied on the letters from her sister. That would have been all she had to keep her connected to her family. But what could have happened to make her leave Los Angeles and go back home to Tindledale, seemingly in disgrace? Maddie recalled Granny's letter to her father about it being a hopeless situation. And why hadn't she kept in touch with Lucia? Especially when they had spent such a wonderful summer together, and Granny had been so happy during her time here. Her grandmother could have written to her friend, stayed in touch, and visited Capri again many times, if she had wanted to. Maddie longed to find out more.

'Thank you for sharing all this, Lucia,' Maddie said. 'It's fascinating hearing about my grandmother's past, but I'm intrigued to know what changed, and why you lost touch with each other?' Silence followed, and Maddie felt concerned now on seeing Lucia free her wrinkled hand from Gio's and place it in her other, clasping and wringing both hands together as if agitated. 'But please, I've not come here to upset you, only to—' Maddie flashed a look at Gio, who gave her a subtle nod before he tried again.

'Nonna, what is it? Did something bad happen? Is this why you lost touch with Maddie's grandmother?'

More silence followed. Maddie and Gio looked at one another. 'Is it something to do with Audrey? You seemed shocked when I said her name to you earlier.' And Lucia stopped moving her hands.

'So much sadness.' Lucia shook her head, her eyelids closing momentarily as if she was remembering another time long ago, trying to work out where to start, or indeed what she could say to Maddie. 'But I think it is better if you talk to your grandmother . . . it is private.' Lucia fell silent once more as she looked away.

'Nonna, it's OK,' Gio soothed, 'Maddie's grandmother has trouble remembering the past, but she has asked for help to find Audrey. This is why Maddie has come to see you while she is here on holiday. Please, if there is anything you can remember . . .' And he flashed a look at Maddie, who quickly mouthed, *Thank you*, in response, grateful for his help and touched by the compassionate way he cared for Lucia. They waited while Lucia seemed to still be locked in another time as she stared with unseeing eyes over her grandson's shoulder and out across the picturesque orchard.

'I'm very sorry, Maddie . . .' Lucia eventually said, shaking her head from side to side before falling silent again.

'I know your friendship with my grandmother was a long time ago, and you may not remember—'

'This is true,' Lucia stepped in, 'it was long time ago, and I do want to help your grandmother remember her past, but it is not my business to talk about Audrey.' And she fell silent again. Maddie nodded in acceptance, respecting Lucia's decision, as it was clear she wasn't going to break her friend's confidence, even if they had lost touch decades ago.

'It's OK . . . I understand, and thank you for seeing me today. I appreciate it and it's been wonderful to hear about my grandmother's life from a friend who knew her as a young woman. A time in history for me to remember . . . even if she can't.' Maddie smiled, masking her disappointment on not being any further on in working out who Audrey was and how she fitted into her grandmother's life. She was curious to know why Lucia had clammed up when asked directly about Audrey. 'Such sadness' – that's what Lucia had said; given that her grandmother had never spoken about her past or her time in Capri in any detail, it seemed Maddie's instinct had been spot on: there was a sad secret in her grandmother's past. But what could it be? And how was Audrey linked? Maddie sat and contemplated for a moment, wondering where to go from here. She so desperately wanted to fulfil her promise and find Audrey, knowing how important it was to her grandmother. Maddie could still see the anguish in Granny's eyes when she'd mentioned Audrey. She couldn't bear to think of her grandmother going to her grave still agitated and asking about the mysterious Audrey . . .

'Your grandmother is a wonderful woman,' Lucia said, seeming more relaxed now that Maddie and Gio had dropped the questions about Audrey. 'I hope she is happy.'

'She is . . . she has her knitting group, and she really enjoys living with her friends in the sheltered housing . . .' Maddie said to be polite, her thoughts still on Audrey and what the sad secret was and if the two were linked. Then remembering the missing photos in the album at Honeysuckle Cottage, Maddie wondered if that was it. Was the sad secret something to do with her grandmother's sister, Patsy, and her baby? Was the baby called Audrey – was it as straightforward as that?

'What is it, Maddie?' Gio asked. 'Do you have another question?' he asked intuitively.

'Well, yes . . . there is something else I've wondered about,' she started, looking at Lucia as she felt her way, not wanting to make her agitated again.

'It's OK . . . please, ask me, and I will answer if I can.' Lucia smiled kindly.

'If you're sure, then thank you.' Lucia nodded for her to continue. 'You mentioned such sadness and so I wondered if this had something to do with my grandmother's family – her sister, Patsy, perhaps? We think they might have fallen out, you see, because there are photos missing from the album—'

'Oh no, no,' Lucia jumped in. 'This never happened – your grandmother loved her sister Patsy very much.' Maddie waited for Lucia to continue, sensing there was something more she wanted to say, but it wasn't forthcoming.

'My mother is tired now.' It was Valerie who spoke next. 'Perhaps you can come another time if you like to talk some more with her?'

'Yes, yes of course . . . and thank you.' Maddie stood up. 'Thank you, Lucia, it has been so nice to meet you.' Lucia nodded, and Maddie could see the elderly woman's eyelids drooping as Valerie looped her arm through her mother's to help her up.

'My joints are creaky,' Lucia laughed as she steadied herself on standing. 'It has been a pleasure to meet you, Maddie, and please come back another time.'

'Of course, I'd love to.' And after hugging Lucia and then Valerie, Maddie said her goodbyes and went to leave.

'Hey, Maddie, hang on.' Gio was at her side. 'It's a long way to walk. I can drive you back on my scooter.'

'Oh, yes please, that would be great.' Maddie grinned, delighted to have the opportunity to wrap her arms around Gio's muscular back again and draw in his delicious scent.

With a veritable spring in her step and mulling over everything Lucia had said, Maddie walked with Gio through the orchard back to the gate where he had left his scooter.

'Is everything OK, Maddie?' Gio asked. 'You are very quiet. Do you not want me to give you a lift on the scooter?'

'Ah, yes, I do . . . I'm just thinking it all through. Hearing about my grandmother when she was a young woman is very fascinating, but it's a lot to take in. And I can't help wondering why Lucia didn't want to talk about Audrey.'

'Yes, I'm sorry my nonna didn't want to tell you the . . . *segreto* . . . how do you say this in English?' he lifted his hands up.

'A secret?' Maddie raised her eyebrows.

'Yes, I think my nonna is keeping the secret about Audrey. And your grandmother's sister, Patsy . . .' He nodded, seemingly deep in thought too now as he dipped his head and pushed his hands into his pockets. As he kicked at a tuft of grass, Maddie couldn't help herself from sneaking a peek at his beautiful face, the beauty spot at the stubble line, his thick dark lashes even more gorgeous from this angle. Yet again she felt an overwhelming urge to move in closer to him. Inhaling sharply, thinking she really must get a grip, she hitched the strap of her camera case further onto her shoulder to distract herself and moved her thoughts back to Lucia and their conversation.

'Why would she do that?' Maddie thought aloud.

'I don't know, Maddie, but it makes me more curious.' And he grinned mischievously. 'It's a mystery for us to solve, yes?'

'Yes, I guess it is. I promised my grandmother I would help her, but I'm not sure what else I can do, to be honest.'

'You say you have letters from the past,' Gio said, then quickly added, 'come on, let's walk this way under the trees before you get sunburnt.'

'Sure.' Maddie turned to carry on walking with him as he cut across to the orchard, inwardly smiling again at his thoughtfulness. 'Yes, that's right, there are lots more letters to read through. Perhaps I'll find something else. I just can't help thinking that this island holds the key, but it's only a hunch, nothing more.'

'A hunch?' he queried. 'What is this word?'

'It means a feeling, a question. There isn't any real proof that I can see, but I wonder why your grandmother didn't want to tell us.'

'Yes, I wonder this too,' he said, then added, 'I can help you with the letters . . . to read them, if you like?'

'Oh, are you sure?'

'Of course . . . I would not offer to if I didn't want to,' he said, folding his arms and studying her. 'I want to spend more time with you,' he paused to gauge her reaction. She smiled as butterflies fluttered inside her. 'And I want to help you work this out for your grandmother – family is important, it's everything . . .' he added touchingly.

'Thank you, that would be wonderful,' Maddie said, loving his candidness, and thinking how refreshing it was after Brad and the games he used to play. She swallowed and pulled back the thought . . . not wanting to make comparisons. More importantly, she wanted to enjoy the moment, be present . . . or whatever it was they said in the self-help podcasts she had listened to. Yes, here, and now with Gio, in this glorious place, she was beginning to see he was quite different to Brad. Or was it her that was different? She certainly felt different here with Gio, as if she was starting to let go of those learned behaviours from her past.

'Good. I must work in the restaurant tomorrow, but it will be quiet in the afternoon so we can do this then . . . I will come to collect you.' And so it was agreed. Maddie grinned and pressed her lips together in glee as they carried on walking.

20

Los Angeles, America 1953

Kelly lifted the lid from the bottle of her favourite Dior perfume and sprayed her wrists, rubbing them together to activate the sensual scent, before applying a liberal spritz underneath each ear lobe and across her collar bones. Inhaling and smiling to herself in the mirror of her dressing table in the bedroom of her apartment in Los Angeles, she thought with anticipation of what the evening ahead had in store for her and Clarke. He would be here soon at her apartment, and she couldn't wait to see him. Capri had been simply marvellous, invigorating and restorative, and she felt happier and more vibrant than she had in such a long time. And with her dear friend Lucia to write to and confide in as well, she felt far less lonely. In fact, Kelly had wasted no time in putting pen to paper; even though she had only been back in America for a few days, she had already started writing a long letter to Lucia. This reminded her, she must finish the letter off and take it for mailing before she started filming tomorrow and was confined to the compound of the film studio. Brushing her platinum curls, Kelly then applied a sheen of delicate rose-pink lipstick, knowing Clarke much preferred it to the thick, gloopy affair the make-up artist used on set. After darkening her lashes with cake mascara, she pinched her cheeks to achieve a flushed, fresh look. Straightening her stockings and slipping her shoes on, she pinned a brooch to her dress and took one last look in the mirror, smiling on seeing her carefully roller-waved platinum hair shining nicely in the lamplight.

Wandering through to the small sitting area, Kelly glanced at the clock and on seeing there were fifteen minutes or so until Clarke was due to arrive, she picked up her fountain pen and red leather writing set – it had been a gift from Dad and Patsy, given to her on the day she departed Tindledale – to add a few more lines to her letter, eager to thank Lucia for passing on the number of the telephone here in the hallway of the apartment block to her cousin, Maribella, in Pasadena. Maribella had called yesterday, and Tammy, who lived next door, had banged on the door and yelled, 'Call for Kelly', which had been most exciting as Kelly had never received a telephone call just for her before. Wasting no time, she had dashed down the stairs and accepted the call from Maribella, who spoke English with a lyrical accent just like Lucia's, immediately transporting Kelly back to the beautiful hills of Capri, sitting on the veranda overlooking the orchard, sipping her friend's homemade cherry chinotto and chatting late into the evening as they watched the hazy Mediterranean sun setting over the sparkling sea. Kelly sighed as she daydreamed, wishing she could bottle all the feelings from her time in Capri to savour forever. Her time there had reminded her of home, in stark contrast to the high-octane atmosphere here in Hollywood. And so, Kelly was delighted that she and Maribella had arranged to meet on Sunday when she had a whole day free from filming. She was very much looking forward to spending time with Maribella and going to church with her and then on to visit their Italian bakery, eager to capture the essence of Capri and Italy once again.

Kelly wrote a few more sentences saying how excited she was to be seeing Clarke this evening and asking about Lucia's romance with Piero, hoping it was going well for them both. Kelly wished her friend luck and was just about to start another sentence with news of the filming that Lucia had asked to hear more of when she heard a knock on the door to her apartment. An immediate swirl of delight pulsed through her as she put down the pen and writing set, swiftly neatened her pink and white striped taffeta off-the-shoulder dress and checked her hair in the mirror again above the fireplace before pulling open the door. Her heart foundered on seeing that it wasn't Clarke. Instead, a telegram delivery boy in a peaked cap was proffering a yellow envelope towards her.

'Telegram for a Miss Rose O'Malley?' he announced, and Kelly's heart lifted once more on realising this would be the news of Patsy's baby. Dad must have sent it as he refused to refer to her as Kelly Sinclair, telling her she'd always be his Rose O'Malley, but that was OK. She was ever so grateful to him, and Patsy too for asking Dad to step in, when as they had rightly predicted, she was most likely run ragged with feeding her new baby and changing nappies day and night. She imagined Dad putting on his best suit and going to the little post office by the village green to arrange for this momentous news to be sent to her all the way from England.

'I'm an aunt,' she proudly told the boy, smiling widely as she pressed the precious envelope to her chest, her thoughts full of Dad and Patsy and now a new baby all the way back home in Tindledale. For a moment, she felt a dart of the familiar homesickness and immediately pushed it away, determined to not let anything spoil this marvellous moment. After thanking the boy, Kelly turned and tapped the door closed with the stiletto heel of her shoe as she walked back towards the sitting room, merrily humming Vaughn Monroe's ballad, 'Blue for a Boy – Pink for a Girl', opening the envelope as she went, keen to see if she had a niece or a nephew.

And froze.

She stopped humming, blood chilling to ice in her veins.

The words merged as she tried to read them again and make sense of this dreadful news.

> Deeply regret to inform you Patsy
> died in childbirth stop Funeral on
> Friday stop Dad

Kelly read the words over and over. Her fingertips instinctively reaching for the gold cross that she had worn on a chain around her neck since her mother passed, but it wasn't there. Instead, it was hidden away, as she had been instructed to do. Damn you, Louis. Damn you. 'DAMN YOU!' she shouted into the abyss of her apartment, shock turning to fear, turning to anger at the helplessness of this moment. Frantically, she pulled at the closet door in the hallway and found her handbag with the cross inside the envelope, needing the cross to comfort her, to hold it in her hand, for it felt as if her faith was all that she had to hold on to. Maybe it could somehow help her make sense of this terrible news. The thought of losing Patsy, her dear forthright and pragmatic twin sister, sensible and bold, her anchor and glorious other half . . . the pain, searing and intense, was like no other she had ever experienced.

'Oh Patsy. What happened to you?' In her chest, Kelly was certain there was a vice tightening around her heart as if to squeeze the life right out of her. Her breathing became shallow and ragged as she staggered along the narrow hallway to slump onto the settee. She stood up. And sat down again. Trembling in shock and utter hopelessness, incapable of knowing what to do as silent tears slid down her face, mingling with cake mascara and landing in large black droplets on the backs of her hands, splashing the yellow telegram still clasped within them, the cross and chain looped around.

'My darling. The door was wide open . . . what happened?' Kelly became conscious of Clarke standing in front of her, concern etched on his face as he crouched down and placed a hand on each of her arms. 'What is it? Did Louis do this? I'm not gonna stand for him treating you this way.' Clarke stood up and paced angrily for a while before bringing himself back down in front of her. 'Sweetheart, tell me what he did to you. I'll have Lenny go right on round there to have it out with him.' Kelly closed her eyes and brought the cross to her lips with her left hand, muttering a prayer as she shook her head from side to side and unfurled the fingers of her right hand to release the now crumpled telegram. Hesitant, Clarke took the paper from her and read the words before letting it drop to the floor. As he cradled her, she could hear soft words coming from his lips, which were pressed tightly into her shoulder as if he was desperately trying to keep her from falling apart completely. She felt his hand smoothing her hair, and his face in front of hers, forehead touching hers before leaning back and gently wiping her tears away with the lightest touch of his thumb. 'Oh Rose, my sweet, dear English Rose . . .'

Three days later, and Kelly had managed to push her feelings of sorrow far down enough to appear on set. While Gwen set about ladling the make-up on to hide the circles beneath her eyes, she'd focused on counting every second until she could go home and cry some more for Patsy, still unable to comprehend that she was never going to see her twin sister again.

She longed to go back to Tindledale to see how Dad and George were coping without Patsy. And to find out what had happened to the baby? The telegram hadn't told her. Kelly was gripped with fear that the omission meant the baby had suffered the same fate as Patsy. If the baby had survived, surely Dad would have shared this news? Kelly had been tying herself in knots over it all. She had sent a telegram with words of condolence and asking after the baby, but so far, only silence. There was no telephone in the hallway of Honeysuckle Cottage, so far away in England, or indeed any of the ordinary houses in the village. She wondered if she might book a telephone call to the landlord of the Duck & Puddle pub on the other side of the village green, so he could fetch Dad to come and talk to her. There were so many thoughts circulating inside her head and all she really wanted was to be with Patsy, laughing and teasing her and talking her out of whatever silly escapade she was currently up to. Only to cry another river when it sank in once more that there would never be an opportunity to do this again.

Trying to hold back the tears, she made her way on to the set. Within minutes, Louis was bawling her out for fluffing her lines. Furious, he then marched her to his office, determined to get to the bottom of whatever was marring her performance. But when she'd told him about Patsy and asked permission to attend the funeral, he roared, 'Send flowers – you going there won't bring her back!' When she dissolved into tears, he changed tack; taking her hand in his and adopting the silky tone he had used in the sitting room of Honeysuckle Cottage, he urged her, 'See the priest. Hell, we'll get a priest brought here to you on set. Or . . . I don't know . . . mix yourself a large whisky, talk to a girlfriend, do whatever it is you broads do.' But when she had been unable to prevent a fresh wave of tears from overflowing, he had reverted to type and bellowed, 'Stop the damn crying! You had all that time off in Capri and now the show must go on. This is Hollywood, time is money! *Big money!*' And then he reached for the silver cutter he kept in his desk drawer, chopped off the end of a new cigar, stuck it in his mouth and began sucking wetly as he swivelled his chair so he was facing the wall. Recognising her cue to leave his office and close the door behind her, she'd fled to the dressing room, gathered her belongings and returned to the sanctuary of her apartment.

*

'I'll swing for him!' Clarke seethed, tearing off his leather motorcycling jacket and slinging it over the back of a chair in frustration. 'Tell me again, doll, what he said . . . He has to let you go home. It's insane to make you work when you're grieving and heartbroken.' He was pacing up and down her sitting room, his shirtsleeves rolled up, his hands alternating between holding his head and settling on his hips.

'It's no use, Clarke, Louis is insistent that I stay here.' She plucked another tissue from a box and dabbed at her raw eyes, clasping the sides of her cardigan tighter together in an attempt to block out the constant chill. Even though the Los Angeles weather was hot and sunny, she just couldn't seem to feel warm since hearing the news of poor Patsy.

'I will talk to him.'

'Oh Clarke, my love, it's no use – he made it very clear that if I go now then I'm done for, finished in Hollywood . . . and to not bother coming back. I must accept that I chose this life, it's my own fault for being so far away from—'

'Sweetheart,' Clarke said, softening now, 'you didn't choose this. You didn't know your sister was going to . . .' he let his voice fade, unable to say the word out loud. 'The guy is a monster. It's not right. Not when you've worked so hard, and you're so close to hitting the big time. You were made for the part, and the film is gonna be a blockbuster—'

'The studio will find someone else – Louis told me that too.'

'Pah! He's trying to scare you,' Clarke dismissed the threat, batting a hand in the air before bringing it down hard on the kitchen counter in frustration.

'Maybe he is. I'll never know. This is the worst predicament of my life. It's disrespectful if I don't go to see my father, and he might need me. Patsy will be buried on Friday and I won't be there. We are so close—' Kelly took a breath, 'I mean we *were* so close. I should pay my respects at her graveside. I wrote to her every week, sometimes twice a week, and she wrote back too. And I liked to do it . . . writing the letters gave me comfort. It made me feel connected to home.'

'You will always have that, my love,' Clarke soothed. 'Relationships don't end when someone passes. They change. You will have a different relationship with Patsy now . . . you can still write to her, put all the news in your datebook and imagine what she would make of it all. You can keep her memory alive that way . . . And I'll send Lenny to talk some sense into Louis, to stop him making you feel bad just for wanting to do your duty . . . to be a good daughter, a good sister.' He broke off and shoved his hands into his pockets and paced some more. 'You know, better still, I'll tell him myself.' Clarke stopped walking and pulled a hand from his pocket to punch a finger into the air. 'I'll go now and make him see sense . . . while you're away, production can shoot all the scenes that don't include you and cut yours in when you return.'

'Clarke, I've already pleaded with him and made this same suggestion, and it had no effect, his mind is made up.'

Sandra had telephoned an hour ago to say that she too had attempted to persuade Louis to relent, brazenly perching on the corner of his desk and leaning across to straighten his bow tie while telling him in a soothing, purring voice that it would be only one teeny tiny week, two at best, that Kelly would be away from filming, only for him to dismiss her with the flick of his hand.

'Louis told me if I insist on going, the studio will file a lawsuit for "wilful violation of contract", and I don't have that kind of money.' Kelly began to sob again, the words ringing in her ears. She felt as if she were back there in Louis's wood-panelled office with the walls closing in on her, squeezing and stifling, making it a struggle to breathe.

'Well, I do have that kind of money!' Clarke thundered. 'And you know what – I'm gonna tell Louis that I'll be going with you to England. I'm done with hiding our love away like a shameful secret! He'll have no choice but to delay shooting the whole goddam film! Bet he'll wise up soon enough when I land him with *that* bombshell!'

And after wrapping his arms around her and kissing her passionately, telling her he loved her and would fix it all, Clarke snatched up his motorcycling jacket from the chair and stormed out of the apartment before she could do anything to stop him . . .

21

The next day in the restaurant, Maddie was sitting on a high stool at the bar with her laptop and an Aperol spritz cocktail that Gio had mixed for her.

'You like this?' he said, gesturing to the glass as he tipped a scoop of ice into his own drink and came around the bar to sit on the stool beside her, his muscular thigh brushing the side of hers as he sat down, making her catch her breath.

'Mmm, yes, it's delicious, thank you. My first aperol spritz and I don't think it will be the last,' she smiled, taking another sip and tapping the screen of the laptop to bring up the folder where all the pictures of the contents of the suitcase from Honeysuckle Cottage were stored.

'Wow, Maddie there are lots of letters,' Gio whistled, leaning in closer to see the screen and treating her to a burst of his gorgeous scent – different to the one he was wearing when they first met – this had a hint of almonds and coconut and fun times. Maddie loved it. And with the seagulls cawing over the sound of the waves below and the slice of orange on the side of the glass and the upbeat house music playing from a speaker behind the bar, she was definitely getting the holiday vibe. She wondered whether she should just give up on trawling through all the photos and admit defeat. She wasn't going to find Audrey, so maybe her hunch was wrong in thinking the island of Capri held the clue, and she should just relish the rest of the time she had here on holiday with Gio and pick up the search for Audrey when she got home.

'This isn't a letter,' he said, breaking her reverie as he clicked on the mousepad and opened the last file on the list. Maddie had been trying to read through all the papers in some kind of order so she could keep track and so hadn't got to many of them yet.

'What is it?' She lifted her shades to get a better look at the screen and saw a picture of an old-fashioned telegram, American by the looks of it, with the Western Union logo across the top. They read the words together. And then both sat back in their seats.

'Oh no, this is shocking . . . poor Patsy, and poor Granny,' Maddie said, reading the stark words of the telegram. It must have come as an enormous shock to her grandmother, finding out from a piece of paper that her dear sister had died.

'I'm very sorry, Maddie,' Gio said, turning his head towards hers, his face mere millimetres from hers, their shoulders touching as he nudged her comfortingly. 'It's sad news for your family . . .'

'Yes . . . and this could explain why Lucia went quiet and seemed agitated when I asked her yesterday about Patsy,' she said softly. 'I had no idea and certainly wouldn't have brought it up if I had. Sorry, Gio, I really didn't want to upset her—'

'Please, Maddie, it's not your fault. I told you my nonna asked me to bring you to see her and she knows her own mind.'

'True, you did . . . but still, it's bringing up painful memories for her.' Maddie considered whether this could be the sad secret that had been hinted at from Granny not having spoken about her past to any of the family. But on reflection, she wasn't convinced. After all, it wasn't really a secret as such, her sister dying. Shocking and desperately sad, yes, so maybe Granny tucked it away as it was just too painful to recount many years later to her son, or granddaughters.

'Maddie, do you think Patsy's baby could be Audrey?' Gio asked. 'It's possible, maybe, that your grandmother has forgotten . . .' He lifted one shoulder and nodded his head.

'I did consider this when I first read some of the letters and discovered that my grandmother had a sister who was pregnant, but if that's the case, then where is she? And why doesn't my dad know Audrey? She would be his cousin, older than him if she was born in 1953 – the date on the telegram – but as far as I'm aware my dad doesn't have any other family.'

'Maybe Patsy's husband took the baby to live far away, and they lost touch with your grandmother?' he suggested. 'We could ask Nonna if she can tell you any more . . .'

'Oh, I'm not sure, Gio. Like I said, I don't want to cause Lucia any upset. And she did say that it was private and that I should speak to my grandmother.'

'Yes, but you know this about Patsy already, so Nonna would not be telling you a secret,' he said, and finished his drink. 'Let's go to the house and see if she will talk to you about Patsy's baby.' Quickly finishing her drink, Maddie packed her laptop away and followed him. Gio cared about his grandmother and seemed to know her well, so if he thought it was OK to ask her, then it had to be worth trying.

*

When they got to the house, Lucia was sitting on the veranda in the sun with her eyes closed and a lovely, contented look on her face. Gio gently took her hand in his so as not to startle her.

'Gio, my dear boy . . . I was dozing.' She smiled and patted his hand. 'Why are you not in the restaurant? Is there a problem?' Lucia sat up in her chair and smoothed down her dress. Maddie hovered at the edge of the veranda, unsure if this was a good idea, but Lucia beckoned her over to come and sit down. Gio explained that they had found the telegram with the terribly sad news of Patsy's death. Lucia sat quietly for a moment, as if digesting what Gio had told her, before making her mind up whether to talk about it.

'Ah, yes, it's true and I'm very sorry . . . I did not think it was my place to tell you about this. It is very sad news for you to hear. But as you know now . . .' Lucia broke off to shrug and nod in acceptance. 'Poor Kelly, she was heartbroken. The bond with her twin sister no longer with her – she felt this pain very much,' Lucia confirmed, moving a hand to the centre of her chest.

It was Gio who asked, 'Nonna, did Patsy die having a baby called Audrey? Is this the reason you said there was so much sadness?'

Maddie waited, holding her breath, hoping this would solve the mystery and she could enjoy the rest of her holiday and then concentrate on finding out where Audrey was when she got home. Perhaps when they found her she might be willing to meet up and help put Granny's mind at rest before it was too late and she had forgotten the past completely, or worse still, had died without ever having found out. Maddie couldn't bear the thought of that for her grandmother, to not know what had become of baby Audrey. Dad may not seem bothered, but Audrey was clearly very important to her grandmother, to ask about her so many times, and so this made her important to Maddie.

Lucia lowered her eyes, before lifting them once more and placing a hand on Maddie's knee.

'No . . . no no no,' Lucia was shaking her head as she spoke, then paused momentarily to gather herself. 'Patsy's babies . . . a boy and a girl – twins – they die too.' A beat of silence followed. Maddie inhaled sharply, a sudden stab of pain for how her grandmother must have felt all those years ago – and an urgent thought raced through the space currently separating her from her own pregnant sister, Sofia. They may not have grown up together and didn't have a typical sisterly closeness, they didn't even really get on for much of the time, with an undercurrent of tension and antagonism marring most of the moments they spent together. And of course, there was constant comparison, the sense of having missed out, and – dare she say it out loud inside her own head? – the jealousy. Maddie knew she had grown up envious of her half-sister, Sofia, but also knew that she had worked hard to make the best of what she had, the family cards she had been dealt . . . as many of us do. But hearing how Granny had suffered somehow helped Maddie to crystallise her feelings towards her sister and she realised that she did care deeply for Sofia and would be devastated if anything happened to her.

Maddie shook her head as if to recalibrate her maudlin, dramatic thoughts, for this was a different time. What happened to poor Patsy was over seventy years ago, and there had been many medical break-throughs since then. Sofia was going to be fine, Maddie told herself. And when they had last spoken, a few days ago, Sofia was her usual matter-of-fact self: the baby was kicking constantly and keeping her awake, and she was sad that Granny had forgotten who she was again but kept asking if Maddie had found Audrey yet.

'Maddie . . . I'm sorry.' Gio leaned in front of her with his elbows on his knees and a concerned look on his face. 'Are you OK? You look sad and tired. Do you want to stop talking and carry on another time? Maddie didn't know what to say but felt as though a rug had been pulled from under her and she was back to square one, wondering who Audrey was and if she would ever be able to find her. And it was true, she did feel sad and weary. Again she debated whether it would be best to give up wondering about Audrey for now and just enjoy being in Capri; she didn't want to ruin her time here by feeling weary and deflated.

'I am sorry you do not know this news already,' Lucia said gently.

'No, no I didn't. This must have been so hard for my grandmother,' Maddie said, thinking it through. 'Was she still here in Capri when Patsy died?' she asked, and inwardly kicked herself. Of course she couldn't have been. Lucia had already said what a wonderful, happy time they had here together, so that would never have been the case if her grandmother's twin sister had died, and her two babies too.

'Ah, no . . . this happened when Kelly, or you prefer Rose? Her real name. They make her change it and she never like it, not really. But it helped her play the part of the Hollywood actress, she told me,' Lucia said as an aside and nodded slowly, seemingly deep in thought.

'Well, she's always been Rose . . . or Granny to me,' Maddie told her quietly.

'*Sì*,' Lucia smiled. 'So, Rose . . . she was in America when her sister died. Soon after she left Capri after our summer together. She wrote to tell me the studio bosses wouldn't let her go home. She never forgave herself for not being there for the funeral, or to see her twin sister for one more time. They were young girls when she left England, barely an adult, and they never saw each other again. It was very tragic.' Lucia fell silent.

'Oh, this is really sad,' Maddie said. She could see now why Lucia had said 'so much sadness'. It must have been so hard for her grandmother being far away from home. No wonder she eventually left Hollywood. 'Do you know when she went back home to England?'

Though Maddie understood that her dad had been right in urging her to exercise caution, that this would be very distressing for Granny, she still needed to understand. No wonder Granny had been reluctant to talk about twins running in the family, when her own twin sister had died during childbirth with twins, and Patsy so young too . . . it must have been devastating. Hearing that her granddaughter, Sofia, was pregnant with twins would undoubtedly have brought it all back. Poor Granny, keeping all that pain and worry to herself, but so typical of her, she wouldn't have wanted to burden any of us, Maddie thought, knowing this is how her grandmother would have seen it.

'No . . . I, er . . .' Lucia fiddled with the cross on the chain at her neck before adding, 'it was a long time ago . . .' and then seemed distracted as she stared into the distance. Instinct told Maddie there was something more, but she didn't want to push it and end up making Lucia agitated. But the mood suddenly changed when Valerie appeared with a flower-patterned box under her arm which she placed on an empty chair. Lucia, on seeing the box, seemed to gain clarity from it; patting her bun, she sat up straighter, crossed her legs and placed her hands one over the other on her knee. 'We lost touch when Rose returned home . . .' And Lucia stared into the distance again. Maddie caught her breath, puzzled as to why this would be. Hadn't her grandmother and Lucia been the best of friends? But then Maddie remembered Granny saying she didn't blame Lucia for forgetting about her . . .

'What happened?' It was Gio who asked. Lucia motioned towards the box on the chair next to Valerie. She passed the box to Lucia, who placed it on the sofa in the space between her and Maddie. After running a hand over the top of the box, Lucia removed the lid and took out a few vintage-style colourful greetings cards and sheets of paper with lovely, neat, old-fashioned flowing cursive handwriting on, written in black ink from a fountain pen, by the looks of it.

'We did keep in touch when she went back to Hollywood after our summer together,' Lucia said, placing the sheets of paper and cards on the lid of the box. Next, she took out a bundle of envelopes tied up in a pink ribbon. 'But when she went home to England, I never heard from her again.' Lucia's voice faltered.

Maddie glanced at the envelopes and saw Honeysuckle Cottage, Granny's address, written across the one on top of the pile in Lucia's hand. But over the address were two angry lines scored deep into the paper. Lucia moved her fingers so Maddie could see the words written next to the address.

RETURN TO SENDER

Maddie caught her breath. 'I don't understand.' She looked at Lucia, who had dipped her head and seemed to be staring intently at the bundle as she untied the ribbon and spread the envelopes, a dozen or so at least, across the lid of the box. All of them with the same red parallel lines scored into the paper, so deeply on some that the paper had holes in it. Whoever had done this had most definitely been very angry.

'I wrote to dear Rose in England, but every time, my letter came back like this, so in the end I had to give up. I had no other way to contact her. It was sad to say goodbye to my dear friend in this way . . . especially after the wonderful summer we had together, and then . . .' Lucia faltered before adding, '. . . all that she endured.'

'Oh Lucia, I'm so sorry.' Maddie touched the back of Lucia's hand before picking up one of the envelopes, and then another and another, placing them on the sofa cushions and sifting through them, seeing the same instruction on each one. 'I really don't understand why my grandmother would send the letters back to you when she spoke of you so fondly; "my dear friend, Lucia", that's what she said, and with such warmth. It was clear you were very important to her . . . there was no anger, upset or bad feelings at all, as these red lines suggest. In fact, Granny said she didn't blame you for forgetting about her.'

'Maybe this is why your granny said she is sorry,' Gio offered.

'But it doesn't make sense,' Maddie said quickly, keen to defend her grandmother. She just couldn't accept that her kind, unassuming granny would do this; she had never known her to be angry, not a cross word to anyone. Granny had even stayed composed that time when Maddie's mum had been nasty to her, having caught Maddie going into Honeysuckle Cottage on the way home from school one day. She'd ranted at Granny for 'poisoning my daughter against me', but rather than engage with her, Granny had dashed inside her house so as not to have a scene in the street, later explaining to Maddie that her mum wasn't to blame, she was 'under the influence' (Maddie hadn't really been sure what that meant at the time), and that kindness was what her mum really needed. So as far as Maddie was concerned, it seemed inconceivable that her grandmother would do such a thing to the friend she had been so happy to meet and spend the summer with, here in Capri, let alone be enraged enough to slash through the envelope of a letter from her and then ghost her in this way. It was a horrible and cruel thing to do. And her grandmother was neither of these. Maddie stared down at the envelopes, her mind racing as she looked at them, searching, as if for a clue of some kind. It was Gio who spotted it.

'See, this one is different.' He picked up one of the envelopes where the words 'return to sender' weren't written in harsh capital letters – still with enough force though to make a little rip in the paper of the envelope – and placed it on top of the pile. 'The letters are slanting and pointy. And this one too . . .' And he put another envelope next to the first one. Silently, Lucia picked up one of the letters Kelly had sent to her when she first returned to Hollywood and set it next to the two envelopes so they could all see the difference in the writing. Maddie inhaled through her nostrils and let out a breath of relief through her mouth.

'The handwriting is completely different!' she exclaimed, tapping the paper. 'When the words were written in capital letters it wasn't obvious . . . but we can see here that my grandmother's writing in this letter is flowing and rounded, not at all sharp and pointed and sloping as it is here.' And she tapped the envelopes to make her point. 'Somebody else wrote *Return to Sender* on the envelopes, but slipped up on these two occasions and didn't use capital letters. My guess is that same person sent them back to you.' She was convinced of it.

Lucia smiled and clasped Maddie's hand, the look of sadness fading from her eyes.

'For many years I missed my friend and wondered how she is . . . and I worried too that she believed I had forgotten about her . . . if she never got my letters,' Lucia said. 'The person who did this sent my letters back to me without Rose knowing, so she must have thought I had abandoned her . . . like all the others did—'

'Others?' Maddie immediately picked up on it, but from the way Lucia shook her head it was clear that she didn't want to elaborate and so Maddie left it, just pleased to have brought some comfort to Lucia after making her agitated before.

'So, I am very happy now to know Rose again,' Lucia continued. 'Maddie, thank you for coming here and bringing her back to me.' Maddie squeezed the elderly woman's hand, wondering who on earth would do such a thing to ruin a wonderful friendship? And more importantly, why would they do this?

'Please, do you have a photo of Rose?' Lucia asked.

'Yes, yes of course.' Maddie immediately reached for her laptop, wishing she had thought of this when she first got here, or better still, had printed some photos to bring with her to give to Lucia. She made a mental note to get some organised as soon as she got home. Maddie opened her laptop and quickly found some of the lovely photos she had taken of her grandmother in Sofia's garden last summer, and turned the screen to show them all to Lucia.

'Ah, yes . . . she looks the same as she did back then, so beautiful. But different now. Her eyes have changed . . . the sparkle is now sadness. I see it there.' Lucia traced a finger over the screen. 'She is thinking about them, yes?' She handed the laptop back to Maddie.

'Thinking about them? Patsy? Who else?' Maddie repeated, closing the laptop, eager to hear more.

'Clarke,' Lucia said.

'Clarke? Yes, I read about the end of the love affair. Granny was heartbroken and returned to England,' Maddie told Lucia, remembering the online record she had found on that website about old Hollywood stars. Lucia studied Maddie for a moment, her eyes searching hers, almost as if she were trying to tell her something without actually saying the words out loud before whispering another name as she dipped her head.

'Audrey?' Maddie repeated gently. Lucia had said the word so quietly, it was barely audible, but Maddie knew she wasn't mistaken. 'Do you know where she is?' Maddie ventured with caution on seeing the apprehension in Lucia's eyes as she glanced up and then away again, hesitant, fearful even. And it was the same look that her grandmother had when she asked Maddie to help her find Audrey.

'No. I do not know,' Lucia said quickly and touched the cross at her neck before looking downward again.

Silence followed.

Maddie looked at Gio, but he shook his head, indicating to let it go.

Lucia gathered all the letters and cards and envelopes together and carefully placed them back inside the box. Then she lifted out another, much smaller bundle of maybe two or three envelopes. Maddie could see the one on the top of the pile had a blue stamp at the corner with a picture of the Statue of Liberty on, *United States Postage* written across the bottom, *25c* at the corner. Lucia's address in Capri was written in similar old-fashioned cursive handwriting, but it wasn't her grandmother's writing . . . no, this writing was bigger and much more flamboyant.

'From my cousin, Maribella in America, she sent these to me . . .' Lucia said, carefully pressing her palm across the top of the bundle as if the letters were precious jewels. She handed the letters to Maddie before giving the box back to Valerie.

'Thank you,' Maddie said, leaning into Lucia as she moved closer to give Maddie a hug.

'You already know your grandmother was heart-broken over Clarke, so I think it is OK for you to read these letters, but the rest . . .' Lucia paused. 'Please be kind to your grandmother when you know this . . . *sì?*' Lucia's eyes searched Maddie's for understanding and confirmation.

'I promise,' Maddie assured her. 'Please know that I love my grandmother very much and always want her to be happy. I give you my word that whatever is in these letters will never change that,' Maddie added, contemplating all that she had discovered so far about her grandmother's past, and the possibility there was more to come too than she had ever anticipated – something bigger and potentially hurtful. She thought of Dad's words of caution again. Of course, he was right about being careful, but his attitude when they had last spoken, his indifference and dismissal of them ever finding Audrey and downplaying the importance of it for her grandmother, didn't feel right to her, now more than ever.

Lucia smiled kindly and glanced at Gio and then back to Maddie.

'The letters, they are in Italian, so Gio will read them and tell you what they say . . .'

22

Los Angeles, America 1954

Four months had passed since the light in Kelly's soul went out and no amount of kind words or sympathy from Lenny or Maribella could ever reignite it. Her darling Clarke was gone for ever. All their hopes and dreams and plans for a future wonderful life together gone with him . . .

On that fateful night he had been riding fast on his way to confront Louis, in the studio, when he had swerved to avoid a Cadillac on a tight bend of Mulholland Drive, a narrow winding road in the Hollywood Hills. The motorcycle had spun in an arc before rolling over the side of the road into a dense thicket where Clarke's head hit a rock. He had never stood a chance, the driver of the car had told Lenny, who had then broken the terrible news to Kelly the following morning when she had arrived at the studio, oblivious, and expecting to see her secret lover waiting there for her. Kelly knew as soon as she saw Lenny's ashen face and his head moving slowly side to side as he had entered her dressing room, closing the door behind him so the rest of the crew wouldn't hear her muffled scream when he gently delivered the words, catching her in his arms as her legs buckled, pressing her tightly into his chest.

'Honey, he's gone.' They stood together, clinging to each other as she sobbed into Lenny, who smoothed her hair with his hand, his own tears falling from his eyes for the lifelong friend, the incredibly talented actor, the handsome, charismatic man they both loved with all their hearts.

The only crumb of comfort that Kelly could comprehend from it all was that her dear sister, Patsy, and the love of her life, Clarke, were together now in heaven. Even though her faith had wavered considerably since that fateful night, and so soon after hearing the news of Patsy, and then the dreadfully sad loss of the twins too – her dad had put it all in a letter that had arrived a week after the telegram – Kelly had to believe they were all together; it was all that she had to cling to. And she needed to keep going for the sake of Clarke's baby that was growing within her. Conceived in Capri from love on that perfect night after their moonlit swim in the Mediterranean Sea underneath a canopy of stars. The joy and gaiety from that time she hoped one day to be able to harness again and relive in her thoughts to remember Clarke by. But she was a long way from achieving this and feared that it may never come as she wore the shame on discovering her predicament, like a cloak of guilt, a punishment for not stopping Clarke from leaving that night. Fired up and angry, how could he have possibly stood a chance when he hadn't been thinking straight? No, she should have stopped him, done more to calm him down. She should have kept what happened in Louis's office that day to herself, instead of blurting it all out to Clarke . . . Kelly had gone over and over the sequence of events from that night a thousand times at least and always arrived at the same conclusion: she was to blame. Kelly had known what she was getting into when she first signed the contract with the film studio, back home in the kitchen of Honeysuckle Cottage, and she should have stuck to the rules – no dating, no marriage and definitely no babies! If only she had been more careful, then Clarke would still be here.

But there was still a chance to make things right, for the sake of their baby. She couldn't allow an innocent child to shoulder the shame of its mother, unmarried and thousands of miles away from home.

Not that Kelly could ever go back home with a baby, it was out of the question. She couldn't ever do that to her dad ... bring shame on him, not after everything that he had endured, losing her mother, brother, and her dear sister Patsy. Now she was all that he had left. She hadn't even had the heart to tell him yet that she had been fired from the film studio and her dream of being a Hollywood movie star was over. She had tried so many times to write the letter to him, knowing that it would break his heart. All she had ever wanted, after a happy life with Clarke, was for her dad to be proud of her. He would have to know she was coming home eventually, when she felt strong enough to post the letter to him. Until then, she had tucked the letter, and the several ones that she had attempted before finally managing to get it right, inside her writing folder, desperately trying to ignore the knot of shame every time it caught her eye.

As for the film that Louis had been so insistent she stay in Hollywood for and not go home to pay her respects to Patsy, it had been canned when Clarke died. The studio had wanted her to start work on another film, but the shock of Clarke's death had caused her to develop a nervous stutter. The physician that Maribella had taken her to said it would probably ease with time, but in the meantime she wasn't able to act and so the studio had dropped her. It would have happened anyway, as soon as she had to loosen her skirts and the bump had made it obvious that she was having a baby, and out of wedlock too. Of course, Lenny had offered to marry her.

'I can't ask you to do that,' Kelly had told him. 'To give up your life to live a lie with me.'

'You're not asking, doll. I'm offering. Let me do the right thing by Clarke,' Lenny had pleaded with her, a hand on each of her shoulders.

But Kelly refused, knowing that his grief for his childhood best friend was muddling his ability to think it through.

'I couldn't do that to Ray. He loves you, Lenny, and it would break his heart. No, there has been too much loss already . . .' Kelly had been resolute. Her own life may have been destroyed but she wouldn't do that to her dear friends. Everyone in Hollywood knew Lenny's secret and turned a blind eye, but this, well . . . this would be too much. They would all blame her and accuse her of trapping him. And what would they say to the baby growing within her? A child that would grow up forever tainted . . . Kelly knew that she could never do that to her baby.

Propping herself up in her bed, Kelly lifted the eye mask that allowed her to manage a few hours of sleep each night before she awoke consumed with emotion. The agony of heartbreak raw all over again as the synapses of her brain connected and she remembered what had happened to her darling Clarke on that fateful night. How she truly wished she had stopped him from leaving . . . the plea going over and over, again and again, wishing she could turn back time, the thought driving her near insane with its relentlessness.

She picked up the letter on the nightstand, from her dear friend, Lucia, in Capri, and read it again.

Dearest Kelly

There are no words that I can write to take away the pain you are feeling but please reconsider my offer. I am sure that we can find a way together to fix everything. Maribella has told me you are not sleeping or eating and barely able to leave your bed. Please come back to Capri and let me take care of you here in the orchard. You were so happy here and I know that you can be again. Maribella will make the arrangements for you to travel, and has said that Lenny will get you a wedding ring to wear on the journey and has offered to chaperone you too, if that would make you feel more comfortable . . .

Kelly folded the piece of paper in half and placed it back on the nightstand before slumping against the pillow, her hands resting over the swell of her stomach. With careful dressing, she would be able to disguise the pregnancy. From the onset of the sickness and by the absence of her monthlies, she reckoned she must be five months along, though the bump was barely noticeable on her tiny frame. Maybe it would be for the best. The studio had said she must vacate her apartment by the end of the week; the place was so full of sadness and painful reminders of that dreadful last night with Clarke, she wouldn't be sorry to leave. At least if she took up Lucia's offer, Kelly could try to start replacing those memories with happy ones . . . of the laughter and love and gay times that she and her beloved Clarke had enjoyed together in captivating Capri. She had felt free there and it would always be the place where she felt closest to him, the man she had fallen in love with and would hold forever in her heart . . . knowing a part of him was going to live on in their child.

23

'Oh Gio, it's so moving . . .' Maddie said as he finished reading aloud the last letter in beautifully accented English and tucked it back inside the envelope. Maribella had written in the letters to her cousin, Lucia, about the crushing devastation Kelly had endured on not only losing her sister, Patsy, but then her lover, Clarke, too, and how this had plunged her friend into a mercilessly, catatonic depression with a terrible stutter. Her lifelong dream of movie star fame had faded as fast as it had brightened when the studio sacked her and evicted her from her apartment in Los Angeles. And then, discovering she was pregnant . . .

Maddie knew that times were different back then and it would have been impossible for a young woman, an unmarried mother, and so far away from home without any family support, but she still couldn't help feeling what a cruel injustice it had all been for her grandmother. And she was in no doubt now that

Audrey was her grandmother's first child, meaning she would be her dad's half-sister. She hoped he would be interested in finding her now there was a tangible connection.

'What do you want to do now?' Gio asked. They had spent the morning together in the Lemon Tree restaurant before it opened to the public at lunchtime, alone apart from the kitchen staff prepping the day's menu. They'd sat drinking refreshingly ice-cold peach juice and enjoying a brunch of pizza spread with sun-dried tomato pesto and topped with salami and creamy mozzarella and handfuls of torn basil followed by traditional Italian sweet doughnuts, or *bombolini*, filled with raspberry mascarpone that Gio had prepared for them. Not that Maddie had much of an appetite . . . the contents of Maribella's letters had been sad and shocking to listen to as Gio had translated, but she had appreciated the effort he had made today and was enjoying getting to know him a bit more too. His thoughtfulness and tenderness as he paused on the more painful parts of the letters was endearing and in complete contrast to the first impression she had formed after seeing him on the party boat.

Maddie had been especially moved by a section in one of the letters where Maribella had explained to Lucia that her dear friend, Kelly, wasn't up to putting pen to paper to write to her herself and she could barely speak for stuttering due to the stress of losing her sister and lover in such quick succession. And then, on discovering she was pregnant with Clarke's baby, the studio fired her for breaking her contract. Maddie had wanted to race home to Tindledale right away and go straight to Evergreens so she could wrap her arms around her wonderful grandmother and tell her how much she loved her. She couldn't bear to even imagine the pain her grandmother had been through.

Maddie shook her head and let out a long sigh of contemplation as Gio looped his arm around her shoulders in comfort. She enjoyed the burst of his now familiar scent and feeling of support as she leaned into his firm chest, but her mind was elsewhere with thoughts of her grandmother and wondering what had happened next for her. The last letter from Maribella to Lucia had said that travel arrangements had been made for Kelly to come back to Capri, but she and Lenny were worried that Kelly might not be up to making the journey . . .

'I honestly don't know,' Maddie lifted her head away from Gio's chest and swivelled in her seat so she was facing him. 'My head is spinning trying to think it all through and wondering if my grandmother did come back to Capri. Was she up to travelling? Did Lenny accompany her, chaperone her, or whatever it was that had to happen for an unmarried mother-to-be to appear respectable back in those days?' She stopped talking to shake her head and sigh, the injustice and cruelty of her grandmother's situation swirling up inside her again.

'We could try asking Nonna,' Gio suggested, picking up his glass and finishing the last of his drink. Maddie immediately shook her head.

'No, I don't think we should,' she said. 'I really don't want to make Lucia feel any more agitation—'

'I understand, but I could ask her if Kelly did come back to Capri. I think this would be OK.' Gio nodded, but Maddie could see that he was wavering, apprehensive about doing this too.

'I'm not sure . . . but thank you for caring, it's touching that you want to help me.' Maddie looked into his eyes, thinking what a thoughtful man he was.

'Of course, I must help you, Maddie. Family is important. And I think you need to solve this mystery and find out where Audrey is. Please, let me ask Nonna. She will say no if she doesn't want to tell me.' And he tilted his head to one side and lifted his eyebrows, understanding how much it meant to her to help her grandmother.

'Maybe,' Maddie thought aloud, 'but I have the impression that Lucia has already told us all that she feels comfortable sharing, Gio. And I am truly grateful, but I really don't want to push her. It's clearly an upsetting memory for her. If my grandmother did come here, pregnant, and unmarried, then I'm assuming it would have been extremely difficult, not only for her but for your grandmother too. They had their faith and went to Mass together in the little church on the hill and, if I'm not mistaken, back in the 1950s being a good Catholic meant not having sex before marriage.'

'True,' Gio agreed.

'Perhaps if there is no other way to know if my grandmother did return to Capri, then you could ask Lucia . . . but I'd really like to take another look at the letters from the suitcase first, just to see if I've missed anything and can work it out for myself,' Maddie said, and finished her drink.

They sat together and looked out at the spectacular view, each contemplating and wondering what to do next.

'I have an idea!' Gio stood up and pushed a hand through his thick dark hair before picking up the key to his scooter from the table and holding out a hand to Maddie.

'Where are we going?' she asked, jumping up too and slipping her hand into his like it was the most natural thing in the world. And she supposed it was, right here in this moment. Plus she was rapidly learning that Gio was very tactile and passionate, with a real zest for life. He didn't hold back or show inhibitions the way she did, and it made her feel confident and able to go with the flow too. She had also replayed him telling her she was sexy in the orchard that day a million times in her head, savouring the sensation it evoked and the person it made her feel she was becoming.

'Chiesa di Sant'Andrea . . .' he said, his eyes widening.

'The little church on the hill,' Maddie confirmed, remembering it from the letters her grandmother had written to Patsy. That was where Kelly and Lucia had first met after going to Mass. 'Yes . . . I'd love to see it, but why now? How can this help us find out if my grandmother returned to Capri?'

'To look for clues . . . if your grandmother did come back to Capri and she is pregnant then maybe she has the baby Audrey here and then she must have her baptised. It has to happen as soon as possible after the baby is born. It is . . . how do you say in English . . . *sacramento.*'

'It's the same . . . sacrament,' Maddie told him, having heard her grandmother talk many times about the seven sacraments of the Catholic church. 'Ah, I get it now,' she nodded excitedly, 'there might be a record of Audrey's baptism!'

'*Sì.*' Gio squeezed her hand in confirmation and went to leave the restaurant.

'But hang on.' Maddie stopped walking and Gio looked at her questioningly. 'Aren't there rules or whatever? We can't just go into a church and look up records, surely. It's all locked away, isn't it?'

'Maddie! Come on . . . let's go, we won't know until we get there,' he persisted, and Maddie couldn't resist. His impulsivity was incredibly attractive, it was exciting and exhilarating, and hadn't she been pondering, only moments ago, on how she liked the feeling of going with the flow?

'Yes!' she said. 'What are we waiting for?' Gio laughed, and she did too as they practically ran to where his scooter was parked.

Arriving at the church, Maddie felt moved by the aura within it after they walked up a small flight of steps and through a dome-topped arched entrance and into the tiny, whitewashed stone chapel. She imagined her grandmother here all those years ago, happy and in love with Clarke, and then . . . was it possible that she had returned with his baby in her arms?

Six rows of wicker chairs were aligned either side

of a short, narrow aisle that led to the pulpit. Three gold-framed paintings depicting scenes from the bible were mounted on the wall. Maddie held back respectfully as Gio blessed himself with the holy water and then went to a door at the side of the pulpit.

'I think the ledgers are kept in here.' He tried the door handle, but it was locked. 'Sorry, Maddie, it was a crazy idea . . . you were right, we can't just look up the records.' And he pushed his hands into his jeans pocket.

'It's OK, Gio . . . thank you for trying,' Maddie said. Seeing his disappointment, she placed a hand on his arm. 'It's nice just to be here . . . this church is a special place,' she said, wandering over to the open, unglazed window at the side of the church and looking out at the breathtaking view, imagining her grandmother coming to Mass, delivered in evocative and beautiful-sounding Italian as she shared the same view that Maddie was seeing right now.

After spending some time just sitting and absorbing the atmosphere, they stood up and turned to leave and had reached the steps outside when a voice called out. Gio stopped walking and went back inside the church, beckoning for Maddie to follow him. Inside again, she saw a priest poking his head out the door that had been locked, a young Italian man, most likely around the same age as her, and who appeared to know Gio as he was shaking his hand and chatting away in Italian as if they were old friends.

'Maddie, this is Padre Alexis,' Gio said, 'he comes to the restaurant.'

'Too many times,' the priest laughed, patting his stomach before speaking in fast Italian to Gio, who after replying, explaining why they were here, Maddie presumed, as he gestured in her direction and said, 'Audrey' and 'Kelly Sinclair' a few times, indicating for her to follow as Padre Alexis led them into the room at the side of the church.

'*Grazie*,' Gio said, shaking Padre Alexis's hand again after he opened a large wooden cabinet where several enormous old ledgers were stored. Maddie caught her breath on realising these must be the baptism records going back many, many years, and she instantly hoped that there might be a record somewhere within these pages to help bring her a step closer to finding Audrey and putting her grandmother's mind at rest.

24

Capri, Italy, 1954

'Kelly, it's time,' Lucia said to her softly. They were the only ones in the Chiesa di Sant'Andrea church, sitting side by side on the chairs with their heads bowed. The same church where her baby Audrey had been baptised a few days after her birth, with just Lucia and her fiancé, Piero, there. Kelly finished her prayer, crossed herself and stood up, grasping her dear friend's hand so as not to stumble when her legs faltered. She was exhausted and quite frail from it all, but knew she must stay strong for Audrey's sake; she owed her this much – a life free from shame and the stigma of having an unmarried mother as her only parent. And it was more than that too . . . Audrey deserved to have everything that Kelly couldn't give her. A loving home with two parents, in a nice neighbourhood, the best schooling and social circle . . .

'Dear Audrey will want for nothing,' the priest had assured Kelly. He had arranged it all with the nuns, who knew of a good Catholic couple – a doctor and his wife who had been a school teacher before she married. They had longed for a child of their own but hadn't been blessed with one and so would cherish Audrey as a gift from God. Kelly had drawn strength from knowing this and hoped one day that Audrey would forgive her if she were ever to be told the truth of her birth.

Lucia placed a hand at Kelly's elbow. 'We can come back another time . . . tomorrow . . . if you are not ready,' her voice faltered. Kelly shook her head and gathered herself before checking in the crib that was stationed on the chair beside her. Audrey's tiny rosebud lips quivered as Kelly stroked an index finger over her cheek one last time and studied her face, storing it away into a recess of her brain as a memory she could access at any time. A kiss curl of dark hair, just like Clarke's, peeping out from underneath her bonnet, long lashes resting on smooth pink skin as she slept contentedly, obliviously, and as it should be. Kelly had dressed Audrey in her best clothes, a beautifully stitched pinafore that Lucia had sewn by hand, with a soft crocheted blanket and her favourite little white fluffy rabbit tucked in beside her. She hoped Audrey's new mother and father would let her keep the rabbit, along with the miniature gold cross and chain that was nestled on a navy velvet cushion inside a jewellery box. Wrapped around the box was the floral-patterned silk scarf that Kelly had bought to wear on that wonderfully happy day at the little secluded cove with Clarke here in Capri, now stowed in the corner of the crib for safekeeping.

'I'm ready,' Kelly uttered quietly, and turned towards her friend, Lucia, who rubbed a hand over the top of her arm in comfort.

'Are you sure?' Lucia checked, sorrow filling her eyes as she looked at Kelly and then into the crib. 'I am so very sorry it must be this way. I thought if you came here then I could fix everything but . . .' Lucia shook her head before bowing it and falling silent.

'Oh Lucia, you have been the very best friend to me, and I wish more than anything that it could be different, but we both know that this is the only option,' Kelly said, remembering how Lucia's parents had reacted when they discovered their daughter's friend, who was staying in their home, was an unmarried mother-to-be.

'*Non può succedere* . . .' They had said, or 'it cannot happen!' And Kelly had heard them, even though their voices had been hushed for fear of anyone else on the island finding out and the family's upstanding reputation being ruined too. She didn't know what all their words meant exactly, but it was obvious what they were saying, and then the looks and falling silent whenever she walked out onto the veranda in her loose-fitting dress had made it very clear. The cloak of shame had intensified then, claustrophobic and all-consuming, culminating in a silent birth, bar the sound of Kelly's tears, in Lucia's bedroom, with only her mother in attendance, monosyllabic as she had told Kelly what to do while Lucia translated and gripped her friend's hand tightly. All three women breathing a collective sigh of relief when baby Audrey had cried on delivery.

'It has to be done,' Kelly said, not wanting to prolong the agonising moment any longer. She had thought of nothing else, and the decision was made. 'It's the right thing for Audrey . . . to have a better life than I could ever give her.' And after letting out a long wavering breath, Kelly neatened her hair, that was now back to its original auburn waves, blinked away a tear and adopted a well-practised technique she had used in the past to overcome stage fright and calm her breathing. Inhale for a count of four and exhale for a count of six, over and over until she was able to step into the hardest role of her life and take the crib towards the door of the vestry.

25

After leaving the church, Maddie and Gio were now on his boat, Maddie with a beach blanket wrapped around her shoulders and Gio's dog, Bella, snuggled at her feet with her chin resting on Maddie's leg, as if to comfort her. Not that Maddie was cold, far from it, the evening air was still gloriously sultry and so she supposed the chill and goosebumps were down to shock, and well . . . the general enormity mingled with an overwhelming sadness on discovering that her grandmother did return to Capri and that baby Audrey was born here. Maddie had found the baptism record in the dusty old ledger for 1954 and had come to the conclusion that the baby Audrey must have been adopted and that her grandmother had been carrying the burden of loss and grief of being separated from her baby for all this time without any of them knowing, and therefore unable to support her. Maddie thought it must have been a very lonely feeling for her grandmother at times over the years, without a soul in the world to confide in for fear of them knowing her shameful secret. And on top of this, thinking her dear friend, Lucia, had abandoned her too when she returned home to England and the letters from Capri stopped coming – or so Granny would have assumed when they were intercepted.

'Thank you,' Maddie said as Gio handed her a drink and sat down beside her. He had been amazing this evening, considerate and kind, when he could see that she was struggling with the enormity of it all. Giving her space when she had wanted to just stand at the side of the boat where it lay anchored in a quieter part of the coastline, gazing out to sea or back at the island. Even in her grief, the sheer beauty of it all had her wanting to take photos, and as she set to work she found the process of checking the lighting and contrast of colours – the sea and sky, the array of pastel-coloured houses tucked into the cliffside – helped her to make sense of all that she had learned today. He had even humoured her and reluctantly stood in a variety of poses – looking out to sea, looking to camera, arms folded, smiling, whimsical and so on. It had been fun and had taken her mind off everything and put her back into holiday mode.

'Do you feel better now? Knowing that your grandmother did come back here?' Gio asked.

'Yes, I think I do. It's comforting to know that my grandmother was with Lucia, when she needed a friend most,' she sighed, glancing at his face. 'It's a lot to think about . . . and thank you for helping me with the letters from Maribella and taking me to the church today. And for everything else too. Being here with you . . . it's been wonderful and has made such a difference.'

'It's no problem, Maddie. I'm happy that you let me do this for you, and we get to know each other more.' He nudged her arm affectionately and wrapped his hand around hers. Maddie had cried earlier, when they first got to the boat, and Gio, who had been sitting opposite her on the deck, had stood up and lifted her from her seated position and put his arms around her shoulders. They had stood together, no words, only the gentle lapping sound of the sea on the side of the boat as tears slid down her face and onto his T-shirt. And since then, something had shifted between them; Maddie didn't know what it was exactly, she couldn't really think about it right now, not when her head was full of feelings for her grandmother and wondering where Audrey was and what she should do with the information she now had. How could she go home to her grandmother and bring up all this heartbreak and sorrow from her past? Maddie wondered how much her grandmother remembered of that time in the 1950s, or if her poor broken heart had blocked it completely from her memory as a way to cope with the enormity of it all. Was this why none of them knew about her life in Hollywood, and how she nearly became a proper movie star? Maybe the shame that Granny had felt from back then in the 1950s had silenced her, made her fearful . . .

Maddie remembered the photo albums in the sitting room of Honeysuckle Cottage that Sofia and she had looked through, the blank spaces that indicated people were missing, erased from the family. Had one of them been her grandmother? Cancelled for bringing shame on the family? But who would do such a thing? Maddie thought of the letter in the suitcase from her grandmother to her dad, apologising and asking for forgiveness. She said that it was a '*hopeless situation, and I am to return home forthwith*' and how she hoped to make him proud of her once again. Could her own father have really disowned her for failing to make it in Hollywood, for falling in love with a man and having his baby? But then in times when honour and keeping up appearances might have been respected more than love, it could very well have been the case, Maddie thought. Her grandmother – or Rose O'Malley, as she would have been on returning home to England – was in disgrace, a fallen woman.

And Maddie thought too of the time a few weeks ago when her grandmother wouldn't come to the phone to talk to her dad, saying, 'should have stopped you . . . and been more careful.' Janice at Evergreens had said that it was entirely possible that Granny might have got in a muddle, thinking her son was somebody else, so maybe she was talking to whoever that person was and not Dad at all. And now that Maddie knew about Clarke and what happened on that fateful night, and Maribella writing to Lucia and saying that Kelly blamed herself for not stopping Clarke from leaving, she wondered if perhaps it was him that her grandmother had been thinking of when she said this. A rush of compassion for her grand-mother made Maddie feel sad all over again. If only they had known about her past, if Granny had confided in them, they could have helped long before now. They could have investigated how to find Audrey . . . As it was, by the time they found her, it might be too late.

With this thought, a sense of urgency hurtled through Maddie. There was no time to waste, not with her grandmother an octogenarian, but where to start the search for Audrey? And would she even want to be found?

'Hey, Maddie?' Gio gave her a nudge. 'Are you OK? You look sad again.'

'Oh yes, I'm OK, thanks . . . I was just thinking about today and the letters and the church and what to do next. I'm not sad . . . more contemplative and wondering how to break the news to my grandmother that it might just not be possible to find Audrey.'

'Why do you say this? You have more letters to read, there could be another clue. If it's true, and Audrey is adopted, then there could be some paperwork,' he suggested, ruffling Bella's fur as she stretched and then snuggled further onto Maddie's lap, as if sensing her swirl of emotions and giving comfort. 'Where is your laptop?'

'Here, and yes, you're right, Gio, it's worth looking again, although I've read through nearly all the papers now and not seen anything to do with an adoption, or even a clue as to what happened to baby Audrey after the baptism.' Maddie let go of Gio's hand and, after putting her drink down, she reached for her laptop and found the folder. Opening it and setting the view so that they could both see a thumbnail of each of the letters and postcards, she started scrolling, discounting all the ones that had already been read. Tapping to open an unread postcard, Maddie smiled on seeing a colourful picture of the Marina Grande in Capri with bunches of pink bougainvillea at the corners. She scrolled to see the other side of the postcard.

'It's nice,' Gio smiled as he read the words.

Dear Patsy

Happy birthday from Capri. I wish you were here to see this paradise place, but I imagine you are having a marvellous time today with George spoiling you. Do have a slice of cake for me! Much love to Dad.

Love Rose x

PS – I have mailed a present that may take an age to arrive!

'Ah, yes, it is paradise here,' Maddie said, her heart lifting on seeing her grandmother's words in happier times. 'I wonder what the present was?' she added as an aside, tapping on through to search for something more.

'Hold on.' Gio lifted the laptop from her. 'Do you mind?' he asked, and moved the cursor until it clicked on the previous thumbnail.

'Sure, what is it?' Maddie leaned over his arm as Gio double-clicked to bring up a small piece of paper with typed words on and an elaborate cross insignia at the top.

'The words are in Italian, but they are hard to read,' he explained, pointing to the first sentence where she could see the ink had faded from the water damage, as much of the other letters and theatre programmes in the suitcase had too. 'So, it's impossible to see who sent this, the address at the top here and name at the bottom here too' – he tapped his index finger to the screen – 'is gone.'

'I can see that it's about Audrey though!' Maddie said, her pulse quickening on seeing the name in the letter.

'Yes. It says: *As we promised to you, here is one photo of the baby Audrey. She is thriving and likes to smile. We trust this satisfies you and that you can put the matter behind you now.*'

'Oh, is that all?' Maddie felt deflated. 'How cruel, to imply that a mother could ever forget about her baby.' She shook her head and swallowed down her anger. 'My grandmother has clearly never forgotten.'

'I'm sorry, Maddie,' Gio said, handing back the laptop. 'Did you find a picture in the suitcase?'

'I did,' Maddie said, remembering the little black-and-white photo of the baby lying on a blanket on the grass.

'And were there any clues in the photo? Could you tell from the background if it was taken here in Capri?'

'No, there was nothing at all, Gio, and I didn't think to scrutinise the photographic paper it was printed on – sometimes in old photos there's a water-mark of the company that developed it,' she sighed, wishing she had brought the photo of baby Audrey with her now. 'But it all points to baby Audrey being adopted here, with the letter written in Italian. What about this insignia at the top? Do you recognise it?' Maddie asked.

'No, I've never seen it before.'

Maddie put the laptop away and gave the back of his hand a quick squeeze. But as she went to move her fingers away, he cupped his hand around hers, weaving his fingers in between her fingers and moving his free arm around her shoulders, drawing her in close to his body.

'How do you feel now?' Gio asked.

'OK. Good in fact,' she nodded. 'I don't have all the answers, yet, but it's a good start. I'll talk it through with my dad and see what he wants to do . . . I'm sure there will be a proper process for tracing a person who was adopted in Italy. I just hope we can make it happen in time for my grandmother.'

'I understand. And I will miss you when you go home, Maddie.' Gio pulled her in closer. 'I wish you could stay . . .'

'Ah, Gio, I wish I could too.'

In silence, she leaned her head against the front of his shoulder, his delicious scent intoxicating now as she felt his chin rest gently on her head, sparking an exquisite sizzling sensation to swirl around her bare legs and up under the hem of her shorts. It was all she could do to resist turning her face up to meet his and planting a long, lingering kiss on his irresistible lips.

'Do you still feel OK?' Gio asked, his voice husky from nuzzling into her hair.

'Um . . . err . . . yes, very OK,' Maddie managed, wondering if he was talking about her contemplative mood, or them being here together with warm, sun-kissed skin on skin – did he even have an idea of how she was truly feeling right now? She stole a glance at his profile, the side of his chiselled face looking straight ahead at the stunning view. Then to the rocky coastline rising from the sea and framed by the sun, and she wanted to do another silent scream of pleasure and pure joy, as she had on the bed in her apartment that time. Cycle her legs up in the air and savour this moment as a memory to revisit again and again – *that time I was draped over the most incredibly hot man I ever met in my entire life on the deck of a boat in Capri surrounded by the Mediterranean Sea –* knowing this memory of how she was feeling right now would most definitely serve her well for many years to come, as her grandmother had said it would.

'So, Maddie, you know more of the person I am now. Not the bad boy you think I am when we first met?' She felt his head lift from hers and so she moved away from his shoulder to see Gio raise an eyebrow as if waiting for her reaction. She grinned and dipped her head to one side.

'No, Gio, I don't think you are a "bad boy" as you say—' She stopped talking on seeing a smile forming at the edge of his mouth. 'Ah, you're teasing me . . . aren't you?' she lifted a hand to tent her eyes from the dazzling sun that was spilling hazy streaks of apricot and gold across the horizon above the shimmering sea.

'Teasing?' he checked, a puzzled look on his face.

'Joking,' she clarified, but wasn't convinced that he really didn't know what this word meant.

'No . . . no, I'm not joking. Today is serious, Maddie. I know this.' And he glanced at the laptop on the deck next to them. 'But I do not like to see you sad, so I want to *cheer you up* – is what you say in England, yes?'

'Yes,' Maddie nodded, 'this is what we say. And being here with you, with this view, everything, has cheered me up,' she told him, the feeling lingering.

More silence followed as they sat together watching the sun sink further down on the horizon and start melting into the sea, the mesmerising ripple of the waves swishing back and forth.

Gio was the first to speak.

'Maddie, you seem very quiet. Are you bored being here?' he asked gently. She turned her head to look at him, surprised that he would ask this.

'No. Not at all. This is wonderful. Being here with you watching the sun set is exactly where I want to be right now.' And she went back to resting her head against the side of his shoulder, thinking how easy it was being with him. Just sitting here and watching the golden Capri sun, the majestic beauty as it faded further into the sea, making the sky a mingle of orange and navy and studded with silver stars. She felt content. Happy. Yes, there was lots to sort out for her grandmother, and her heart still ached for the pain she had experienced in her past, but right now, right here, with Gio, was incredible. She felt alive. Exhilarated. Excited. Intoxicated with anticipation of what the rest of this night might bring. With the spectacular view, the sound of the waves, and the blissfully warm feel of the sun-drenched deck beneath the fluffy white towel she was lounging on. The heady mixture of Gio's aftershave, saltwater and sandalwood teasing her senses, muddled with the red-hot heat firing from his fingers still wrapped around hers, his index finger tracing a delicious path up and down the inside of her thumb.

'Are you sure?'

'Yes, of course. Why do you ask?' Maddie sat upright and swivelled her body so she was facing him now. Their hands were still entwined.

'My girlfriend said I'm boring because I like to be quiet and calm here on the boat . . . to watch the sun setting. And not always be busy at parties.' He flicked his eyes away.

Maddie leaned forward.

Her mouth fell open.

She closed it and then opened it again, trying to wrap her head around this revelation, and the juxta-position from feeling wonderful with him to utterly panicked, bamboozled and completely foolish, and couldn't wait to get off the boat quick enough. Even Bella picked up on the sudden tension and stood up, her ears going down and her tail tucked in between her back legs as she looked pensively from Maddie to Gio and back again.

'Oh . . . your girlfriend.' Maddie said the words, but it was as if they had come from somewhere else, a vortex that had drained all her thoughts and feelings, rendering her stunned and incapable of saying a proper coherent sentence. She dropped his hand and jumped up. Of course, he had a girlfriend, a stunning one no doubt, just like him. And they must have only recently met, Maddie assumed, because he couldn't have taken her to meet his family yet . . . why else would his own mum and sisters have thought that Maddie was his girlfriend and then say that he needed a 'nice girl-friend'? No, they clearly didn't even know about Gio's stunning girlfriend. Whoever she was. Maddie felt her face flame, sparking a prickly, mottled rash of shame to spread across her neck. Not that anything physical had really happened between her and Gio, thankfully, but it could have, so very easily . . . not that she would intentionally do that to another woman, if she had known there was another woman! But something had shifted between them. She knew it. There was a connection, a flirtatious, yet emotional connection, and that was just as bad, worse in fact, if feelings were involved. And Gio telling her she was sexy! Sun goddess. He really was a giant player, after all. And she was a giant fool for falling for it. Her first instinct had been right. She cringed at the memory of telling

293

him he was hot, very hot . . . For crying out loud, why hadn't he mentioned this tiny yet *very* significant detail about his love life until now?

There had been a moment earlier today when Gio had leaned a little closer and she thought he was going to kiss her, or was it her imagination? Wishful thinking? She didn't think so. And what about the hand holding, the finger stroking, the arm around her shoulders, pulling her into his chest . . . it was very provocative, and who does that when they have a girlfriend? Gio, it seems. Or maybe for a moment he'd just felt sorry for her so moved in closer but decided a pity kiss wasn't on the cards, after all.

'I should go,' she muttered. 'Yes, that's what I should do.' And she quickly picked up her laptop and camera case and threw off the beach blanket that had got caught up in the waistband of her shorts.

'What are you doing?'

'Going. I'm going away from here. I'm getting off the boat!' Maddie winced at the shrill edge to her voice, closed her eyes momentarily, took a deep breath and added, 'Look, thank you for all your help, Gio, . . . and for all this too,' she glanced at the empty prosecco glasses, 'but, I can't do—' She broke off to gather the rest of her stuff up into a big bundle in her arms, shoved her feet into her sliders and ran to the other side of the boat, stepped on to the towpath and went in search of a taxi to take her away as fast as possible.

26

Back at her Airbnb room, Maddie was sitting on the balcony with a glass of red wine, looking out at the gold lights twinkling in the night sky across the island, and thinking about all that had happened today, when a FaceTime call appeared on her phone.

'Mads, how are you? . . . So tell me, I'm dying to know what happened on the boat?' Cynthia asked, to open the conversation from a sunny California, complete with palm trees for a backdrop and a large cup of frothy green liquid in her hand. 'Ugh, this stuff is disgusting . . . wheatgrass and matcha, no thank you! Give me a full-fat almond croissant any day!' She dumped the cup on a table to the side of her and leaned in: 'I'm intrigued to hear more about your hot Italian guy,' she winked.

Maddie picked up the wine glass and wandered inside to sit on the bed where it was more private, and she wouldn't run the risk of being overheard from the street below.

'Are you OK?' Cynthia looked concerned. 'Oh, no . . . you're not, are you? Oh, Mads, what is it?' Five minutes later, having told Cynthia about what happened with Gio and him dropping the girlfriend bombshell and how she had legged it off the boat, Cynthia held up a hand. 'What a rat!' she declared indignantly and puffed out a long breath of air. 'Sorry, Mads . . . I did say he sounded a bit like a player.'

'Hmm, well, yes you did, but you also said, "You're going to be on a boat with an incredibly sexy man who is clearly into you, and you fancy the pants off him – so who cares! You're on holiday so go for it and have glorious, no-strings-attached sex, because what happens in Capri stays in Capri!"' Maddie grimaced, recalling the text chat she'd had with Cynthia last night.

'Ah, yes,' she pulled a face. 'Well, I might have said that. But, in my defence, that was based on him being a player, as we thought at that time, with his flirty send-a-limoncello-cocktail-over-to-the-table action, and not an actual cheating-on-his-girlfriend rat! As we know he is now.'

'Well, either way, I've made a massive fool of myself.'

'How do you work that one out? Listen, Mads, you are not the home wrecker here . . . he is! He's the fool, not you.'

'What do you mean?'

'For having a girlfriend and blowing his chances with you – the best woman he could ever dream of meeting.'

'Well, I wouldn't go that far. Besides, you're my friend so you have to say stuff like that.' Maddie found herself grinning at Cynthia's cheerleading.

'That's better: a smile on your face. Honestly, Mads, forget about it.'

'I'd love to, but it's not as easy as all that. I'll have to see him again, if only to return the letters that Maribella sent to Lucia. I can't just keep them. I've got to take them back to Lucia, and he could be there.'

'What does it matter if you see him?'

'I feel embarrassed . . . for running off like that. I should have been breezy and nonchalant.'

'Oh hang on, Mads,' Cynthia said sternly, leaning closer to the camera on her phone. 'You are enough – don't ever think you need to change and be bloody breezy or whatever. It's too much, all this pressure we put on ourselves to be a different way. It's OK to be yourself and absolutely bloody fine to be annoyed and leg it off a boat.'

Silence followed as Maddie pondered what her friend was saying.

'Hmm . . . maybe when you put it like that.'

'No *maybe* about it. Come on, Maddie, you are fine exactly as you are.'

'It a shame though, as I had such a wonderful holiday, and on the boat today we were holding hands and snuggling, I felt relaxed with him, and I so wanted to kiss him. I genuinely thought I might be developing feelings for him.' She looked away. 'But still, how could I have got it so wrong?'

'You didn't get it wrong. He did. He was flirtatious. Anyway, ignore me, I'd have kissed his face off, girl-friend or no girlfriend.'

'Cynthia!'

'What! It's just a kiss,' she replied, a wicked glint in her eye. Maddie gave her a look, eyebrows raised.

'OK, OK . . . let's just agree to disagree . . . My moral compass isn't as functional as yours,' Cynthia laughed. 'Seriously though, Mads, I'm sorry. I was really rooting for you having a wild, passionate holiday fling with a gorgeous, sexy Italian man.'

'And you know . . . I think I would have really liked that,' Maddie said, remembering the moment on the deck when she was in Gio's arms watching the sunset together.

'Anyway, let's change the subject: have you found out anything about Audrey?' Cynthia asked.

'I have actually . . . quite a lot, in fact.' Maddie then told her everything she had discovered.

Cynthia stared into the camera, agog. 'Wow! Your lovely granny . . . I can't even—' And then her face turned sad, her bottom lip pulled in and her eyebrows knitting together. 'Oh God, I might cry . . .' She flapped a hand underneath her eyes before dabbing the corners so as not to ruin her expertly applied make-up.

'I know, it's awful, isn't it. And what is my dad going to say on discovering he has a half-sister he never knew about?'

'Good point . . . gosh, I don't know.' Cynthia slowly shook her head. 'It's huge news. When are you going to tell him?'

'When I get home.' Maddie had decided.

'Really? Why not right away?'

'I just thought it might be something I should say face to face.'

'Hmm, maybe . . . but then he might feel hurt, knowing you sat on such big news without telling him. Didn't you say he was hurt when you discovered your granny had a whole other life in the Golden Age of Hollywood that he knew nothing about?'

'Yes, yes, he was. He had no idea. She had never talked to him about it and nobody else had ever said anything to him. You'd think there would have been rumours, gossip or whatever in the village, wouldn't you?'

'Er, yes . . . I agree, everyone knows your business in Tindledale – isn't that why we left all those years ago?' Cynthia smiled wryly.

'Ah, yes! So, I'm assuming my grandmother must have come back home to Tindledale and resumed her old life as Rose O'Malley.'

'Oh God, I can't begin to imagine what that must have felt like for her. All the movie actors I've worked with spend years training, working hard in fringe theatre or off Broadway and doing the rounds of casting calls trying to make the big time, and so to lose it all when it was there within reach . . .' Cynthia sighed. 'Maybe your dad could find out why she never told him any of this. Not now, I mean . . . I'm not a total monster, I know your granny's memory is going, but I mean years ago when she was younger. Why did she never mention it?'

'Maybe she just wanted to put it all behind her after it didn't work out. And I guess she would have felt ashamed being an unmarried mother. It was the 1950s, after all.'

'Guess so,' Cynthia shook her head. 'But if you tell your dad ASAP, then he can talk to your granny about Audrey's adoption and see if she remembers any more details while you are still there in Capri. Or could you talk to Lucia . . . or what about her cousin, Maribella? Maybe she knows more.'

'Ah, Gio told me that Maribella died about ten years ago,' Maddie said.

'Oh, that's a shame. So, are you going to call your dad now?'

'Yes, I'll FaceTime him. But not until tomorrow, when I've had time to think it all through and work out how I tell him. It's bound to be a shock. Plus, it's not really my business . . . it's Granny's private and very personal business—'

'But you can't exactly phone her and tell her what you know. It's too much, too painful, potentially. No, she needs your dad with her, holding her hand, so I say tell him first.'

'Yes, yes she does. A phone call wouldn't work . . . she might not even remember who I am,' Maddie said quietly, hoping this would never happen, but realistically, it was sadly inevitable.

'Then even more reason why Audrey must be found. She might want to meet before her birth mother's memory fades completely,' Cynthia said. 'Surely, Audrey should have the option. I mean, fair enough if she doesn't want to meet, but for all we know, she could have been searching for your granny for years.'

Cynthia was right, it wasn't just about Maddie's wishes, or her dad's, or indeed her grandmother's. No, the person at the centre of all this was Audrey. This was her life and Maddie had no way of knowing what that was like for her. But one thing Maddie did know was that she needed to make sure Audrey was respected, and her wishes appreciated. It was entirely possible that she might not know that she was adopted. And if she was born in 1954, then she would be in her sixties now, most likely with her own family and happy life that she might not want disrupted. Was she still living in Italy? Had she ever tried to contact Granny? A trillion questions were flying around in Maddie's head. She only hoped they could find something, anything, to give them a chance of finding Audrey . . .

27

Early the next morning, with the sun already searing, having enjoyed a delicious breakfast of fresh fruit and pastries with the best coffee she had ever tasted from a traditional trattoria a few streets away, Maddie was now sitting on the balcony to her apartment. Admiring the spectacular view of the now familiar lush green landscape, with bursts of pink bougainvillea and pastel-coloured villas, she thought how truly picture-postcard perfect it was here, and wished she wasn't going home tomorrow. She would love to have more time here, to explore and take more pictures and really imprint the feeling of being here on the island in her memory forever.

She'd always have the orchard and sitting on the veranda with Lucia, just as her grandmother had, decades before, but Maddie wanted more. Maybe she could come back after the Italian job she had lined up later this year and stay longer next time. Even after yesterday's fiasco and running away from Gio and the boat, Maddie had enjoyed her holiday in Capri and so was going to ask Jona if she could book in for her return. A part of her was wishing she'd come here with her dad as a child, just as Sofia had. She had even dreamed about it last night, a strange mixture of splashing about in the sparkling sea as a child, feeling excited and happy, with Dad lifting her and swinging her around laughing and carefree, but then she was an adult again and Brad appeared with his back to her. As he walked away, she ran after him, but when he turned around it was Gio's face she saw, walking towards her, smiling, and telling her she was sexy, a sun goddess and he wanted to get to know her . . . but she was the one turning and walking away this time. Maddie had woken up at this point, with an overwhelming feeling of confusion, yet relief, knowing there was no point dwelling on what might have been with Gio. Or indeed fantasising about a fictional childhood she could have had with her dad in Spain.

From here on, it was all about now and the future. So she had written all her thoughts in her journal and amazed herself with how calm and serene she felt. Lighter and unencumbered – and she wanted to keep it this way. Coming away on holiday by herself had given her the headspace she had hoped it would, the time to work through her thoughts and let go of the ones that didn't serve her well. It was thrilling. Very thrilling, and she had also started putting together a plan listing all the practical changes she wanted to make in her life when she got home. Like pursuing her photography career. And travelling more – starting with Spain, to see where her dad lived, spend time with him there. It shocked her that she still hadn't been. With her mum never allowing her to go to see her dad in Spain, and then Brad talking her out of it whenever she had mooted the idea of them going together and making her doubt whether she'd like, or even cope, with travelling on her own, time had trundled on without it ever happening. Plus, her dad hadn't actually invited her to come and stay with him in Spain, not since that time as a child when he had offered to pay for her flight and her mum had refused. The realisation shocked her.

But she was free of all that constraint and control now and could go wherever she liked. It felt great. She quite fancied going to Los Angeles too and seeing the apartment block where Granny had lived in Hollywood as Kelly Sinclair; the Italian bakery in Lincoln Heights mentioned in the letters that her grandmother had never got to visit before her world fell apart when Patsy and Clarke died. Maddie wanted to capture it all and preserve it forever. Already she was looking forward to showing her grandmother the pictures of the orchard in the hope that they might spark something for her and she'd find comfort in remembering happier times there with her friend, Lucia, who never did forget about her. And she'd keep copies for herself too. Maddie thought it a wonderful record of the start of her new life full of adventures. Yes, coming to Capri had freed her from the confinement she had felt as a child and then in her relationship with Brad. And in a way, she had her grandmother to thank for it. She wouldn't have come here if she hadn't found the postcard from Capri inside the dust-covered suitcase on top of the wardrobe.

Maddie closed her eyes and tilted her face up to the sun as she sat back in the chair and just enjoyed the moment, savouring the warmth and letting herself relax as she listened to the sound of the cicadas and inhaled the sweet scent floating up from the buckets of flowers on the pavement outside the florist shop below.

Moments later, a buzzing sound woke Maddie from her reverie. It took her a few seconds to register her phone skating across the tabletop.

'Dad,' she answered, on seeing his name on the screen. 'You got my WhatsApp message . . .' Pulling a robe on over her bikini, Maddie pushed the phone into the crook of her neck, tied the belt and walked inside where it was cooler, and sat on the end of the bed. She had messaged him as soon as she woke up this morning to ask if he could call her when he was on his own and had time to talk. Maddie hadn't wanted to phone him and come out with such big news of a sister he never knew about, figuring it best he be prepared for more than just a general chat beforehand.

'Yes, I did. Is everything OK? You said you had some big news to share with me,' her dad said, cutting straight to the chase.

'That's right . . . I do,' she started, and then, sensing something a bit off in his voice, 'Are you all right?' She heard him sigh. 'What is it, Dad?'

'It's nothing, love . . .'

'Is Sofia OK?' Maddie checked.

'Yes, all fine here – no sign of the baby.'

'And Granny, she hasn't had another fall, has she?'

'No. She misses you though, and has been asking for you. When is it you're coming home?'

'Tomorrow, Dad.' Maddie stood up, distracted. Why was he being like this? He knew it was tomorrow. No, something was definitely up. 'Are you sure everything is OK?'

'Yes, like I said, it's nothing, love.'

'Well, it doesn't sound like it. Have I done something wrong?' Maddie asked, and instantly wished she hadn't. She thought back to the last conversation they'd had; he'd been a bit quieter than usual then too, when she had told him about meeting Lucia. In fact, he hadn't said much at all, almost as if he wasn't really interested. Had she inadvertently upset him?

'Not that I know of,' he laughed, but it was hollow sounding, forced. If he wasn't going to tell her what was up, then she had no choice but to drop it. 'Why don't you just tell me what it is that you have to say?'

'Oh, um . . . OK then . . .' Maddie sat back down on the bed, took a breath, and did as he asked. 'I've found out about Audrey . . .'

Silence followed.

'Found out about her?' he eventually said 'What do you mean?'

'That's what I need to talk to you about, Dad, and it might be a shock, but it could be really wonderful too. Audrey is Granny's daughter.' Maddie waited to let the news sink in. And waited. 'Dad . . . are you still there?' She found herself holding her breath and wondering why he wasn't saying anything. 'Did you hear me . . . it means you have a sister, a half-sister because her dad was an American man called Clarke who—'

'I know what it means,' he said flatly.

'Oh . . . yes, sure, sorry, of course you do,' Maddie said, confusion swirling. Why was he being like this? Was he disappointed that Granny had never told him? The same way he was when they had found out about her going to Hollywood. Was he in shock, perhaps? Or crushed on finding out he had a sister he'd never known about and had never met. She knew he only had Granny when he was growing up, being an only child, and his dad dying when he was a teenager must have been devastating for him and poor Granny. Hadn't the poor woman suffered enough loss in her life. No wonder she had asked for Maddie's help to find Audrey.

Dad still wasn't saying anything and so Maddie talked to fill the gap.

'I'm going to find her, Dad. I promised Granny I would, and I will. Please don't blame Granny for not telling you. We'll find Audrey together. I know she was born in 1954 and I've been to the church where she was baptised. I was thinking we could find out what the process is to trace someone adopted in Italy. We could always do one of those DNA things on an ancestry website. Audrey could very well already be in one of those databases looking for Granny. A biological match. Or we could contact that programme – *Long Lost Family* . . . yes, Dad I've got lots of ideas. And I'm sure Granny will be over the moon too when she knows that I've met her old friend Lucia and that she never forgot about her either. And I have photos to show her, of Lucia and the orange and lemon orchard that Granny wrote about all those years ago in her letters to her sister, Patsy—'

'Why would you do that?' Dad jumped in. Maddie stopped talking, stunned. Her mind was racing, trying to work out what he meant.

'Um . . . the pictures? Well, I thought it might be a comfort for Granny to see something nice and maybe it could jog her memory and she would remember more about her past – she did write in the letter that she loved it there in the orchard and Lucia has told me they had such a marvellous summer together, and—'

'The church!' Dad cut in again, his voice cold and monotone.

'Oh, er . . . why wouldn't I? We want to find Audrey, don't we? For Granny . . . she asked me to help her,' Maddie said, her mouth and throat suddenly dry. She put the phone on speaker and placed it on the bed while she grabbed a bottle of water and took a big gulp. Her cheeks were burning and just like that she had regressed straight back to her childhood in those weekly phone calls with her dad where she had been so keen to be on her best behaviour. So much for feeling lighter and all the promises she had made to herself when writing in her journal. She had wobbled at the first hurdle.

Standing up again, she put the bottle on a coffee table in the centre of the room and paced up and down, cupping her hands around her curls to scoop them up into a big ponytail while she tried to work out what was going on. Why was he being so cold? Why did he sound cross with her? What had she done wrong? Why hadn't he tried harder to see her? Why hadn't he invited her to come and stay with him in Spain? Why not? What was wrong with her? All her thoughts and insecurities swirled into a massive soup inside her head, merging and mingling together until she had completely lost sense of the moment and what was happening. She carried on pacing. Waiting for him to say something. To tell her why he was being indifferent and sounding like he wasn't bothered and obviously annoyed with her.

And then the proverbial penny dropped.

He didn't want her to find Audrey.

He had been evasive about it right from the start. When her grandmother had first asked for her help, he had tried to put her off, saying not to drag up the past and to let it be. Why didn't he want Granny to have peace of mind? Why didn't he even seem interested in discovering he had a half-sister, let alone excited or curious or . . . well, anything, to be honest. Instead his reaction had been clinical and unemotional. It didn't make sense. Surely he'd have *some* thoughts on finding out he had a sister he never knew about. Yet it was as if he didn't care at all.

And then it did make sense.

Maddie took a deep breath and closed her eyes in a desperate attempt to calm her runaway thoughts and gain clarity.

'You already knew.' The words came out quietly but hung ominously in the air between them. Maddie sat back down and waited, the sound of silence deafening as she wondered why he hadn't said anything, why he hadn't spoken up and said he knew all about Audrey? In fact, he had purposely tried to put her off helping her grandmother. He knew how upset and distressed Granny was getting about it, always asking where Audrey was, and it had been going on for well over a year now . . . And all along he'd known that she was Granny's long-lost daughter? How could he do this to his own mother – prevent her from finding her lost daughter? And to Audrey too. Had he prevented Audrey from knowing about Granny? Had he been in touch with her? Did he already know where she was?

Maddie pressed her palms to her cheeks in a bid to cool them and slow her racing thoughts. She was angry and hurt and feeling very let down by him. Again. It struck her. She had tried for years to push the feeling away, not wanting to feel this way about the dad that she had adored.

He coughed to clear his throat as if preparing his defence. But she couldn't help herself and jumped in.

'How could you do this? How could you watch Granny suffer and not do anything to help? Why didn't you tell me? Instead of letting me go off and try to piece it all together from a pile of old letters and a postcard from Capri?'

'Maddie, please,' he started, before falling silent.

'What did Granny ever do wrong? She's the loveliest and kindest person – she doesn't deserve this. She deserves better. And so do I—' Maddie stopped talking. The enormity of what she was saying sinking in and terrifying her. She had told him. At last. And there was no going back now. She wasn't on best behaviour with him any more.

'I know,' Dad said quietly. Maddie stared at the phone still on the bed.

'Um, pardon?' she managed, picking it up and switching the speaker off. 'Know what? Know about Audrey, or that Granny deserves better, or . . .' she took a beat to inhale through her nose and then said it again, feeling far stronger this time: 'that I deserve better?' her voice cracking momentarily.

'Yes, you do,' Dad validated, and Maddie felt tears scratch in the corners of her eyes. 'Of course, you do, love. I should have made more effort when you were younger . . . and in recent years too. I should have made you more of a part of my life.'

'Why didn't you?'

'Guilt, I guess . . . and shame. I had an affair, love.' He let out a long puff of air, and Maddie caught her breath; this was the first she'd heard of it. 'Yes, and then I left your mum and you, and . . . well, I was a fool who didn't deserve you. I had made my bed and had to lie in it – I thought you were better off without me.' She heard a heavy sigh.

'But you have a lovely life in Spain, you are happy and—' Maddie felt overwhelmed, the image she had always painted inside her head now distorted and different. Plus, this still didn't explain why he had kept quiet about Audrey.

'I was at the start,' he continued, 'yet sometimes the grass isn't always greener, love . . . Maria and I split up. We should have done it many years ago, really, but we stayed together thinking it best for Sofia and, well, I had already wrecked one marriage and one little girl's life . . .' A beat of silence followed. Maddie licked a salty tear from the side of her mouth. 'Then, when Sofia settled down with Ben in Tindledale, it became all too apparent what needed to happen. Maria and I agreed to go our separate ways . . . Anyway, enough of that. I am sorry, Maddie. I'm sorry I let you down. I've wanted to talk to you about it for years and I think I put it off because I was too afraid of what I might hear. It seemed easier to paste over the mistakes I had made and make the best of the relationship I did have with you. I never wanted to risk losing you completely.'

'Oh Dad,' Maddie said, staggered by his openness and wishing she had waited until she was home so she could give him a hug. Her feelings of frustration and disappointment in him had subsided. It took courage to come out with all this. 'Why would you think you'd lose me?'

'Well, the fear of rejection can be a tough thing to face, especially from your own child. And I guess, I thought you had your own life . . . and when you didn't come out to Spain—'

'You never invited me,' Maddie said, and instantly regretted the accusatory tone. Dad was baring his soul here; she didn't need to make him feel any worse than he already did. 'I'm sorry, Dad, I didn't mean it to come out like that. I could have asked to come and visit you, I can see that now.'

'You don't need to ask, love, you're welcome any time. I guess, I should have made that much clearer. I just assumed, you know—'

'I think we have much more in common than we realise . . . I've felt the same way, Dad. I've wanted to talk to you about it for years too. And I've always put it off, telling myself it was never the right time,' she told him, purposefully leaving out all the negative thoughts that had percolated inside her head all these years, how she had felt abandoned, and it had shaped her life and then her relationship with Brad, because her intention wasn't to hurt him. She had already chosen to focus on now and the future, and a big part of that was to build a better and more open relationship with her dad. But she did need to find out why he had kept Audrey's existence a secret. She was about to ask him, but he spoke first.

'It's always the right time, darling. I love you, and please, from now on let's make sure we keep talking. We have lots of gaps to fill in. I'd really like that, Maddie, if you would to?' he said, his voice full of hope.

'I would, Dad,' Maddie said, laughing a little bit through her tears. 'And I love you too.'

'And I really am very sorry I let you down, love,' he said, 'it's why I didn't say anything about Audrey, why

I didn't want the past raked up . . . I never imagined you would actually find Lucia or discover all that you have about Mum's other child. I thought you'd go to Italy – I should have said how proud I was of you getting the photography job in Naples by the way – and that you'd then have a fantastic holiday in Capri and come home again none the wiser.'

'But I don't understand, Dad. Isn't it a good thing for Granny to know about Audrey? At least to know if she is well and had a happy life? And aren't you curious? And what did you mean when you said, "it's why you didn't say anything about Audrey"?'

Silence followed. Maddie waited for him to answer.

'Well . . . I always knew there was another child,' he eventually admitted.

'Did Granny tell you?'

'No, not exactly . . . but I remember Mum telling me when I was about six or seven that there might be a big sister out there for me. Of course, I didn't really understand what she was saying at the time, but as I grew up and put the pieces together . . . her tears on the same day every year—' Maddie heard him puff out a long breath of air.

'What date was this?'

'March twentieth . . . it stuck in my mind with it being the same day as my dad's birthday and I used to assume it was because she missed my dad, but one year I overheard her crying quiet tears in her bedroom. The door was ajar and so I peeped through the crack by the doorframe, instinctively knowing that I shouldn't disturb her, and she was looking at a black-and-white photo of a baby.'

'Could it have been the little photo I found in the suitcase?' Maddie asked.

'Possibly. I saw Mum kiss her fingers and press them on the photo, saying something like, 'my girl, Audrey, happy birthday darling . . .' It was emotional to see, and I felt ashamed for spying on her and wished I could say something to comfort her. And I did one time. I remember asking who Audrey was, and Mum flew into a panic. I'd never seen her like it before. The colour completely drained from her face and then she was yelling at me to stop it. I was never to say Audrey's name again – nobody must know, I wasn't to tell a soul. She made me promise. And I did. I felt scared and grew up with the sense of it being a secret that I had to keep. That Audrey, my big sister was a secret. I thought I was protecting Mum because it was her business and I wanted her to trust me. I was all she had, and vice versa. Looking back, I see now that she probably felt ashamed, or was made to feel ashamed. It was all very different back in those days.'

'Oh Dad. That must have been difficult for you, but it makes sense. When Granny asked me to help her find Audrey, she looked so wary and frightened. And it's heartbreaking that she would feel this way after all these years.' Maddie sighed.

'It is,' her dad agreed. 'I asked her once about the missing photos torn from the albums that were kept in the sideboard of the sitting room—'

'Oh yes . . .' Maddie said.

'Mum told me her dad had done it. He had spiralled into a depression – she didn't say why exactly, only that he had suffered terribly with his son dying in the war followed by his wife. Most likely it was PTSD – that's what we would know it as now. He had become angry, and she bore the brunt of it, being the only one left after her sister died, her mum and brother too . . . Granny's dad lost his mind towards the end and refused to even talk to her.'

'How sad . . . I wonder why?' Maddie said, wondering if Granny's dad had been responsible for the angry red lines on Lucia's letters and sending them back to her. 'Could he have found out what happened in Capri? That his unmarried daughter had a baby before she returned home to England and so didn't want her to keep a connection with Lucia? Could he have thought that his daughter had been corrupted when she went to America and

Capri? Or perhaps he was just disappointed that she hadn't made it in Hollywood,' Maddie suggested, thinking it all through and trying to work out what it must have been like for her grandmother back then.

'Maybe he did find out. Maybe all of what you've said is true, or maybe he was ill, love, mentally ill with PTSD and grief . . . remember, he had suffered heartbreak and loss too,' Dad said, sadly.

'Yes, it's very sad. And it must have been hard for Granny on her own . . . I hope she went on to find happiness with your dad.'

'She did, love. All my memories of them together were very happy and with lots of laughter. Dancing to the Beatles in the kitchen . . .'

'That's good to hear, Dad . . . Granny has had a hard life with all this loss and sadness, she deserves to have some happiness too, don't you think? Especially now . . . She wants to know where Audrey is.' Maddie waited a few seconds before asking him outright: 'Do you know where Audrey is, Dad?'

'No, no I don't . . . I only knew there was another child, nothing more, I promise you, love.'

'OK. But why are you reluctant to look for Audrey? For Granny . . . And what about Audrey, shouldn't we at least give her the chance to decide? She could be searching for her birth parents.'

'I don't know, love,' Dad sighed. 'I've gone over it a hundred times since this all came up but I just keep going round in circles . . . It's fear, I guess.'

'What do you mean?'

'Well, it could happen again.'

'What could?' Maddie asked.

'Love, your grandmother was very happy with my dad . . . but there was a time after he died when she wasn't,' he paused, and Maddie waited quietly for him to continue. 'You see, she had to go away for a while.'

'Away? What do you mean?'

'I was a young lad . . . a teenager, so my memory of it all is a bit hazy, but I stayed with a neighbour, and I can remember her saying it was Mum's nerves. It happened a couple of times . . .'

'Oh Dad, do you think Granny had a breakdown?'

'I think so, love, and I guess this is why I didn't want the past raked up, in case it happened again. Granny is elderly, the last thing any of us wants is for her to be unhappy at her time of life, or worse still, have another breakdown . . . even though it hasn't happened again in thirty years or more, that I'm aware of, I just didn't want to risk it—'

'Of course, I understand, Dad. And I'm sorry.' Maddie inhaled sharply, a stab of disappointment rushing through her for not even considering that her dad wasn't being deliberately obstructive. 'I can see now that you were just worried about your mum; that you were acting out of love in trying to protect her.'

'Maddie, love . . . you have nothing to be sorry for. You didn't know any of this and you were acting out of love too. Your grandmother asked for your help, and you've done everything you can.'

'I've tried, but we still haven't found Audrey, and that's what Granny wants. Are you reluctant for us to try to trace her?'

'I'm not sure, Maddie. Bringing a complete stranger into our lives . . . I'm just not sure.'

'Why does that bother you, Dad?'

'What if she comes and takes it all away.'

'Takes what away? And Audrey isn't a stranger, she's your sister, Granny's daughter! What could she possibly take away? She might not even want to know us – she might not even be alive. We just don't know, Dad.' Maddie waited again, but he was quiet for ages, until eventually he spoke, his voice wavering.

'The house! Honeysuckle Cottage.' Maddie heard him draw in a deep breath and then exhale. 'It's for you.'

'Me?' Maddie gasped, and with closed eyes she turned her head from side to side, trying to take it all in.

'Yes. Sofia will have the house in Spain when I'm gone.'

'But Honeysuckle Cottage is Granny's house, her home, she lived in it since she was a child.' Maddie didn't want her grandmother's house if it meant never finding Audrey, and her grandmother never knowing what had become of her daughter.

'It's your home too,' her dad said. 'And one day . . .' he paused momentarily before carrying on, '. . . when your granny is no longer with us, the cottage will come to me. When it does, I'm passing it on to you. And well, I've given you so little, love, and I didn't want Granny's will contested and the house taken away from you . . . potentially.'

'Dad, please . . . I'm so sorry I brought all this up and then telling you what I had found out without even thinking about how you might be feeling—'

'Don't be daft, Maddie, you acted with best intentions, to help your granny, to make her happy – unlike me, I'm ashamed to say, trying to deter you and thinking about an inheritance instead of the fact that I have a half-sister out there somewhere.'

'Dad, you're only human, flawed like everyone else. As far as I can see, you were just worried, you had good intentions – misguided, maybe, because I can't imagine Audrey would just turn up and claim any inheritances. Like I said, she might not even be alive, or want anything to do with us . . . And you know, she could actually be a very nice person.'

'Yes, you're absolutely right, Maddie. I'm glad it's all in the open now,' he said, sounding considerably lighter than he had earlier. 'I'll wait for you to get home and then we can chat to Granny about it all together and you can show her the photos you've taken of Lucia, and the orchards too . . . it sounds wonderful.'

'It really is, Dad, and I can't wait to come back here another time.'

'Maybe we could go together,' he suggested, 'have a bit of a holiday, and spend some quality time together, as they say.' She heard a smile in his voice. 'Only if you'd like to?' he then asked, sounding tentative now.

'I'd like to very much,' Maddie grinned to herself. 'Will you tell Sofia about Audrey? Or shall I?' she asked. 'Let her know that she has an aunt somewhere in the world . . .'

'I'll talk to her,' he said, 'and I do have some explaining to do – let her know why I kept quiet, I hope she understands.'

'I'm sure she will when you explain it all to her.'

'OK. And Maddie . . .?'

'Yes, Dad?'

'I'm glad we talked.'

'Me too.' She smiled.

'And Maddie, when you take the letters back to Lucia, perhaps you could ask if she'd be willing to resume corresponding with Granny . . . I think she might like that.'

Maddie ended the call and went back out to the balcony to sit in the sun and look out across this very special place, her grandmother's words echoing in her ears. She knew the memory of how she felt right now in this moment, the shift in the relationship with her dad making way for a new closeness and a deeper understanding was very freeing and would serve her well for many years to come . . .

28

Her last day in Capri, and Maddie had returned the letters from Maribella to Lucia earlier this morning and then spent some time with her chatting and sipping more cherry chinotto. Lucia had been delighted at the prospect of corresponding again with her friend, Kelly Sinclair, or Rose Williams, as she was now, and Maddie had promised to set this up. She was now on her way to the marina from where the ferry departed, with her rucksack on her back and dragging her silver wheelie case along.

Maddie left the tunnel after getting off the funicular train and walked out into the glorious sunshine. Smiling, she thought about all that had happened and changed since she first arrived here. It felt like a lifetime ago – certainly a lifetime of lessons had been learned, that was for sure. She was different, coming to Capri had changed her, and she'd always be grateful to the island for that.

She walked past the vibrant waterside cafes and restaurants with their colourful awnings and warm aroma of tangy garlic and herbs, the sweet scent of gelato too from the ice cream parlour floating in the air again as it had on the day she arrived in Capri. Walking on, she looked at her watch and saw there was plenty of time to take a few more photos of the marina, the cafes and sailboats bobbing in the shallow sea water, the view towards Naples out across the Mediterranean to add to her Capri Life portfolio, and so stopped and lifted her camera. Adjusting the lens, she focused on the marina first and took some wonderful pictures of the sea view, and then turned the camera to capture the street view: tourists milling around, excited people everywhere chatting and laughing. And then she stopped. Put her camera down to take another look, and then lifted it again, magnifying to zoom in on the middle distance over at the far end of the marina. A guy on a scooter waving. And he had parked up now and was running directly towards her. Removing his crash helmet as he got closer and closer. Maddie moved the camera down away from her face. What was he doing here?

Gio was now standing in front of her, wearing a white T-shirt and jeans, a little breathless as he pushed his dishevelled dark hair away from his beautiful face.

She went to turn away, because, despite everything Cynthia had said yesterday, and Maddie had agreed with it all and had sworn not to feel like a fool ever again . . . right now, right here, she was melting, her face flaming and her whole body tingling with a mixture of annoyance at the game he was playing, and overwhelming attraction to a man she had absolutely no right to feel this way about. Packing her camera away quickly, she grabbed the handle of the wheelie case and turned to walk away.

'Please, Maddie, don't leave without talking to me . . .' Gio gently caught hold of her arm as she brushed past him, having no choice but to move in closer to him as a group of tourists spilled out from a nearby restaurant and filled the pavement. She glanced at his face and saw the same baffled look he had displayed when she had run away from him on the boat.

'What are you doing here and how did you know where I was?' she asked quickly and quietly, irritation flooding her voice at his sheer audacity. She slipped her shades over her eyes as a mask as they moved into a quieter space, a pretty, little, narrow tile-paved street leading away from the main marina. Gio indicated towards a small courtyard where there was a bench beside a blue and white mosaic-tiled fountain flanked by two pink bougainvillea trees. Maddie checked her watch again; still plenty of time, the flight wasn't until much later tonight and so, after slipping her rucksack from her back and putting it on top of the camera case, she sat down at one end of the bench, Gio at the other.

'*La signora*, the lady in the flower shop,' Gio said. 'She told me you were coming here and so I come here too. Maddie, I must see you before you go home.'

'But why?' Maddie looked at him, he was leaning forward with his elbows on his knees and his head dipped down.

'Because I like you. I told you this already. From the moment I first saw you, there was an instant attraction. But it's more than that . . . I can't stop thinking about you. I want to get to know you properly and for you to know me. I want more time for us together.'

'You have no right to though!'

'Maddie, why do you say this? And why did you leave the boat so quickly? I put Bella away to stay safe inside the cabin but when I got to the towpath you were going in the taxi. I called out to you but the car drove away . . .' He looked up at her.

'Gio, I couldn't stay . . . I felt like a fool!'

'Why. What's the problem?'

'You have a girlfriend, that's the problem,' Maddie snapped. 'What is she going to think about . . .' she paused before adding . . . 'all this?' She felt unable in this moment to work out exactly what 'this' was, only that it was something, or so she had thought. 'The day on your boat. The closeness, our connection . . . the cuddling and hand-holding and—' She stopped short of saying 'the kiss that very nearly happened' and how she had developed feelings for him and might actually have started falling for him as they had connected on both a physical and emotional level. Not to mention him saying she was sexy! That's a bold compliment to give to another woman when you already have a girlfriend.

'She thinks nothing!' And Gio lifted his head and shook it from side to side before moving along the bench a little closer to her. 'Ah, Maddie. I make a mistake . . . I said it the wrong way. My girlfriend – she's not my girlfriend now, we split up a long time ago – a year or more.'

'What? Um, but you said *my girlfriend*.' Maddie swivelled so her whole body was facing his.

'*Sì* . . .' he nodded. 'I'm sorry, I got this wrong. My sisters have already told me I'm a stupid idiot and to . . . how do you say? To mend it with you. So this is why I have come to find you.' He smiled wryly and Maddie tried to keep a straight face as she imagined all his sisters yelling and telling him off in animated

Italian, his mum, Valerie, giving his arm a smack, no doubt.

'So, you really don't have a girlfriend?' she double-checked, and felt like a fool all over again for running off right away instead of challenging him at the time, but he had said so . . . Yes, it was a silly mistake for him to not say 'ex-girlfriend' and it was feasible that it just got lost in translation, but, still, she had to admit that she was shocked by her strong reaction at the time. It was insane, intense, and not like anything she had experienced before. Maybe she had been over-wrought, it had been a very emotional day, but even now she could feel herself tingling with the intensity of being in such close proximity to him and the feel-ings she had been developing for him, and had since tried to pack away, were now making an overwhelming return.

'No, Maddie,' Gio said gently. 'I promise you . . . I really don't have a girlfriend. I am not the type of man who would do that. I have been hurt by this too . . . my girlfriend, sorry, my *ex-girlfriend*, she cheated on me . . .' his voice tailed off momentarily, 'and my sisters . . . my mother, Nonna, they would never allow me to behave this way.' He laughed and pulled a scared face. 'Please get to know me some more and find out for yourself.'

'Oh . . . well, that's OK then,' she said, stunned, and moved along the bench, so they were sitting close together, and instantly became very, very conscious of the warmth emanating from the side of his thigh and the quickening of her pulse. The physical attraction was intoxicating. And he was right, there was something more happening between them . . . much more, and so yes, very much yes, she wanted to find out for herself.

They sat together in silence for a while, both staring ahead and considering this unexpected development in their fledgling friendship, until Gio said, 'Maddie, please don't go . . .' And moved his hand around hers, his fingers linking through hers.

'But my flight is tonight . . . I can't just stay, even though I'd love to,' she told him, and they sat side by side, contemplating quietly for a while longer.

'I know,' Gio said softly, nodding in acceptance as he squeezed her hand.

'I'm coming back though.'

'You are?'

'*Sì*,' she laughed, tilting her head, and shrugging in the same way she had seen him do. 'Next month, actually,' Maddie added, having been delighted when she went to ask Jona about coming back to Capri in the autumn and she had booked her in and then told her about a cancellation that had literally come through minutes earlier, meaning the apartment was going to be unexpectedly free for a fortnight from the middle of next month. 'I was going to wait until the autumn, when I have another photo shoot in Naples, but I think I might have fallen in love with this island . . . and so, well, I'm not sure I can wait that long to discover what else might be here . . .' she paused and looked into his gold flecked brown eyes, '. . . and explore this further.'

'This is a good plan. Maddie. I want to do this too . . . explore this further, as you say.' And he tenderly touched a finger to the side of her face, before standing up and holding out his hand to her. 'Come on . . .'

'Where are we going? I have to get on the ferry soon,' Maddie protested, pulling up the handle of the camera case and manoeuvring it into position behind her, ready to pull along. She was planning on spending the day in Naples before heading to the airport for her flight tonight.

'I have another idea . . .' He swung her rucksack over his shoulder in one swift move and led the way.

An hour or so later, Maddie was sitting next to Gio behind the steering wheel of his friend's Riva speedboat with the saltwater spray tantalisingly invigorating as they rode the waves of the Mediterranean. With the mist capped mountains of Capri left behind, for now, and the sun dazzling up high in a perfect cloudless, cerulean sky, the experience was utterly thrilling and one that Maddie knew she would cherish forever.

As the coast of Naples came into view, Gio expertly slowed the speedboat and steered them into a bay in a secluded part of the marina, then turned his body towards Maddie.

'You like the ride?' he asked.

'Yes, very much,' Maddie laughed, dabbing at her cheeks, which were wet with droplets from the sea spray. She looked into his eyes that seemed to have darkened as they searched hers, then glanced away. 'Gio, I'm sorry I overreacted yesterday and didn't give you a chance to explain. I should have at least spoken to you about—' Maddie was stopped from saying anything more as his lips were on hers. Warm and soft, the lightest touch, sparking the most intense sensation deep within her. And then he suddenly sat back and lifted his arms away from her. 'Um,' she managed, utterly confused now, touching her fingertips to her mouth, which was still tingling from his touch.

'Now I am the one who is sorry.' He put his hands back on the steering wheel.

'No, please, Gio, you most definitely don't have anything to apologise for.' She touched his forearm, yearning for his lips to be on hers again. The tingling sensation was still there. Her breathing quickened until she was practically panting. She inhaled through her nose in a desperate attempt to still herself, to calm down, but it was hopeless. She could feel Gio's breath on her cheek as he gently lifted a lock of hair that had fallen into her face before bringing his hand down and linking his fingers through hers again, sending another spark of electricity straight up her arm and on to circle her heart, teasing and making her pulse quicken so fast she felt lightheaded and giddy.

'Maddie, I have wanted to kiss you from the first moment I saw you, but it was not the right time. You were sad and emotional from all that you had found out about your grandmother.'

She studied his face. His eyes softening. She moved in closer and slipped her arms underneath his and around his muscular back, and gently pulled him towards her.

'Are you sure, Maddie?' He lowered his head until his face was mere millimetres from hers.

She nodded.

And kissed him right back.

A long, lingering kiss. His hand at the nape of her neck sending a shiver all the way down her spine. Her fingertips traced a path along his bare back below the bottom of his T-shirt, touching his irresistibly warm skin as a swirl of hot Mediterranean sea air furled around her bare legs, making her melt into his embrace. Wishing she could stay in this moment forever, she arched her back, already yearning for her return to the magical island of Capri . . . It couldn't come fast enough.

29

Capri, Italy, six months later

Rose remembered her friend as soon as she saw her standing there in the same spot on the veranda of the terracotta-coloured villa with her arms outstretched in greeting. With curious eyes, and a kind soul, although her hair wasn't dark and glossy as it had been back in the summer of 1953 when they first met on the road leading from the church after Mass one Sunday. They say a scent evokes a memory, and Rose thought the orchard looked exactly the same, with vibrant bursts of yellow and orange amongst rich green leaves, the warm Italian air with the glorious scent of citrus mingled with mimosa, giving the same tranquillity and sanctuary that it had all those years ago, and it was as if she was a young woman again, vivacious and consumed with a zest for life . . . before the darkness took over.

'Lucia, my dear friend,' Rose said, as she reached the veranda, her son fussing beside her, but she didn't mind, he meant well and was just worried she might have another fall. They were always worried about a fall, Jim and the girls, her granddaughters Maddie and Sofia, but Rose had never felt as fortified and energised as she did in this moment. Coming back to Capri was a dream she never imagined would be possible again. Not at her age. An octogenarian. It always caught her by surprise. How was it possible, when inside, in her heart and mind, she still felt the same as she did as a young woman. Wiser, yes, but with the spirit and dreams she had back then, although her memory was failing her on occasion – but not today. Today was a good day, and she remembered everything from all those years ago as if it was only yesterday and not a lifetime ago. The fun she'd had with her darling Clarke, swimming in the moonlight, partying and dancing with Lenny and Ray, the Lemon Tree restaurant, looking out at the sumptuous view . . . and then coming back again, mired in sadness . . .

Maddie looked over at her grandmother sitting on the sofa next to her dear friend, Lucia. The two elderly women were laughing as they reminisced about that summer of 1953. It had been an emotional reunion when her grandmother and her dad had first arrived in Capri a few days ago, and a long time in the planning, everyone wanting to be sure that her grandmother was up to the trip. The doctor at Evergreens had said Rose was in remarkably good physical health, even if her forgetfulness was progressing and becoming more apparent these days. She'd issued strict instructions for her not to overdo it or attempt to climb any of the rugged mountain roads in Capri, but had recommended that Rose take the trip and have a thoroughly wonderful time. So, Maddie and her dad had made all the travel arrangements – he was living mostly in Tindledale these days to be close to his mum. And closer to Sofia too; with three children under three, her dad wanted to be around to babysit and see his grandchildren growing up. He didn't want to miss out as he had when Maddie was a child. Sofia and Ben weren't here today as they had taken the twins and their new little sister, Rose, named after her great granny, to Spain, to meet Maria, Sofia's mum. They would all be coming out to Capri next week.

Maddie, on the other hand, having finished the autumn fashion shoot a few weeks ago, was spending as much time as she could here. The month after her first trip, she'd returned for two wonderful weeks where she and Gio had got to know each very well indeed.

And she'd flown back twice more as their initial feelings of physical attraction had deepened into love.

Maddie sighed contentedly as Gio waved to her. He was walking through the orchard, in between two rows of lemon trees, with the autumnal sun still hazy and casting a golden glow all around him, making her heart skip a beat as it always did on seeing him approach. Bella did her usual stretch and stood up, trotting off to greet him with her tail swishing from side to side in pleasure. Maddie waved and left the veranda to go and join them.

'How did it go?' she asked, after giving Gio a kiss and then slipping her hand inside his.

'It went very well . . .' And he glanced over his shoulder to where two elderly men and a very stylish woman with red bobbed hair and an exquisitely cut, navy-and-white jumpsuit on with gold strappy sandals, and her arms looped through theirs to support them, were slowly making their way through the orchard. 'Come, let me introduce you.'

Gio turned around and took Maddie to meet her aunty.

Audrey was here, in Capri, and Gio had just travelled down to the marina in a taxi to collect her from the ferry. Audrey had wanted it this way, no fuss, and with a moment to catch her breath before meeting her birth mother and the rest of her family for the first time. Audrey wanted to thank Rose for giving her and her parents a very happy and loving life together. And now here she was, in Capri, ready to do just that.

Maddie felt overjoyed as she walked over to Audrey, who unlooped her arms from the two gentlemen's elbows so they could hug.

'Maddie, this place sure is beautiful . . . and the perfect location for a reunion! You weren't exaggerating when you told me all about it,' Audrey said in her now familiar accent, although a little more nervous sounding than she had been in their many calls, Maddie thought, as she stepped back. Taking a proper look at Audrey, she could truly see it now: the remarkable resemblance to her grandmother, especially in the eyes. Then she recalled the picture of Clarke she'd found in her Google search: the fine bone structure and aquiline nose. She could see those features reflected here in his daughter, Audrey.

'I'm so pleased you made it. Granny is elated to be properly meeting you at last,' Maddie smiled, so grateful to have found Audrey and for her grandmother's mind to finally be at rest, knowing her daughter was happy. Audrey had told them she'd had a wonderful life growing up in Naples. Her adopted family had been loving and generous, providing her with everything she could ever have dreamed of. She had always loved films and the creative arts, realising now that she knew who her birth parents were, that it was most likely in her genes, inherited from Clarke King and Kelly Sinclair, and so had made the move to Los Angeles in her late twenties to pursue her career. She was now a very successful movie scriptwriter. And this happy, successful life was everything that Rose O'Malley, aka Kelly Sinclair, had wanted for her baby on that day in Chiesa di Sant'Andrea, when she had carried the crib into the vestry. 'Although Granny is still very anxious too . . .' Maddie added, 'and has been saying again that she hopes you will forgive her. I think she has forgotten that you have already talked about this together on the phone, several times.'

'I know,' Audrey said tenderly, placing a hand on Maddie's arm in reassurance. 'It will be fine . . . I'll take good care of her, Maddie, I promise you . . . just as she did for me when she put my needs before her own all those years ago.'

Silence followed as Maddie and Audrey hugged again.

'And I will too.' One of the elderly men wearing gaberdine trousers and a blazer over an open-neck shirt with a stylish polka dot cravat at his neck, came over to join them as Maddie stepped back and stood next to Gio, who put his arm around her shoulders and pulled her in for a comforting cuddle. 'It's the least I can do when Kelly . . . sorry, Rose,' he smiled, 'took great care of me a very long time ago when she turned down my proposal and stopped me from doing something, that, with hindsight . . .' he broke off to chuckle and shake his head as he considered this. 'Isn't that a wonderful thing – hindsight!' They all nodded and then he continued, 'Well, it would have been wrong . . . and most likely made both me and her miserable for many years.'

'Oh, this is Lenny,' Audrey said, as an introduction. It was there in Los Angeles that Lenny had crossed paths with Audrey at an awards ceremony. Recognising the name, and struck by the extraordinary resemblance to his childhood friend, Clarke, he had immediately made the connection. Lenny had made sure to keep his distance, of course, not knowing if Audrey was aware of her background. Nevertheless he had kept watch over the years and may have even opened a door or two in Hollywood for his friend's daughter. It wasn't until recently, when he saw a piece that she'd written for the *Los Angeles Times* about her Italian heritage, adoption and connecting with her birth mother and her family, that Lenny had finally reached out to her.

'It's a pleasure to meet you at last, Maddie,' Lenny said, his rheumy eyes twinkling as he beckoned the other man over. 'And this is my husband, Ray . . . He wants to thank Rose, too.'

'This is amazing . . . I'm so pleased to meet you, Lenny, and you too, Ray. I know my grandmother is going to be over the moon to see you both again.' Maddie shook their hands. It was wonderful to finally meet them in real life. 'She knows you're coming too . . . I've explained that Lenny looked out for you, Audrey, made sure you were OK—' Maddie smiled, looking at Lenny, and then to Audrey.

'Always . . . Clarke was my best friend, it's what he would have wanted,' Lenny said, giving Audrey an affectionate smile and placing a hand on her arm.

'And thank you again, Maddie, for making this happen,' Audrey said. 'Without your persistence in working out where the adoption agency was in Naples—'

'Ah, I can't really take the credit for that,' Maddie said. 'It was Gio who came up with the idea of showing the old, faded typed letter to Padre Alexis to see if he might recognise the insignia. He immediately directed us to the convent in Naples, and from there we were able to discover details of the adoption the nuns arranged for Kelly Sinclair's baby all those years ago . . .'

'Thank God you did,' Audrey said, 'I had been

searching for a woman called Kelly Sinclair for some time, without any luck, when it was Rose O'Malley, now Williams that I needed to find . . . And well, now it is finally happening, and I can't wait any longer,' Audrey said, pressing her palms together before opening her handbag and pulling out a scarf, an exquisite floral-patterned silk scarf with Capri embroidered at a jaunty angle on the corner – a gift from her mother who she was very much looking forward to meeting at last . . .

Acknowledgements

Thank you to Rowan Lawton, for the generous support, guidance, kindness and friendship and for being the most diplomatic, tenacious and calm agent any author could ever want.

Thanks to Kate Bradley, for being a fantastic editor and friend, and for the pep talks and chocolate care packages and for making this book a million times better than it originally was. Thanks too to Anne O'Brien for the very intuitive copyediting and to Lynne Drew, Charlotte Ledger and all the incredibly hard-working team at HarperCollins.

Thanks a million to my husband, Paul, aka Cheeks, the calm to my catastrophising, and for the top drawer room service of cake, tea and the perfectly shaken-not-stirred French Martini to my office when the deadlines were looming. An extra special thank you to my darling girl, QT, for bringing joy to every day and for coming up with the very best plot ideas and twists within seconds, and often when I've already spent hours trying to figure them out.

To my dear Caroline Smailes, as always, for everything. My wonderful, inspiring, funny friends Carmel Harrington, Rachel Noble-Forbes, Tracey Capelett, Cathy Bramley, and Mark Ennis for the help with sailing times. Special thanks to my incredibly warm, welcoming, generous, supportive and inspiring SW ladies, I'm so happy to have found you.

My biggest thanks go to you, my wonderful readers from all around the world. I love chatting to you on social media and reading your emails and messages, and I feel very grateful and humbled by the trust you place in me when you get in touch to share personal accounts of how my books have been a comfort or a welcome escape during a difficult time in your lives, or when you've chosen one of my books to read in your precious holiday time. You mean the world to me and make it all worthwhile. Thank you so very much for loving my books as much as I love writing them for you.

Luck and love,

Alex x

Valerie's Cherry Chinotto cordial

Ingredients

800g pink grapefruit

2kg oranges

3 cups cherries

3 sprigs of rosemary

3 tbsp coriander seeds

3 sticks cinnamon

4 whole nutmegs

8 cups sugar

2 litres water

Method

1. Slice the citrus into 1cm slices and arrange on 2–3 roasting trays lined with baking paper.

2. Scatter over the cherries and then the herbs and spices.

3. Roast at 220°C (200°C fan) for 30–40 minutes, until the citrus becomes blackened at the edges.

4. Bring the sugar and water to a simmer, stirring until the sugar is completely dissolved, then allow to cool to room temperature.
5. Transfer the contents of the roasting tray to a large preserving jar and pour over the sugar syrup.
6. Allow to steep at least overnight but preferably for a week or two, then strain the syrup into bottles.
7. Serve over ice, diluted with soda water.

If you enjoyed *A Postcard from Capri*, read on for an extract of Alex's escapist and heartwarming novel, *A Postcard from Paris*...

1

Tindledale, in rural England, 1916

Beatrice Crawford craved adventure. Yearning to escape the confines of her provincial young ladyhood and find her purpose, to be a positive influence in the world. A woman of substance, just like Lady Dorothy Fields, the inimitable, flame-haired woman who had ignited the dimly lit village hall earlier this evening with a very rousing speech. Beatrice had listened intently as Lady Dorothy had talked about her nursing work with the Voluntary Aid Detachment, or VAD, carrying out her patriotic duty to look after the brave soldiers fighting in fields far away for King and Country in the Great War.

After buttoning up her cotton nightie, Beatrice sat at her dressing table and brushed out her ebony curls then, securing them away from her face with a tortoise-shell clip, she pressed cold cream over her cheeks and neck, sweeping down and across her collar bones. Going over in her mind the events of such an extraordinary evening, she recalled with wonder the atmosphere in the village hall. It had been quite thrilling. An audience of young women just like her, suffragettes too, with little tricolour brooches pinned to their lapels, sat shoulder-to-shoulder, all united in their desire to do so much more for the war effort than endure a stifling life made up of endless tedious occupations such as light domestic work or embroidering samplers in silent drawing rooms. Her younger companion, Queenie, the housekeeper's niece, who was already doing her bit by working in an ammunitions factory in the nearby town of Market Briar, had almost missed out on hearing Lady Dorothy's speech. Queenie had arrived late and in a fluster, discreetly brushing a sheen of fine raindrops from her wool beret and gloves, whispering a grateful, 'Thank you, Trixie,' before sliding onto the chair that Beatrice had saved for her at the end of the row. Exchanging a clandestine glance, Beatrice had pressed her friend's hand in reply, both of them knowing and secretly delighting in their small act of defiance. For Beatrice's stepmother, Iris, had forbidden Queenie from using 'Trixie' as a suitable pet name for her stepdaughter, citing it 'undignified, and quite common!' But Beatrice liked being Trixie: it made her feel more alive, jolly and without constraint, and so the two friends had continued with it whenever Iris was out of earshot.

Beatrice and Queenie had forged an unlikely friendship five years ago when Iris had insisted that the then 13-year-old Beatrice 'must be perfectly fluent in at least two languages if she were to be a refined debutante and catch a suitable husband.' Eight-year-old Queenie, known to be a quick-witted and fast-learning young girl, with a tumble of auburn curls and sparkling, impish green eyes, was brought in from the village each day to be taught French and High German, in order that Beatrice might practise her own conversational skills. As for Beatrice's rudimentary French and German writing skills, they had been deemed beyond hope and were to be forgotten about forthwith. Even though Beatrice's stepmother was French, she was far too engaged in a hectic social life – which frequently took her to glamorous parties in London, Paris, Monte Carlo and beyond – to idle away her time on academia, especially when, according to Iris, Beatrice hadn't 'shown enough flair in her younger years'. Iris had also declared that revision was a tedious waste of time, and that Beatrice should show humility and recompense for her shortcomings by learning alongside an uneducated and much younger village girl, who would most likely pick it all up in half the time that it had taken Beatrice. 'So that ought to keep you on your toes!'

So, together with her French and German conversational skills, thanks to her insistent stepmother and Swiss governess, Miss Paulette, there were now only ten lectures and ten lessons in first aid and nursing standing between Beatrice and her ambition to help the soldiers fighting on the front line in France. Not that it was imperative to have language skills, but Beatrice thought it might give her a little something extra to offer, and Lady Dorothy had explained that it wasn't only English-speaking soldiers who required nursing. There were Frenchmen too. Some German soldiers, prisoners of war, as well. Of course, she would need practical first-aid training. A hospital in London perhaps, that's what Lady Dorothy had recommended, to get a foot in the door and to show her mettle. And they really were rather keen to recruit volunteers.

Drawing her knees up to her chest and placing her slippered feet on the edge of the velvet cushioned chair, Beatrice wrapped her arms around her legs and hugged the feeling of possibility into her, for she could see a way forward now. It was as if a light had been switched on deep within her, sparking a frisson of hope that she felt barely able to contain. Not that the bleak battlefields of France were a cause for elation. Certainly not. No, it was very much more than that. She had to do something. The newspapers were full of lists. The names of soldiers killed in the trenches. Pages and pages of men, some only mere boys. Thousands on the very first day of the war in 1914 and it had been relentless ever since. Fathers. Sons. Cousins. Uncles. Nephews. Her own dear brother, Edward, having enlisted at the start of the war, had mercifully been missing from the lists so far. But for how much longer? Beatrice carried a perpetual sense of foreboding that seemed impossible to shake off. Although, for the first time in her life, she felt that she also had an opportunity, a sense of purpose.

Of course, Father would protest, preferring she marry Clement Forsyth, the odious son of his banker in London, but how could she when her heart was with another? A secret love. Because Bobby worked in the stables, mucking out and tending to the horses, and so would never be suitable husband material as far as Father was concerned. Beatrice's heart had almost broken in two when Bobby had gone away to fight for his country, and not a moment went by when she didn't think of him, wrapping an imaginary shield of safety around his beautiful body so he would return to her arms once more. The only comfort being that Bobby and Edward were together in the same PALS battalion.

Queenie's older brother, Stanley, too, along with many of the other men from the village, with their camaraderie to keep their spirits up until they could return home. Beatrice treasured the photograph of Bobby that she kept hidden inside her diary, alongside the pages where she had written about her endless love for him.